MW00412529

Chapter
1

Viper

I SET MY DUFFEL BAG on the floor and shut the front door as quietly as I could, praying no one had heard me come in. Thankfully, the house was dark and quiet, just like I'd been hoping. I locked the door and tiptoed quietly up the stairs, cringing as they creaked beneath my feet.

The Minnesota Wild had just finished our first road trip of the season and my plane had landed about an hour before, but instead of heading home to *my* house, my car seemed to drive itself straight to Michelle's. It was pretty late and I knew that she was probably sleeping, but the thought of waking her up for I-haven't-seen-you-in-five-days sex was too good to pass up.

I was hungry, but not for food.

Her bedroom door opened slowly revealing her motionless body lit by the small lamp on her nightstand. The low hum of her breathing filled the room. So did the smell of coconut from her shampoo, which meant she'd showered just before bed.

Even better.

I lifted my knee onto the bed, hoping to slowly crawl across and surprise her, but the bump of the mattress made her flip around quickly.

"Viper!" she whispered loudly. "You scared the hell out of me!" Her eyebrows were pulled in tight with an angry glare and a few strands of her damp blond hair clung to the side of her face. She'd never looked hotter.

Without saying a word, I gave her a wicked grin and started crawling again. Her expression softened instantly and she lay back on the bed, opening her arms for me.

"Sorry," I apologized half-heartedly just before I crashed my mouth against hers. She kissed me back, her lips parting as she invited me in. I gladly dipped my tongue into her mouth and shoved my hands into her hair, gripping tightly. Being on the road was nothing new for me, but having someone waiting for me when I got home was.

She tucked her hand inside the waistband of my sweats, slowly moving up and down my hard shaft. "You don't *feel* sorry." She giggled.

"I tried to be sorry—it didn't work. Now take your clothes off," I said gruffly.

I trailed kisses down the side of her neck, pulling eagerly on the neckline of her T-shirt.

"Really?" she teased. "No 'hello'? No 'how was your week'? Nothing?"

I sat back and pulled her up to a sitting position, dragging her T-shirt over her head. "I've been waiting all week to have these in my mouth." I took her nipple in between my lips and sucked hard. She let out a gasp just as I let go. "But if you really want to we can chat instead?"

"No, no. That's good," she said breathlessly. "Keep doing that."

The corner of my mouth lifted in a smirk as I turned my attention back to her chest. One of the things I loved most about Michelle was her body—her *real* body. A body that had given birth to two amazing kids. A body that wasn't stick thin. A body that had curves in all the right places. A body that was strong enough to do the job of both a mother and a father and never complain about it. Best of all, a body that was my playground for the next several hours. I just had to decide where I wanted to play first.

"I missed you," I said before I gently pushed her back on the bed and kissed the soft skin on her stomach.

A sexy grin spread across her lips. "You did?"

"Mmhmm. A lot." I kissed her stomach again.

"Prove it."

With those two words, my head lifted slightly and I stared her straight in the eye. She waited a second and arched one eyebrow, challenging me. Without taking my eyes off of hers, I licked my lips and grabbed her shorts and panties at the same time, pulling them down hard and tossing them off the side of the bed. I licked my lips one more time and dipped my head between her legs, but just before I could taste her, I heard the dreaded...

"Moooooooommy!"

I froze and lifted my eyes to hers.

"Shhh. Pretend you didn't hear him." She waved her hand toward the door before gently pushing my head back down.

"Mooooooooooooom!"

Michelle sighed and dropped her hand on the mattress in frustration. "I love that little man, but he has the *worst* timing."

I laughed and sat back. "Let's make a deal. You stay right here—just like this—and I'll go see what he needs."

She sat up, shaking her head. "You don't have to."

I put my hand on her shoulder, stopping her before she could stand. "I know I don't *have* to. I *want* to."

"Really?" she asked skeptically.

"Yeah," I shrugged as I stood. "You're not the only one I missed."

Her eyes softened as she chewed on the corner of her lip,

BETH
EHEMANN

trying not smile.

"I mean it—stay right there. Just like that," I ordered. "Actually . . . wait. You were more like this." I opened her legs a little wider. "There. Perfect. Don't move."

Her cheeks turned pink and she lifted her hand to her mouth, trying to stifle her laugh.

"Uh . . . wait a sec," she called out as I started toward the door. I turned back and her eyes moved from my face to my cock as she lifted an eyebrow. "You wanna do something about that? That's a conversation I'm not ready to have yet."

I looked down at the bulge in my sweats. "Oooh, good call. We don't want The Viking to scare the poor kid." I shot her a wink and tucked my boner in the best I could as she rolled her eyes. "I mean it—don't move. And for the love of God don't fall asleep."

"Got it, boss," she joked, nodding obediently as I turned and left the room.

Boss, huh? I could get used to that.

"Moooooooommmmmmmyyyyyyy!" Matthew called one more time, just as I got to his door. The glow from the hallway moved across the room as I pushed the door open, eventually lighting up his face. He squinted and covered his eyes with the back of his hand.

"What's up, buddy?" I greeted with a loud whisper.

His mouth fell open and he dropped his hand. "Viper!" he shouted excitedly. He climbed to his feet and jumped from the bed into my arms, wrapping himself around me like a monkey.

I squeezed him back, hard. "I missed you."

"I missed you, too! Did you have a good trip?"

"I did—"

"I watched your games," he interrupted. "There were four of them. You played really good for three and kinda sucked for one."

4

I let out a quick laugh. Gotta love the honesty of a five-year-old. "I did suck for one of them, didn't I?"

"Yeah." He nodded as he pulled back but didn't take his arms off me. "I told Mom that and she said not to say 'suck.'"

I rolled my eyes and chuckled under my breath. "Of course she did."

He stared at me for a second, his big blue eyes traveling all over my face, before he cracked a tight-lipped smile and squeezed me again.

"What's this one for?"

"I just missed you," he muffled into my shoulder.

I closed my eyes and tightened my arms around him. "I missed you, too, bud. That's why I came over tonight. I wanted to be here when you got up in the morning."

"Do you have hockey tomorrow?" he asked as he wiggled out of my arms and sat on the edge of his bed.

"Nope, we have an off day."

"Yay!" he cheered, pumping his little arms in the air. "Can we do stuff?"

I sat down on the bed next to him. "Sure. What did you have in mind?"

He shrugged. "I don't know. Go out for breakfast, go to the park, go to the zoo, maybe the circus? Then lunch, the library, play catch in the backyard—"

"Wait a sec." I looked at him in amazement. "You want to do all of that *tomorrow?*"

He nodded proudly. "Then if we have extra time, can we get ice cream?"

I shook my head incredulously. "Buddy, if we're gonna get even *half* of that done, we both need to get some sleep." I stood up and reached around him, lifting the blankets for him to crawl under.

I pulled the quilt up to his chin and then tucked the sides in nice and tight. "I'll tell you what . . . you close your eyes and get a good night's sleep and I'll see what I can do about that list of yours. Deal?"

"Deal," he agreed with a grin.

I leaned down and kissed his forehead before heading back down the hall to Michelle's room.

As I pushed her bedroom door open and saw her curled up with her back to me, my poor dick wept with disappointment.

"No, no, no," I whined as I crawled across the bed and tried to wake her. "How did you fall asleep that fast?"

"Hmmm?" she answered in a sleepy moan without opening her eyes.

I rocked her back and forth. "Come on, it's been five days."

"That's fine, just put it on the counter," she slurred, sounding like the weird little sleepy mouse from *Alice in Wonderland*.

I sighed, grabbed the remote, and leaned back against the headboard.

Apparently the only balls that'll be bouncing tonight will be on SportsCenter.

Chapter
2

Viper

LIGHT KISSES TRAVELED DOWN THE back of my neck, setting every nerve in my body on fire and making my dick even harder than it already was. I fought through a sleepy haze to open my eyes just as Michelle lay back on the pillow next to me, flashing me a sexy smile.

"Good morning," she said.

"Morning," I growled into the pillow before closing my eyes again.

"Wait," she exclaimed sadly. "You're going back to sleep? Your eyes were just open."

"That's because you were kissing my neck so I thought I was getting laid. You stopped so I'm going back to sleep." I opened one eye halfway, peeking at her, just as she pouted and rolled her eyes. "Plus, I'm mad at you," I added.

"Mad at me?" Her voice rose in surprise.

"Yep."

"Why?"

I lifted my face off of the pillow just slightly. "I believe your response was 'Got it, boss' when I told you not to fall asleep last night. Less than ten minutes later, I came back in here ready to bury my face in between your legs and you were sawing logs."

Her bottom lip popped out in a pucker. "I'm sorry. I was so tired, I couldn't keep my eyes open."

"Mmhmm."

"Well, the kids are still sleeping . . . I can make it up to you right now," she said seductively, sliding her hand in between my stomach and the mattress. She gripped my morning wood over my sweats and her eyes grew wide. "Wow! Someone sure woke up ready to go."

"I'm always ready to go when you're around. I walk around with a constant hard-on, ready to strike at any moment, just in case you decide you're in the mood."

She planted a soft kiss on my cheek as she kept massaging my dick. "As cute as that is, we both know it's not true. If you walked around all day with *that,* people would definitely stare . . . and talk."

"Oh, yeah?" I rolled over, giving her easier access. "And what would those people say?"

"Hmmm . . . probably that Viper's girlfriend is the luckiest woman in the whole world."

"Well, I can't argue with that." I sat up and kissed her neck. "I'll be right back. *Don't. Move.*"

She giggled as I walked over to the master bathroom. "What are you laughing at?" I called out.

"You. That. I don't know how you pee when it's like that."

I leaned back and shook my head. "It fucking sucks. You think Matthew has bad aim? Come look at the bathroom wall in here in about a minute and you'll see what I mean."

She let out another small giggle as I closed the bathroom door. I wasn't *really* mad at Michelle, but I wasn't kidding about wanting her so bad. Over the last year since we started dating, it had been a learning process, mostly on my part. I'd been used to going to the bar on Friday nights and leaving with whomever I wanted to. When we'd gone out on the road for away games, I didn't think twice about taking a hot little puck bunny back to my hotel room for a few hours. Women were constantly shoving their phone numbers in my face, and a year ago I would have taken them all home and put them in my kitchen drawer. Now . . . I threw them away. I went back to my hotel room after the games and called Michelle, and I almost never went to the bar, unless I was meeting up with Brody or something. Michelle had changed my life drastically . . . for the better.

I pulled my sweats up, washed my hands, and hustled back to the bedroom, ready to finally finish what I'd started the night before. Just as I crossed through to the bedroom, I froze. Michelle pressed her lips together and gave me a sympathetic smile as my eyes traveled down next to her . . . to Matthew curled up in my spot.

My mouth dropped open. "Nooooo!" I whispered loudly.

"Sorry," she said quietly. "He came running in and said he wanted to snuggle, then fell right to sleep. What was I supposed to say?"

"I don't know, how about: 'I know you want to lie here, sweetie, but Viper's penis has been a very lonely guy for the last six days, so I'm going to keep it company and rub it for a few minutes until it spits back at me. Now hurry back to bed, little cock block.' That probably would've covered it just fine."

"Shhhh! He'll hear you," she scolded through a giggle as she looked down at Matthew, who hadn't moved a muscle.

"So? You're never too young to learn about the importance of getting your rocks off as often as possible." I walked over to the bed and plopped down with a sigh.

"I'm sorry," she said as she reached out and rubbed my cheek with the back of her fingers. "I promise, promise, *promise* I'll make it up to you tonight."

"Sure you will," I groaned.

"I mean it. Free reign. Anything goes."

My face flashed over to hers and I raised one eyebrow. "Free reign? Anything goes?"

"Anything goes," she repeated with a nod as she licked her lips.

"You're gonna regret saying that." I shook my head as I stood. "You're also not gonna be able to walk tomorrow."

"No walking? Sounds good to me. I'll just lie in bed and read all day while you do all the chores and parenting," she said with a wink.

"Deal."

"Wait, where are you going?" she asked as I turned and headed out of the room.

"I'm starving. I'm gonna make the kids pancakes. Want some?"

"No." She leaned over and grabbed her cell phone off the nightstand to look at the time. "I actually have to get them up and moving. We have a breakfast date with Gam."

"We do?"

She nodded. "I talked to her yesterday and she asked us to come over. I had no idea you'd be home already, so you should come."

I sighed. "I've been trying to come for like twelve hours now."

Her mouth fell open as she grabbed a pillow and threw it at the door, just as I closed it.

"Lawrence!" Gam called out, crossing her yard with open arms as we climbed out of the car an hour later.

"How's my favorite girl?" Gam's larger-than-life personality made me forget how small and frail she really was, but when I put my arms around her and squeezed gently, it was a sharp reminder that she wouldn't be here forever.

10

"I lived to see another day, so I'm great." She pulled back and looked up at me but didn't let go, her tiny hands holding mine. "This is a nice surprise. Michelle didn't tell me you'd be home already."

"She didn't know." I shook my head. "I got in late last night and surprised her and the kids."

"Well, I was already excited to see her and my favorite kids, but now I get to see my favorite grandson, too. What a great day!"

"Gam," I said dryly, "I'm your *only* grandson."

"Whatever." She waved her hand at me. "Shut up and take a compliment, would ya?"

She said hello to Michelle and Matthew and gave each of them a big hug before she bent down to Maura, who was sitting happily in her stroller, trying to pull the little pink bow out of her hair. "And you . . . I've missed you so much, my sweet Little Mo."

Michelle's lips spread into a wide grin as she looked from Gam to me and back again with a twinkle in her eyes. We had no idea where it came from, but a while ago Gam had started calling Maura "Little Mo," and it was Michelle's favorite thing. Matthew and Maura still saw Mike's parents whenever they came into town, but with them living on the other side of the country, Gam was their only consistent grandparent. But I knew the twinkle in Michelle's eye wasn't just for Little Mo. Michelle loved Gam, and Gam loved Michelle. They had an instant, intense connection that I couldn't quite put my finger on, but sometimes I was pretty sure if Gam was forced to choose one of us, I'd be on the outside looking in.

"You guys come on in." Gam waved her arm, walking toward her house. "I made your favorite. Blueberry breakfast cake."

"Yay!" Matthew threw his arms in the air excitedly.

As we stepped onto her creaky wooden porch steps, something off to the right caught my eye.

"That's cool. Where'd you get that?" I said, taking a couple steps closer to the new, brightly painted coffee table that sat in front of her white wicker couch.

"You like that? I made it," she said proudly.

"What?" I looked at her incredulously. "No, you didn't."

She nodded. "I sure did. Got a bunch of those pallets from the dumpster behind the grocery store and followed a plan I found on Pinterest. I made it, then I painted it. Voila."

I looked back and forth from her to the table a couple times, processing what she'd just said.

"What?" she asked defensively after I didn't respond.

"I just . . . wow. I can't believe you did that. You're almost ninety. Shouldn't you be rocking in a chair, knitting your handsome grandson a sweater?"

"I would, but I don't think it would fit past that swollen head of yours," she joked as she turned and opened her screen door.

I leaned down, close to Michelle's ear. "Speaking of swollen heads, I have two . . ."

She let out a quick gasp seconds before I took a sharp elbow to the ribs.

We followed Gam through the door and instantly . . . it smelled like home. Her house was small but cozy, and it always smelled like cinnamon and sugar.

"Mmmm," Michelle hummed with a smile on her face. "It smells amazing in here."

"Thanks!" Gam replied proudly. "I couldn't sleep, so I got up and made a double batch at four o'clock this morning."

Michelle pulled her brows down low. "You what?"

"She's always done that, didn't you know?" I answered with a laugh. "When she can't sleep, she cooks. Sometimes it's meatballs, sometimes it's spaghetti. This morning, I guess it was a double batch of blueberry breakfast cake."

Michelle looked from me to Gam in amazement, her eyes

wide. "I had no idea!"

"Eh! Stupid insomnia." Gam waved a quick hand. "I just figure instead of lying in bed, staring at the ceiling, why not wake up and cook?"

Michelle giggled. "I don't even want to cook when I *should* be cooking, let alone when I should be sleeping."

"I don't know why you're not tired at night," I said in an accusatory tone as I picked up a piece of paper from her kitchen table. "What's this about?"

Gam glanced at the paper and let out a tiny chuckle. "That's nothing."

"What is it?" Michelle craned her neck, trying to read over my shoulder.

"It's a letter. 'Dear Ms. Finkle . . . We are writing to alert you of an official complaint we've received from a neighbor about you and another individual driving human transporting vehicles through his or her flowers.'"

"Human transporting vehicle?" Michelle asked in a confused tone.

"I think it's a Segway," I answered dryly.

Michelle's mouth dropped open, her blue eyes as wide as they could go as we both looked up at Gam in unison. She stood at the sink with her back to us, her shoulders shaking slightly.

"Are you laughing?" I asked in disbelief.

As she turned slowly, she reached up and wiped the corner of her eye with a tissue. "Sorry. It's just so funny."

"Wait. This is for real?" Michelle exclaimed. "When did you get a Segway? And who were you with? Whose flowers did you ruin?"

Gam walked across the kitchen and handed Matthew an oatmeal cookie, then broke another one into small pieces for Maura and set them on her stroller tray.

"It wasn't that big of a deal. Marge 'I-Haven't-Had-A-Boyfriend-In-Forty-Years' Cooper got her undies all in a bunch

BETH
EHEMANN

and called the office on me and Regina for having a little fun."

"You skipped the part about getting a Segway," I grumbled, feeling more like her overprotective father than her grandson.

"Phil's grandson sells them. We got a great deal," she answered nonchalantly.

I held my hand up. "Wait a second. Who's Phil?"

Gam stared at me blankly before her eyes shifted over to Michelle. "You didn't tell him?"

"Tell me what?"

"I didn't have a chance yet," Michelle answered Gam, ignoring me.

I let out a heavy sigh, my frustration growing. "Someone better tell me what's going on right now before I—"

"Oh, calm down, you big baby," Gam interrupted. "Phil is my friend. He comes over often and has dinner with me. Sometimes we watch movies. Sometimes we go for a walk."

"Sometimes they hold hands," Michelle added with a little giggle.

"You have a boyfriend?" I roared.

Gam put her hands on her hips and glared at me. "He's not a boyfriend, he's my *friend*."

"You're almost ninety years old. What do you need a boyfriend for?" I complained, completely ignoring what she'd just said.

She looked straight at me, raising her eyebrows slowly. "I don't know, Lawrence. What do *you* need a girlfriend for?"

My stomach rolled as Michelle let out another giggle. I decided to stop asking questions about Phil right then and there.

Chapter
3

Viper

AFTER WE VISITED WITH GAM for a while, went to the zoo, had ice cream, and went to Matthew's favorite train restaurant for dinner, we all went back to Michelle's house for the night.

Maura's sweaty little head rested on my shoulder as I carried her into the house and up to her room. It was barely dark out but she was already having trouble keeping her eyes open.

"You tired, baby girl?" I asked as I changed her diaper and slipped pajamas over her head.

She yawned and rubbed her eyes, her cheeks pink from the sun. When she was dressed, I picked her up off the changing table and walked over to her crib. As I started to pull her away to lay her down, she whimpered and gripped me tighter. Closing my eyes, I wrapped my arms around her and laid my head on the top of hers and rocked back and forth.

After a couple minutes, I heard the door push open against the carpet and Michelle quietly walked up next to me. "Well aren't you two the cutest thing I've ever seen."

"She didn't want to lie down yet, so I thought I'd rock her for another minute."

She leaned her head against my biceps. "It must have worked. She's sound asleep," she whispered.

"Seriously?"

She nodded.

I cradled Maura's head in my hand and gently laid her down in her crib. She sighed and immediately rolled onto her side as I covered her with her fuzzy pink blanket.

Michelle stepped up next to me and stared down at her. "Isn't she just the cutest thing you've ever seen?"

"She really is." I nodded before looking over at her. "Where's Matthew?"

"He was out before I left the room."

I arched an eyebrow. "Oh, really?"

"Yeah. Why?"

I wiggled my eyebrows up and down before picking her up and tossing her over my shoulder.

"Ahhhh!" she squealed. "What the hell are you doing?"

"Shhh! Don't wake the kids," I warned. "It's been six days and at this point, even if they wake up they're just gonna have to sit in the hallway and wait until we're done."

She chuckled the whole way down the hall to her room. Once inside, I kicked the door shut with my foot, set her down, cupped her face in my hands, and clamped my mouth over hers. She leaned into me and moaned in satisfaction as our tongues met. Without breaking our kiss, she walked backward toward the bed, pulling me with her by the waistband. My hands left her face and found the button of her jean shorts, undoing it as quickly as I could.

As we reached the foot of the bed, her shorts fell to the floor and her lips left mine so that she could pull her T-shirt over her head.

"I hate being away from you," I said, wrapping my arm

around her waist and lifting her onto the bed.

"I hate it, too," she said, pulling me down on top of her.

I took a deep breath, trying to steady myself. "If you don't slow down, I'm not gonna last very long."

"I don't want it slow," she said, pulling my shirt off. "Six days is a long time for me, too. Now show me how much you missed me."

Her words made my heart thump hard against my chest and adrenaline shoot through my body. Michelle didn't talk like that often, but when she did, it did crazy things to me.

As I lowered my mouth back down to hers, my hand dipped in between her legs and I could feel how much she missed me.

"My God," I said against her mouth. "You're already ready to go."

"Then what are you waiting for?" she panted back.

That's all it took. I couldn't wait anymore. Her mouth fell open and she let out a low groan, digging her fingers into my shoulders as I pushed myself inside of her slowly.

"That's the last time I'm gonna be soft tonight," I warned playfully, kissing the corner of her mouth.

"Good," she said breathlessly.

I studied every inch of her beautiful face as I moved in and out of her. Everything about Michelle was intoxicating to me— her body, her voice, her smell—but nothing, and I mean *nothing,* turned me on more than the faces she made when we were having sex.

She pinched her eyes shut tight as she bit her bottom lip.

"Open your eyes," I ordered. "Look at me."

"I can't. I'm gonna—Oh God."

"Now. Open them. I want to watch you."

She flicked her eyes open and raised her hips off the bed, grinding against me.

"Oh, Viper," she groaned as I pumped faster, the sound of

our skin slapping together filling the room. I grabbed her shoulders and pulled her against me, every thrust bringing me closer and closer to finishing.

"Oh God!" she called out, arching her back as she squeezed her thighs around me. That was it. That was her sign. When she clenched and every muscle in her body tightened up, I knew that she was there.

"Don't look away," I grunted, not far behind her. Staring straight into her hazy blue eyes, I pushed harder. "I need to watch you as I fill you."

One last push and I stilled. My cock contracted, releasing six days' worth of cum and tension. I moved one hand down to her hip, holding her tight as I groaned and thrusted slowly a few more times.

Michelle lifted both hands, cradling my face. "I love the hell out of you, you know that?"

"I do know that." I lowered my head and gave her a quick kiss on the tip of her nose. "And I love the hell out of you, too. Be right back." I stood up and walked to the bathroom, returning with a towel for her. I cleaned up quickly and hopped back into bed without getting dressed.

She rolled onto her side and eyed me suspiciously.

"What?" I asked defensively through a laugh.

"Can I ask you something?"

"Yep."

"A serious something. No joking, okay?"

"Oh boy. Okay . . . hit me."

"You do that a lot when we're having sex—wanting me to look right at you—but I've never asked why."

I stared up at the can light in the ceiling, trying to figure out how to answer her question. I knew the answer, but I wasn't sure how to say it to her.

"Do you really want me to answer that? Honestly?"

Her eyes widened as she swallowed nervously. "Of course."

I took a deep breath and rolled on my side to face her. "I've been with a lot of women in my life, especially the last few years, and you already know that most of them were one-night stands or quick fucks in a car outside of the bar or whatever."

Her eyes dropped to the bed.

"Don't do that." I reached over and lifted her chin. "You don't even know what I'm gonna say, so stay with me."

She lifted her face and nodded.

"Anyway," I continued. "When I was with them, I didn't care about them. I didn't know anything about them . . . their favorite color, what they did for a living, even some of their names. I didn't *want* to know about them, and I certainly didn't want to look them in the eye when I was inside of them because they were just a fuck, simple as that."

She recoiled, pinching her eyes shut at my harsh words, but quickly reopened them and came back to me.

"But when you and I got together, it was different. From the very first time it was different." I reached out and tucked a stray blond hair behind her ear. "You were the first girl I loved before I had sex with her. Hell, you're the only girl I've ever loved, period."

Her lips curled into a tiny smile. "Really?"

"Really. And not only did I want to learn every single thing about you, I wanted to look at you. All the time I wanted to look at you. I still do. And when you come, and you're looking into my eyes, it does things to me, Michelle. It makes me primal, animalistic. Like I want to climb up on the roof, pound on my chest, and tell the whole world that you're mine."

"Wow, that was not the answer I was expecting."

"What were you expecting?"

"I don't know,"—she shrugged—"but not that. Just when I think I have you all figured out, Lawrence Finkle, you show me a whole new layer that I didn't even know existed."

I let out a quick laugh. "What can I say? I'm a complicated

asshole."

"You are complicated, but you're definitely not an asshole. Not even close."

Leaning forward, I gently grabbed the back of her head and pulled her lips to mine. "I love you."

"I love you, too, Viper," she said, with as much sincerity as I'd ever heard. "Now let's talk about this professing your love from the rooftops thing a little more. You know I'm totally okay with that, right?"

Chapter

4

Viper

"**G**OOD MORNING, BOYS!" I BELLOWED, holding my arms out straight as I walked through the doors of the Wild's locker room. Most of the guys looked up quickly, then immediately went back to what they were doing, but Brody stared at me with raised eyebrows.

"Why are you in such a good mood?" he asked, then shook his head quickly. "Never mind. Forget it. I probably don't want to know."

Louie slipped his foot in his skate and shook his head. "He probably got laid this morning or something."

Ignoring my young, annoying teammate, I walked up behind Brody and slapped my hands down hard on his shoulders, shaking them slightly. "Why not be in a good mood, Mr. Murphy? Life is amazing!"

Brody chuckled and shook his head as he bent down to buckle up his leg pad. "Yep. He definitely got laid."

"I did," I admitted proudly. "Last night I had amazing, mind-blowing sex with the hottest woman in the world, and I'll

21

probably do it again tonight, so fuck all of you."

Louie rolled his eyes and headed out of the locker room toward the ice. Once he was out of earshot, I bent down close to Brody. "That's not the only reason I'm in a good mood though."

Brody jumped up from the bench and whipped around. "Let's agree never to whisper something like that that close to my ear ever again. Deal?"

"Shut up, asshole," I snapped back, wadding up a towel and throwing it at him.

He caught it as it bounced off his face.

"I had a dream," I said excitedly. "About you and me—"

He held a hand up in the air. "Seriously, dude. Stop. I don't want to hear any more."

"Listen! I had a dream that we opened a bar. Together. And it was fucking awesome."

"A bar?" He raised his eyebrows in surprise. "Like a drinking bar?"

"No,"—I rolled my eyes—"a sleeping bar. Yes, you idiot, a drinking bar."

He shrugged his shoulders and tossed the towel into a big bin in the corner of the room. "Why would we do that? What's the point?"

"We're not getting any younger, man. Let's strike while the iron's hot. Why wait until we're old and no one gives a shit about us anymore?" I set my bag in my locker and started pulling practice clothes out of it.

"Wait a minute." He straightened up and blinked a couple times. "Are you being serious right now? I thought this was just a dream."

"It was a dream, but it made me think. Let's do it! Let's open a bar together."

"Holy shit, you really aren't kidding."

"I'm not! Think about it—it would be a badass sports bar

with sports memorabilia and signed shit all over the place."

"And while that sounds awesome, a lot more goes into owning a bar than cases of beer and signed hockey sticks, Viper."

"I know, but I just have this gut feeling."

He stared at me for a few seconds before taking a deep breath and letting it out slowly. "Last time you had a gut feeling, I ended up in Buckingham Fountain and you had to bail me out of jail, remember?"

"This is a different gut feeling. A good one. That whole fountain thing was . . . fucking stupid. I don't know why you ever listened to me on that."

He pressed his lips into a hard line and glared at me as he pulled his practice jersey over his head. "Let's just go practice."

"Think about it. Promise me you'll at least think about it," I called after him.

Without turning around, he lifted one glove in the air. "I know you can't tell, but I'm flipping you off in here."

"That means you're gonna think about it!" I shouted as he disappeared around the corner.

I spent the entire three hours of practice skating close to Brody every chance I got, calling out, "Sports bar," until finally he stuck his stick out and tripped me, making me fall flat on my face.

"Thanks for tripping me with your stick, asshole. That was a little uncalled for," I complained playfully as we walked back to the locker room.

"So was you annoying the shit out of me for three hours."

"I wouldn't call it annoying. I would call it being persuasive."

He shot me a hard glare but said nothing.

"Did you think about it?"

"No, but if you'll shut up for five minutes, I will."

I grabbed my phone from my bag. "Deal."

He grimaced as he took his skate off. "My knee is bothering me. I'm gonna go sit in the hot tub for a while. You stickin' around?"

"Yeah, I probably—" I looked down at my phone and froze at the series of texts from Michelle.

M: Are you on the ice?

M: Call me ASAP.

M: I'm meeting the ambulance at the hospital with Gam.

M: Viper, please call me NOW!

Fear shot through my body as every other noise drifted away. I hit the call button on my phone and started ripping my uniform off.

Michelle's phone went straight to voicemail.

"Fuck!" I yelled out, silencing the whole locker room.

"What's going on?" Brody asked.

I ignored him, my hands shaking as I tried to send Michelle a coherent text.

What's going on? I'm leaving now. Call me.

"Yo! What is it?" Brody called out, panic lacing his tone.

"It's Gam. I gotta go." I finished taking my clothes off and tossed them into my bag, throwing my regular clothes on as fast as I could.

"What happened?"

I turned and jogged toward the door. "I have no idea. I'll call you later."

My hands wrapped around the steering wheel, squeezing it so tight I worried I was going to pull it right off. I didn't have much family, and Gam was without a doubt the one I cared about most. The thought of something serious happening to her made my throat close up and my eyes sting.

Don't cry.

My tires screeched against the blacktop as I pulled into the hospital parking lot. I yanked the wheel, turning into the first parking space I found, and broke into a full sprint for the main entrance. As I rushed through the automatic doors, I froze, frantically looking left to right as I tried to figure out where to go.

"May I help you?" A woman's voice caught my attention. I turned to my right and saw her smiling at me from behind a desk.

"Yeah, I'm looking for the emergency room—I think," I stuttered, realizing that I wasn't even sure where Gam would be. "Well, maybe not. I'm trying to find my grandma. Gam—uh, Elizabeth—Finkle."

"Just one second. Let me see what I can find out," she said with an annoying grin as she typed into her computer. She squinted and leaned in closer to the screen. "Okay, here she is. Looks like she's still in the ER. You're going to head through those doors over there—"

"Viper!" I spun around as Michelle hurried toward me. "I called you back, but you didn't answer. Follow me."

I gave the woman at the desk a quick wave and caught up to Michelle. "What's going on?"

Her tiny legs were moving so fast I practically had to jog to keep up with her. She let out a heavy sigh. "I got a call from Regina a little bit ago—"

"Regina?" I interrupted.

"Gam's friend."

"Oh, right."

"Don't yell. Promise?"

"What?"

"You have to promise not to yell."

"Michelle, are you kidding me right now?"

"Fine." With a heavy sigh she pushed another set of doors open and turned right, following the red arrow toward the emergency room. "Regina said they went out on the Segways after we left and there was an accident. Gam went over a curb that was too big and fell off."

"Holy shit. Is she okay?"

Michelle shook her head slightly. "She's not critical, but she's not great. They're doing X-rays right now. They think she might have broken her hip and possibly her femur. She's in a *lot* of pain."

We got to the crowded waiting room and walked to two open seats in the far corner. A couple of people stared at me, but I avoided eye contact with everyone except Michelle.

If anyone has the nerve to ask for an autograph right now, they'll be needing a room of their own.

"Are you okay?" Michelle asked in a shaky voice as we sat down. She rested her hand on my knee and my heart rate instantly slowed a little.

"I don't know what I am. I'm glad it wasn't more serious, but a broken hip isn't a small thing either. She's going to need round-the-clock care and nurses and meds and I'm just at the beginning of a new season—"

"Hey," she interrupted softly, giving me a tiny smile. "Calm down. Take a breath. I'm here. I can handle whatever you need me to handle, okay?"

I studied her thoughtful blue eyes. The same thoughtful eyes that had saved me so many times when it really should have been *me* saving *her*. "I don't know what I would do without you, you know that?" I put my hand on top of hers and squeezed.

"I know exactly how you feel because I feel the same about you." She closed her eyes and leaned into me, resting her forehead against my cheek.

I closed my eyes against her skin. "Where are the kids?"

"Taylor is with them. They're fine."

Before we could say anything else, a woman's loud voice called out, "I need the family of Elizabeth Finkle!"

We both stood quickly. "That's us," Michelle said, gripping my hand tightly.

"Come with me, please." The nurse turned and pushed open a set of double doors, leading us down the hall.

As we followed her through the sterile-smelling halls of the hospital, she started quickly filling us in on Gam's condition . . . but her words clogged my brain and my mind drifted. I found myself staring at her shoes. There was nothing special about the pink and black gym shoes, but I couldn't look away.

"Viper!"

The sound of my name broke through my thoughts. Michelle was standing in the doorway of a hospital room, staring at me with her eyebrows pulled down low. "What's going on? Are you okay?"

"Yeah." I nodded. "I'm fine."

She eyed me skeptically and waved for me to follow her.

The instant I stepped into the room, the familiar hum of machines made every muscle in my body tense up at the same time. I hadn't been in a hospital room since I said good-bye to Mike, and hearing those same beeps, smelling those same smells, and seeing those same blue curtains made my stomach churn violently.

I stopped in the doorway and ran my hand through my hair, desperately trying to slow my breathing. "Uh . . ."

Michelle took a step closer to me, wrapping her arm around my waist. "What is going *on?*"

"Nothing," I lied. "I'm fine."

The sound of metal scraping on metal filled the room as the nurse pulled the curtain back. Gam was lying in the hospital bed, half sitting up, half lying down. When she saw us, her face lit up in a big, goofy grin.

She pointed at us. "Hey! I know them!"

The nurse shot Michelle and me a look. "The pain that comes with a broken hip is excruciating, so your grandmother will be on heavy pain meds until surgery—"

"That's my cute grandson," Gam cut her off. "His name is Lawrence, but that name is pretty stupid, so his friends call him Viper, which is even stupider because he's not a snake. I'm gonna call him Bob instead."

The nurse looked from Gam to me and rolled her eyes. "*Really* heavy pain meds. I'll be back in a few minutes." She stepped past us, out into the hallway, and disappeared.

"Come here, Bobby!" Gam raised her arms and tried to sit up.

"No, no. Don't move. We don't want to make anything worse, okay?" I said sternly as I walked over and gave her a hug.

"I don't think it can get any worse," she said, shaking her head. "I just hope the horse is okay."

Michelle narrowed her eyes. "What horse?"

"The one I was riding!"

"Gam, you weren't riding a horse," I answered with a laugh.

"Oh yes I was," Gam insisted. "A big brown one named Cinnamon. We were galloping through the neighborhood, looking for Phil, and she got spooked by a little bastard squirrel and bucked me right off. And now here I am. Ta-da!"

I gaped at her in amazement before looking at Michelle, who was having trouble keeping a straight face at that point.

"You were on a Segway, not a horse," I corrected her.

"No, it was a horse," she said adamantly.

"I promise it wasn't."

Her eyes grew wide as they darted around the room. "Well then who the hell was I feeding carrots to?"

Chapter
5

Michelle

ONCE GAM WAS DONE WITH stories of imaginary horses and instigating squirrels, she passed out until it was time for surgery. Thankfully her surgery went great and she came out on the other side with four shiny new screws in her hip. Her surgeon, Dr. Chams, met with Viper and me in the waiting room and said that if Gam's health hadn't been as great as it was, that fall could have easily had a very different outcome . . . a grim one. When he said that, I could practically feel all of the air leave Viper's lungs.

We were able to see her for a few minutes after surgery but she was pretty out of it, so Dr. Chams suggested we go home and get a good night's sleep. We were both so exhausted that it didn't take much persuading.

We walked through the door and dragged ourselves up the stairs, straight to my bedroom. When Regina called me earlier that day, Taylor, Mike's youngest sister happened to be over playing with Matthew and Maura. She wasted no time offering to sit with the kids while I rushed to the hospital. Then when we found out that Gam was going to need surgery, and since we were most likely going to be home late, she packed up bags for them and took them to her house for a sleepover. While I wasn't used to being away from my babies and missed them terribly, the thought of having several hours of uninterrupted sleep, snuggled up next to Viper, made me giddy.

He collapsed on top of the covers and let out a heavy sigh.

"You okay?" I asked, immediately regretting my question. "Of course you're not. That was stupid. Is there anything I can do for you?"

Without saying anything, he waved me over.

I set my purse down and lay next to him on the bed, curling up in the nook of his arm.

"That's perfect," he said.

I rolled onto my side and rested my hand on his chest. "What are you gonna do about tomorrow?"

"I already left a message for Coach Collins to call me. He's gonna be pissed that I'm missing practice, but I think he'll understand. I'll be at the game on Tuesday. I just need to make sure she's okay tomorrow."

I nodded. "She was pretty funny today, with the horse thing."

"She *was*," he agreed, "but she scared the hell out of me, Michelle. I don't ever want her riding that thing again."

"I know—"

"No. I'm serious," he cut me off. "She's the only *real* family I have, and I can't stand the thought of anything happening to her."

Ouch. That stung.

"I get it," I responded softly, trying hard to ignore the lump that had formed in my throat. "Let's go to bed so we can head to the hospital early, okay?"

A minute went by and he didn't respond.

I lifted my head to look at him just as a single tear fell from the corner of his eye and dripped down toward his temple. Scurrying to sit up, I held my arms out. "Hey, come here."

"No. I'm fine," he said gruffly, pushing my arms away as he stood. "I'm gonna take a quick shower. Go ahead to sleep, I'll be out in a minute."

"Viper, wait—" I called after him.

"Just stop!" he snapped angrily without turning around.

My heart sank as he walked to the bathroom and slammed the door. The day must have been horrible for him, and I knew that, but I wished more than anything he would let me in. Even just a little.

But . . . I wasn't surprised.

That was Viper.

He was really good at expressing his feelings when they were good, but when they were bad . . . not so much. He was a runner. An ostrich. He buried his head in the sand and pretended the bad things weren't happening until they eventually just went away. I'd seen it more than once over the last year, but I kept hoping that if I stayed by his side and never wavered, it would get better.

The shower turned on as I walked over to the closet and changed into pajamas. Without saying any more to him, I quickly brushed my teeth and hopped into bed, fighting back my own tears. Just as I started to drift to sleep, I felt the mattress dip. He scooted right up behind me and wrapped his big arm around my waist, pulling me tight against him.

His chest rose and fell with a deep, troubled breath. "I'm sorry about before," he said against the back of my neck, sending shivers down my whole body.

"It's okay," I lied. It wasn't okay—not even a little okay—but I just wanted him to be normal again. "I'm kinda used to it at this point," I added, sounding snottier than I'd meant to.

He loosened his grip on me and lifted his head. "What's that supposed to mean?" he asked defensively.

"Nothing." I grabbed his hand and pulled his arm back down around me. "I don't want to fight tonight, okay? It's been a long day for me, too. Let's just go to sleep and talk more in the morning."

He didn't argue back, but he didn't hug me the same way either. I instantly regretted opening my mouth. It was the wrong time. I knew it was the wrong time, but I did it anyway.

I took a deep breath and laced my fingers with his, thankful that he didn't pull his hand back.

The next morning, I woke up with the night before not far from my mind. Viper, on the other hand, didn't remember anything.

"Morning, sexy," he said cheerfully, slapping my butt as he passed me at the bathroom sink. "I didn't even hear you get out of bed."

I shrugged. "You looked comfy so I snuck out and hopped in the shower early."

"Should've woke me. I would have joined you."

I raised an eyebrow at him in the mirror.

"Ya know, to conserve water. Gotta save the planet and shit."

Pinching my lips together, I tried to stifle a laugh.

"So what's the plan for today? Hospital, kids, dinner, then sex?"

As annoyed as he made me at times, I couldn't stay that way for very long . . . especially when he gave me his signature shit-eating grin. I smiled back at him and rolled my eyes. "Sounds like a plan."

Gam was awake by the time we got to the hospital, and the scowl on her face showed us exactly how she was feeling.

"What's wrong?" I asked as we were barely through the door.

She slid her eyes over to us but didn't change her expression. "I want to go home," she complained.

"Gam, you just had major surgery last night. It's going to be a couple days," Viper said as he walked around the other side of her bed.

"Then I'm going to starve to death. These people don't know how to cook." She waved toward her breakfast tray that was sitting off to the side. "Runny eggs and rubber bacon. Mmmm, delicious." The tone of her voice was dunked in sarcasm and covered in scorn.

Viper let out a chuckle as he bent down and set a soft kiss on her forehead. "Good to see you haven't lost your sense of humor though, huh?"

"Are you in any pain?" I asked as I walked over and wrapped my arms around her shoulder.

"No." She shook her head. "I can't really feel anything at all . . . except my stomach growling."

I sat down on the bed next to her and held her hand. "Want me to get you something?"

"Yeah—out of here," she barked back.

Viper stood and walked around the bed, brushing past me. "I'll be right back."

"Where's he going?" Gam asked.

I followed him to the door, then shrugged and looked back at her. "No idea. Okay, all joking aside. How do you feel?"

"Like shit." She sighed. "I hate this. I like to do things by myself and not depend on other people. This isn't gonna work for me."

"I know," I said quietly, trying to calm her irritation. "This is definitely going to be a change for a while, but you're strong and you'll battle back. I know you will. And I'll be there to help you every step of the way."

She tilted her head to the side and pursed her lips. "You have those two sweet kids to take care of and a household to run. The last thing you need to be worrying about is taking care of your boyfriend's grumpy old grandma."

I squeezed her hand again. "I happen to love my boyfriend's grumpy old grandma. And it would be my pleasure to help you out."

"We'll see about that," she answered, her red-rimmed eyes dropping to her lap. In that moment, I wasn't sure if she was upset about her situation, or if she was sentimental because of what I'd said and just avoiding her feelings like her grandson.

I stretched my neck to sneak a peek at the paper on her tray. "What's this?" I asked, picking it up.

"Ugh," she groaned, waving her hand dismissively. "That's the menu they gave me."

I raised my eyebrows and looked at her. "Oooh, really? It looks good!"

"That's the key word. It *looks* great, but it tastes more like they have Tweedledee and Tweedledum cooking the food down there."

Shaking my head, I let out a small laugh. "I have a feeling nothing would be good enough for you when it comes to food though. If there's one area you're the master of, it's that."

"Damn right it is." She nodded proudly. "In my opinion, serving bland food should be a crime punishable by law."

"Oh, Gam. You would *hate* my kitchen."

"I thought Viper was teaching you how to cook?"

"He was. He did . . . kinda. Then we started dating, and now he just cooks for us," I said with a quick laugh. Gam was important to me, and not just because she was my boyfriend's grandmother, but because over the last year I'd grown to love her . . . a lot. She wasn't just his family, she was my family, too.

"Maybe he wasn't the right teacher for you."

"What do you mean?"

"Sometimes you need to let the master teach you in order to *really* learn."

"You?"

"Yes, me!"

My eyes traveled down her body and back up to her face. "How would that work now?"

"My mouth still works, doesn't it? I'll sit at the kitchen table with my whiskey and tell you what to do." She shrugged. "Sounds like a perfect plan to me."

"What sounds like a perfect plan?" Viper bellowed as he walked back into the room, making us both jump. "You two conspiring to take over the world?"

"Maybe," I said in a facetious tone.

"What's that?" Gam asked as he set a white box on the end of her bed.

"I ran to the bakery at the corner. It's a blueberry muffin, a piece of lemon poppy seed bread, a cinnamon scone, and an éclair—your favorite."

Gam's mouth dropped open as she stared up at Viper in amazement. "You went and got this for me?"

"Of course I did." He smiled back as he handed her the box.

She quickly lifted the lid and peered down into it. "There's a bear claw, too."

"That's Michelle's. They're *her* favorite." He shot me a quick wink.

"And three key lime tarts?"

"Mine. I'm starving. Don't judge." He snatched the box back from her and started pulling the pastries out, setting them on the tray one by one.

"This is really sweet of you," Gam said, watching him closely.

"What can I say?" He held his hands out as a big grin spread across his lips. "I'm an amazing human being."

"We'll see how amazing you are." Gam raised an eyebrow at him.

He dropped his arms and stared at her blankly. "What's that supposed to mean?"

She covered her mouth and let out a small laugh. "It means what am I getting for lunch and dinner?"

Chapter
6

Viper

GAM WAS UP AND WALKING that day and back home a week later. Though she complained about the food every chance she got, she handled the rest of the week like a champ. But boy was she glad to be home.

Unfortunately for me, the day she came home was also the same day I had to head out of town for a quick three-day road trip with the Wild. Michelle assured me she had everything with Gam under control. What I didn't tell her is that I had Andy Shaw, my friend and agent, ask his assistant look into hiring a full-time nurse to help Gam out around the house. I didn't tell Michelle, or Gam, because I knew they would both argue, but it was the right thing to do.

Michelle had the kids to take care of already and spending most of her days and some nights at Gam's just wouldn't work. And if I told Gam, she would just say that she was fine and possibly end up hurting herself again. That was a risk I wasn't taking. Period.

"Hey!" Brody smacked me in the hand. "Why are you so

serious today? What's up?"

"I'm not serious," I said, pinching the bridge of my nose and squeezing my eyes shut. "I just have a headache."

"No shit. I would too after all you've been through."

"It's been a long week. Everything hurts . . . my back, my head." I arched my back off the airplane seat, trying to get some relief for my tense muscles. "I need a vacation."

"Yeah, well . . . the season just started, so you're gonna have to wait eight months for that. Hopefully nine."

"Nine would be nice, wouldn't it?" I sighed. If we were still playing in nine months, that meant the Wild made the play-offs. Not only did I want to still be playing in nine months, I wanted to be winning. We all did. We'd been working our asses off, and we deserved it.

"It would," he said, probably thinking the same thing I was about play-offs. "And then—I'm serious—you drop those kids off with us and take your girl on a great vacation. A *real* vacation. None of those rent-by-the-hour shady ass places that comes with its own semen-filled pool right there in your room."

My shoulders shook as I laughed. "I haven't been to one of those in a long time, but oh the memories."

"Disgusting."

"Don't knock it till you try it," I joked, looking over at him just as his lips curled and his eyes widened.

"No thanks. Those STDs can stay right where they are." His eyes slid over to me. "And you better not even be thinking about taking her there. She deserves better, especially for putting up with your dumb ass on a daily basis."

"She really does, doesn't she?"

Without lifting it off the seat, he turned his head to face me. "Between you and me, I think she deserves a ring."

"A ring?" I sputtered, scowling at him.

"Yes, a ring," he repeated. "A big, fat diamond one."

I shook my head, crossing my arms over my chest. "You've

clearly lost your fucking mind. I'm not buying anyone a ring—ever."

"Oh come on," he said, rolling his eyes dramatically. "You guys have been together for a year now. It's seriously never crossed your mind?"

"It seriously never has," I responded with a shrug.

"Why not? It's the natural progression of things."

"Maybe it was natural progression for *you*. For me, it's a death sentence."

"You have things backwards, my poor, stupid little friend. Let me teach you." He turned in his seat and leaned in close. "You don't date a woman who has two kids for a year if you never plan on marrying her. *That* is a death sentence."

"No, it's not," I scoffed. "Michelle is awesome. She feels the same way I do."

"She does?"

"Yeah."

"You've talked about it?"

"No, because she's not a needy leech like most women."

Brody turned back in his seat, facing forward again. "It was nice knowing you," he said dryly.

"Shut up," I nudged him hard with my elbow. "I do agree on one thing though, she *is* pretty fucking awesome . . . and supportive of everything. For example,"—I mentally put on my salesman hat—"she thinks this bar idea is amazing."

"Oh my God." He stared straight ahead at the back of the seat in front of him. "Don't. Just don't. I really don't want to be known as the crazy hockey player who snapped and threw his best friend out of a plane, but if it comes to that . . ."

"You promised you'd think about it."

"I did think about it."

"And?"

"And . . . now's not the time or the place." He raised a finger and pointed to the row in front of us where Louie and a couple other guys sat.

I waved my hand. "Fuck them. Come on, tell me. What do you think? Honestly?"

"Honestly?" He raised his eyebrows and then let out a heavy sigh. "It sounds like a lot of work and a lot of money."

Fuck.

I nodded slowly and sat back against my seat feeling defeated. While I understood his apprehension, I was still disappointed with the answer. I'd thought about that bar at least a hundred times over the last week or so, and every time I let myself get a little more excited.

"But," he continued, and my head snapped toward him, "it also sounds like a lot of fun *if* we can make it work."

"Wait. Seriously. You're in?"

"Here's what I'll commit to . . . we're going to take this in stages. Right now, I'll agree to talk to people and do some research on start-up costs and shit. If I like what I hear, we'll move to the next stage and I'll agree to scout places with you. If I like what I see, I'll agree to move to the stage after that. Got it?"

"Got it," I agreed with a big, stupid smile on my face. "But I have one question."

"Okay?"

"Is there a stage when we get to give each other a celebratory hug and hold on for an awkwardly long time?"

He closed his eyes for a quick second and shook his head. "Yes. It's right before the stage where I hack up your body into little pieces and bury it somewhere."

Once the plane landed and we got to the hotel, I called Michelle just to check in. The phone rang a couple of times before someone picked up.

"Hello?" a tiny voice said on the other end.

"Hello? Who is this?" I asked, knowing exactly who it was.

"This is Matthew. Hi, Viper."

"Hi, buddy. How are ya?"

"Good. Guess what?" The excitement in his voice practically came through the phone and punched me in the cheek.

"What?"

"I was riding my bike outside today and I totally wiped out. I had to go to the hospital and everything!"

"Wait. You did?" I wasn't too concerned because he sounded happy about it, but a trip to the hospital isn't what I was expecting to hear from him.

"Yep. I had a big cut on my knee that wouldn't stop bleeding, so Mom took me."

"And what happened?"

"Well," he said, his tone turning gloomy, "they used glue to close it up."

"Okaaaaay. Is that a bad thing? You sound sad."

"Kinda. I really wanted stitches. I've never had stitches before."

I let out a hearty laugh that bounced off the walls of my empty hotel room. "Buddy, you're young. You still have plenty of time for stitches. Trust me."

He let out a small sigh. "I hope so."

"Is Mom close to you?"

"Yeah, she's sitting right here shaking her head. Bye. I love you."

"I love you, too, kiddo," I said, smiling to myself. "I'll call later."

The line was quiet for a minute and then I heard a heavy sigh. "That kid is something else, isn't he?"

"He really is," I said through a chuckle.

"I've never heard of a kid being mad because he *didn't* have to get stitches before."

I lay down on the bed and switched ears. "Oh, I totally get it."

"You do?"

"Hell yeah. Boys love battle wounds. As much as it hurt, he was probably excited to go to school Monday and show his friends his stitches."

"But he still has the cut. Isn't that good enough?"

"No way. Stitches look tougher."

Another sigh. "I don't think I'll ever understand boys."

"Trust me, we feel the same way about you girls," I teased.

"So, how was your flight?"

"Good. I mean, Brody wouldn't keep his hands off me, but other than that it was fine."

She let out a quick giggle. "Ya know, if you weren't such a hornball all the time at home, I might seriously wonder about the two of you."

"We did talk about the bar thing though."

"Oh, yeah?"

"Yeah, he's willing to at least check some things out with me."

"I talked to Kacie for a while this morning and she said that he'd been thinking a lot about it. I'm happy for you."

"Did she say anything else?"

"Not really. We laughed about how different the two of you are. You want the bar to have a super fun place to hang out, but Brody is looking at it as an investment opportunity for when he's not playing hockey anymore."

I waved my arm in the air. "Psh, that's because Brody isn't planning on playing forever like me."

"You're gonna play hockey forever?"

"Hell yeah. I'm immortal."

"Did you inhale plane fumes or something?"

"I'm not kidding," I defended.

"Viper, you're almost thirty and not getting any younger."

"Yeah, and I'm gonna be the oldest guy to ever have an NHL contract, you watch."

She let out a small chuckle and I wasn't sure if she was laughing with me or at me. "I hope you're right," she finally said. "I can't imagine being any prouder of you than I already am, but that sure would bump it up a notch."

"Thanks, babe." I let out a heavy sigh. "I sure miss you guys already."

"We miss you, too," she said in a soft, sexy tone. "But thankfully this is only a quick road trip and you'll be back home soon."

"I can't wait. I hate being away, especially now with Gam just coming home and stuff."

"She's totally fine. We were there with her all day, except for our little detour to the ER. We helped her take a bath, she read a few books to Maura, and she taught me how to make skirt steak. Then she wanted to take a little nap, so we came home to pack overnight bags."

I'd known Michelle was an amazing person for a long time and she'd been *my* amazing person for a year, but she continued to surprise me with the way she cared for me, and now Gam. I was overcome with gratitude and not sure how to process it all.

"Are you still there?" she asked a couple seconds later.

"Yeah, sorry." I cleared my throat. "It's just that . . ." My voice trailed off and I took a deep breath.

"Viper, what is it?" she asked softly.

"It's just that I love skirt steak so much, and knowing that you know how to make it now is overwhelming me."

"Oh, you're such an asshole!"

"What?" I exclaimed defensively. "I really *do* love skirt steak."

Chapter
7

Michelle

WHILE I HATED VIPER BEING away, thankfully it was an easy transition. I was already used to that lifestyle from being married to Mike. I handled it all in stride. The kids, the house, life in general. It all balanced out. Now I had the added task of helping Gam out, and while it wasn't *that* big of a deal, it worried me a little. She lived about half an hour away from my house, so it wasn't that easy to just zip over if she needed me. Most days we went over in the morning and hung there until bedtime. A couple nights we'd even slept over just in case she needed anything during the night.

I spent the morning at her house and then Regina came over to visit with her daughter and grandkids. Feeling guilty that I had to be there so much, Gam told me to head on home since she had people there. I probably should have argued more, but I was happy to have a day to do some other things. I gave her a kiss good-bye and told her to call the minute Regina left.

Just as I was loading the kids in the car, my phone beeped, letting me know a text had come in. I clicked Maura's buckle shut and grabbed my phone from my back pocket. It was a text from Brody's wife, Kacie.

K: Hey! What are you guys doing today? I know you're busy with Gam and stuff, but I was wondering if you wanted to come up here and swim while we still have a few nice days left?

I let out a heavy sigh and looked back and forth from Matthew to Maura. I had a million things to do at the house, but those two had been such troopers about going with me to Gam's every day, they deserved a little fun. Plus, the thought of having another mom to chat with for a while sounded more exciting than a bubble bath and a glass of wine.

"Hey, you want to go to Kacie's and swim with the kids?" I asked Matthew.

His arms shot straight up in the air. "Yay!"

I mumbled under my breath as I grabbed the bag behind the passenger's seat. "Wait. Let me just see if I have—Bingo!" I pulled their wadded-up bathing suits from the bag and held them up. "Guess it pays to leave your junk in the car for a couple weeks, huh, Matthew?"

He grinned and nodded.

I sent Kacie a quick text.

You have no idea how bad I needed this today. On our way!

Kacie and Brody lived about an hour away, but the kids were ready for a nap anyway, so the timing was actually perfect. They slept in the car while I drove along, bopping my head to the soft music.

We pulled onto the long dirt road that led to Kacie's house and drove slowly through the trees until her house came into view. Lucy, Piper, and Emma were running around the front yard and Kacie was sitting on the big porch swing with Grace in her arms. She stood and waved as we pulled up.

"I still can't believe you live here," I called as I unbuckled Maura from her car seat. Brody and Kacie had built their dream house just a hundred yards or so away from her mom's place, The Cranberry Inn, and it was beautiful. An enormous, white country-style house with the most massive front porch I'd ever seen. In the back was a huge deck that looked out over their large yard that butted right up to the lake. It was a dream.

"Sometimes I can't believe it either," Kacie said as she came down the steps to meet me. "Hi, sweet girl." She leaned over and planted a kiss on the side of Maura's sweaty head before wrapping her arms around me, too. "How *are* you? Brody told me about all of the craziness with Gam."

"I'm good." I shrugged with a smile when she pulled back. "It does add a lot of work to my day, but nothing I can't handle."

"Come on in. I made lunch," she said cheerfully, waving us to follow her.

"Matthew, I'm gonna go inside with Kacie. You stay by Lucy and Piper, got it?" I asked him in that way that moms do, where it's more telling than asking.

"Yes, Momma," he answered quickly before turning around and chasing Emma across the yard.

"Lucy and Piper?" Kacie called out.

"We got him, Mom," Piper called back.

We climbed the wooden steps of her porch and went through the door. Kacie's house was bright and open, yet warm and inviting. The strong smell of cinnamon invaded my nose and I closed my eyes and inhaled deeply. "That smells *so* good. Are you baking?"

"No way," Kacie shook her head with a laugh. "It's a candle. I hardly cook at all when Brody's out of town. I'm the worst."

"I hardly cook when Viper's *in* town. *I'm* the worst."

We both laughed as I sat down at the kitchen table, letting

Maura loose on the floor. She immediately waddled over and plopped down next to their black lab named Diesel, who was sleeping quietly. "She's okay over there, right?"

"Oh yeah," Kacie nodded. "He's the most gentle creature you've ever met in your whole life. If living with these four crazy girls hasn't made him snap yet, I'm pretty sure nothing will. Plus, he's in his happy place."

Without saying anything, I tilted my head to the side, not sure what she meant.

"He's lying on top of the air conditioning vent," she added.

I let out another quick laugh as she turned and headed up the stairs. "I'm gonna lay her down real quick. Be right back."

The floor above my head creaked as she walked across the second floor to Grace's bedroom.

"Momma. Goggie!" Maura said excitedly.

"I know." I grinned at her. "Is that a doggie?"

Her little head bobbed up and down as she looked back at Diesel, who'd opened one eye and was watching her cautiously.

A couple seconds later, Kacie came back down the stairs with the baby monitor in her hand. "Okay," she said with a big sigh. "What can I get you to drink? I have water, sweet tea, pink lemonade . . ."

"I would love a glass of pink lemonade, actually."

"Coming right up." She took a pretty aqua glass out of the cabinet and set it on the island. "Okay, so let's get to it. How are you really?"

"I'm good," I answered.

She stopped pouring and glanced at me skeptically, raising one eyebrow.

"I promise I am," I reassured through a chuckle. "I mean, I'm not sure what day it is, but I'm good."

"You have a lot going on right now, Michelle."

"I know, but I love Gam so I don't mind."

She set the glass down in front of me. "I know that, but just because you love someone doesn't mean taking care of them isn't exhausting."

"I'm definitely exhausted, I'll give you that. But it's nothing I can't handle yet." I didn't really want to talk about Gam and my exhaustion any more. It just made me more tired. "So what's going on over here with you guys? We didn't get to talk long the other day."

"Not much." She shrugged her shoulders as she sat down across from me with her own glass of pink lemonade. "Just settling back into our routine of having Brody gone half the time. That's always an adjustment."

"I'll drink to that." I raised my glass before taking a big gulp of the tart juice.

"And every year I feel bad. As summer ends, he gets so excited to start a new season, but for me it's bittersweet because that means he's going to be gone . . . a lot."

"Same here." I nodded.

"And lately he's been hinting to maybe wanting another baby, and honestly . . ." Her voice trailed off as she shook her head, staring outside.

"Are you really thinking about it?"

"I don't know. Part of me would love to try and see if I can give him a son, but then I think maybe we're just meant to have four girls." She looked back at me and stuck her bottom lip out dramatically. "My uterus is tired."

I tossed my head back and let out a loud laugh. "I can only imagine."

"What about you guys?"

My laugh stopped like someone turned it off with a light switch. "What about us?"

"I don't know. Marriage, mini-Vipers . . . any of that on the horizon?"

I swallowed hard, wanting so desperately to be honest with

49

Kacie about how I *really* felt about all of that, but decided it wasn't the right time. "I have no idea. He's not exactly the marrying type, ya know?"

"He wasn't until he met you."

"I'm still not sure, but who knows. I guess stranger things have happened, right?"

"Stranger things *have* happened. Like me catching Brody loading the dishwasher last week. If that can happen without me even asking, I'm pretty sure nothing is impossible."

I let out a quick laugh. "Hey, I meant to ask you. Have you talked to Darla lately?"

"I have, actually. Her and Neil are settled into their apartment and she says it's perfect. She starts her new job next week."

"Good," I said with a nod. "I miss her."

"Me, too." Kacie's mouth turned down.

We spent the rest of the afternoon talking about everything and nothing while the kids splashed in the lake and built sandcastles on the shore. Those couple of hours with her felt like my soul had plugged itself in for a recharge of epic proportions. I didn't even know I needed that afternoon, but it was completely refreshing.

As the sun was starting to set, I was sad to start packing up the kids to leave.

"You know"—Kacie craned her neck to see the clock—"their game starts in about half an hour. Wanna give the kids a bath, throw them in some pajamas, and they can play while we watch the game? Maybe order pizza and sleep here?"

My need to go home and catch up on laundry was quickly trumped by my need to have a sleepover at Kacie's house with all the kids.

"That sounds awesome, just let me check in with Gam. If she needs me, I'm gonna have to go." I fished my phone out of my bag. "I'll be right back."

I stepped into the other room and dialed Gam's number.

The phone rang . . . and rang . . . and rang. My heart started pounding faster as horrific scenarios zipped around my brain.

Finally she answered. "Hello?" she said through a laugh.

"What are you doing?" The words rushed out of my mouth in a scolding tone.

"Are you okay? Why do you sound like that?"

I took a shaky breath. "I was just scared because you took so long to answer."

"Michelle, I just had hip surgery. I'm not quite marathon ready just yet," she answered sarcastically.

"I know *that*. Anyway, what are you guys doing? Do you need anything?"

"Nope. We had lunch and Regina's daughter brought some of her old home movies over, so we watched those and have pretty much been laughing all afternoon. I think we're gonna have dinner and as soon as they leave, I'm hitting the sack. I'm beat."

"Are you sure you don't need anything tonight?"

"I'm fine. What are you up to?"

"I actually drove out to Kacie's. The kids have been swimming in the lake, building sandcastles, and eating more junk food than I thought humanly possible."

"I bet they're having a blast. You're a good mom, Michelle."

Her words were the cherry on top of my afternoon sundae. Having no family of my own was as tough for me as it was for Viper, which was why I clung so tightly to Gam. Every mom thinks at some point in their children's life that they're screwing them up royally and doing every single thing wrong, but having someone there to give you a hug and tell you that you're doing a good job makes all that self doubt just disappear.

"Thanks, Gam. That means a lot . . . especially today."

"Anytime you need to hear it, honey, you just call me."

We talked for another minute and I told her I'd call first thing in the morning.

I walked back into the kitchen and Kacie had her cell phone pinched between her ear and her shoulder, with Grace and Maura in each arm, balancing on her hips.

"Okay, thanks," she said into the phone before strategically dropping it into her open hand. Her eyes met with mine. "Sorry, I was snooping and could tell you're staying and I'm starving so I ordered dinner."

"With two children in your hands? You really *are* Supermom."

"I had twins, remember?" she laughed.

Before the pizza came, we quickly bathed the lake water, sand, and sunscreen off the kids and put them in clean jammies. Again, not cleaning out my car came in handy because I still had a clean pair for both kids in my overnight bag for Gam's. The doorbell rang just as I finished brushing Maura's curly blond hair. We set the kids down around the table and starting cutting pizza and passing out plates like we were feeding hungry animals at the zoo. Once the kids all had pizza, apple slices, and milk in front of them, Kacie and I finally made our own plates.

"Ooooh, the game is starting!" Kacie mumbled through a mouthful of pizza. She grabbed the remote off the coffee table and found the game on TV. They were zoomed in on Brody's face as he took a few chugs of water from the Gatorade water bottle on his net. Kacie beamed with pride as the announcers talked about how he'd had three shutouts in a row and the team was looking really good early on in the season.

"Maybe this is our year?" she said with a shrug.

"That would be awesome, wouldn't it?" I added.

Lucy, Piper, Matthew, and Emma ate fast and scampered off to play Ping-Pong in the basement while Grace and Maura toddled around the family room, chewing on everything they could get their hands on.

"Want a glass of wine?" Kacie asked as she put the last of the pizza in the fridge.

"Um . . . nah. I've been fighting a headache all day and that would just make it worse."

Kacie nodded and filled her wine glass with Riesling. She grabbed a water bottle from the fridge and balanced the drinks carefully in her hands as she stepped over our makeshift baby gate of pillows and an ottoman.

"Thanks." I took the bottle from her, ready to relax and watch our boys play. The second period was just starting and the Wild were already up 2—0.

I didn't think the day could get much better.

Kacie plopped down roughly, giggling when she spilled a little wine down the front of her shirt. "Oh well." She shrugged and took another sip.

"Thanks for tonight, Kacie. You have no idea how much I needed this."

"Oh my goodness, don't mention it. It's been so fun. I think this should be our new road trip tradition."

"I'll drink to that," I said as I held my water up in the air. She grinned and immediately leaned over, touching her glass with my bottle.

We relaxed back into her oversized couch happily, while our babies played and boys kicked ass on TV.

Just before the second period was ending, there a breakaway play and Viper was all alone, dribbling the puck down the ice toward the goal. Kacie and I both sat forward in our seats, praying for another Wild goal. He skated along the boards, nearing the goalie, when out of nowhere Ricky Young from the St. Louis Blues barreled into him, sending him crashing into the glass.

"Holy shit!" I jumped up and covered my mouth.

Hard hits were nothing new in hockey, but that one was brutal, and it was obvious by the way his body flew that Viper had no idea Ricky was even near him.

"He's okay. He's totally fine," Kacie tried to reassure me, taking a step closer as she put her hand on my arm.

But . . . he wasn't okay.

Within a couple of seconds, the station cut to a commercial break and fear exploded inside of my chest.

Not again. Oh God, please not again.

Chapter
8

Viper

"FUCK!" I ROLLED AROUND ON the ice, trying desperately to give my knee some relief. Any relief. The burning sensation was overwhelming. Within seconds, half of the team and the ref stood over me.

"You okay?" a bunch of them called out and a few knelt down next to me, but I was in too much pain to answer.

Within seconds Pete, our trainer, was by my side.

"What's going on? Talk to me."

"My knee. I hit the board and felt a huge fucking pop," I growled.

"Your knee actually hit the wall?"

"No," I shook my head. "My leg was straight but that leg went straight into the wall."

His eyes widened and he quickly wiped sweat from his brow. "Okay, we have to get you off the ice."

The look on his face ignited a fear inside of me that spread like wildfire through my body, every nerve prickling with anxiety.

"Okay," I answered gruffly, trying to stand.

"Wait, wait. Just wait. I need you to move *slow* and not put *any* pressure on that leg. Got it? No pressure."

I nodded, grimacing as I tried to stand. Once I was upright, the audience started clapping. Ignoring the pain the best I could, I took off one of my gloves and gave them a thumbs-up. The clapping grew into a thunderous roar that shook the whole building. Choked up that they cared more about me than the away jersey I was wearing, I gave another wave as I slung one arm around Pete's neck and the other around my teammate Rex Craig's. They skated slowly off the ice and I was careful to keep my right leg just above the ice, practically dangling along behind me. As I got to the doorway of the bench, one of Pete's men stood waiting for me with a wheelchair.

"Seriously?" I groaned toward Pete.

"Shut up and sit," he answered without looking back at me.

With Pete's hand tucked under my armpit, I carefully turned and sat in the wheelchair. He quickly unlocked the wheels and hurried back to the small medical clinic within the arena. Dr. Houston, the St. Louis Blues team doctor, was already in the room waiting for us.

"Do you need help lifting him?" he asked as Pete wheeled me over to the exam table.

"No, I'm fine," I answered before Pete could.

Pete's eyes slid from the doc's to mine and back again. "This one is a live wire. I can handle him. If you don't mind, I'm also going to be the one to examine him."

"Of course," he said with a nod as he took a step back and folded his hands in front of him. "I do have to stay in the room because of liability, but do your thing."

The next several minutes consisted of Pete doing an assessment of my knee, asking things like "Does this hurt here? What about here? How about now?" as he touched different places. Some of the movements made me cringe in pain. Others didn't hurt at all. His eyes darted up and down my leg as his jaw clenched.

"What are you thinking?" I asked, not really sure I wanted to hear the answer.

His nostrils flared as he inhaled slowly, still looking at my leg. "It's gonna swell fast. I wanna get an X-ray. Now."

The enormous knot in my stomach hurt way worse than my knee, and the way Pete was avoiding eye contact with me didn't help. He took his phone out of his pocket and stepped into the hallway.

Lying on that table, staring up at the fluorescent lights in the ceiling, I took a slow, deep breath in through my nose and did something I hadn't done in a *very* long time.

I prayed.

Hello, up there. It's me, Viper . . . Lawrence . . . whatever. You and I haven't always seen eye to eye, and I know I've done a lot of shi—stuff that has probably made you roll your eyes, but I'm desperate here. If you help me out, I promise to quit sending pictures of my junk to Michelle and no more Icy Hot in Brody's underwear. In all seriousness, please, please, please do this for me. Hockey is my life. I'm nothing if I can't play. I'm begging you to make this a minor little tweak and let me back on the ice in a day or two. I can't not play hockey. I don't know how. Amen.

"What are you looking at?"

My head snapped quickly to my right where Pete stood again, staring up at the ceiling. "Oh, sorry." I cleared my throat. "I didn't hear you come back in."

"Obviously," he said sarcastically. "Ambulance will be here in a minute. How are you feeling?"

"Nervous."

"I can tell. You've never been injured on the ice before, have you?"

"Nothing major." I shook my head. "A busted lip here and there, lots of stitches, but nothing like this."

"This might be nothing major, too. Let's wait and see what the X-ray shows, okay?"

I nodded but didn't say anything.

"And while we wait, use this," he said, handing me his phone.

"For what?"

"Trust me. I've been doing this a long time. There are people watching that game on TV who love you and are worried sick right now. Call them."

Shit!

I was such an ass. Calling Michelle hadn't even crossed my mind yet. I'd been so wrapped up with myself that I totally forgot that she might be freaking out. I quickly dialed her cell number as Pete and Dr. Houston stepped out of the room.

"Hello?" she answered quickly in a shaky voice, obviously not recognizing Pete's number.

"Hey, baby. It's me."

"Viper!" she called out, her voice cracking. "Are you okay? What's going on?"

"I'm okay. I got hit and slid into the wall. It's my knee."

"Is it broken?"

"No, I don't think so. I can move it a little, but it hurts, so I'm gonna head to the hospital just so they can take a closer look."

"Okay," she said quietly.

"Are *you* okay?"

"No," she squeaked out before soft sobs filled the phone.

"I'm sorry, honey."

"It's just that you got hit, then you slid into the boards. It was like Mike and—I couldn't breathe," she rushed out in between sobs.

"I know, baby. Where are you? Are you alone?"

There was shuffling for a second and then I heard another woman's voice. "Hey, Viper. It's Kacie."

"Oh! Hey! Is she okay?"

"No, but she will be. Watching that obviously scared the crap out of her, but I think now that she's talked to you, she'll be better. I took the phone so she could get a drink of water and catch her breath for a minute."

"Thanks. Are you at her house?"

"Nope, her and the kids came here to swim and hang out. They're gonna sleep over, too."

I nodded. "Okay, good. I was hoping that she wasn't going to drive home tonight."

"Nope, I got her. Hang on . . . here she is."

Their low voices spoke to each other for a minute before she came back on the line. "Hi. Sorry."

"Don't apologize," I said. "I know this must be horrible for you—"

Pete's head popped into the room. "Hey! Ambulance is here. Sit tight. We'll come get you in one second."

"Okay," I called back with another nod.

"Huh?"

"Nothing. That was Pete telling me the ambulance is here. I'll call you later, okay?"

"Okay," she said sadly. "Please do. I'm not gonna be able to sleep tonight anyway, so it doesn't matter what time it is."

"All right. I'll call you as soon as I can. I love you."

"I love you, too." She sniffed. "A lot. Viper, I love you a whole hell of a lot."

"Back atcha, babe."

We hung up just as the EMTs got there. They hurried into the room and moved fast, talking to Pete and sliding me carefully off the table onto a stretcher. Before I knew it, they were rolling me down the concourse and out to the back parking lot.

Once we got to the ER, everything moved in hyper speed. The doctor came in, examined my knee for about ten minutes, and sent me off to X-ray. Those came back quickly and confirmed what Pete already knew. Nothing was broken. The doctors and nurses stabilized my knee and the Wild front office put me on the first plane back to Minnesota, where I could see our team doctor the next morning.

It was a long, exhausting night and my plane didn't land until about two o'clock in the morning. I was groggy from pain meds and beyond thankful when Samantha, who handles most things for the Wild, texted me that she'd arranged a car to drive me home since driving was obviously out of the question for at least the next few days.

I exited the plane last, slowly making my way up the cold, quiet hallway from the plane to the airport on my crutches. It had only been a couple of hours and I was already sick of those fucking things. They annoyed me more than they helped me. I was constantly getting them caught on the ground or banging them against things, like the leg of the guy sitting next to me on the plane. I swear if he glared at me one more time, I was going to shove my crutch so far up his ass that it would knock out all of his teeth from the inside.

I finally reached the desk at the end of the concourse and a woman in a navy blue suit greeted me with a smile.

"We've been waiting for you," she said cheerfully.

"Sorry," I mumbled. "Takes me a while with these things."

She reached out and touched my arm. "No worries. We've actually arranged a ride for you the rest of the way."

"A ride?"

"Yep," she said as she stepped back and waved toward a small man who looked to be in his mid-forties, smiling at me from behind a wheelchair.

"Uh, thanks, but that's not really necessary." I shook my head.

I didn't think Tiny over there would be able to push me anyway.

The woman gave me a tight-lipped smile and clasped her hands together. Something told me I wasn't going to win that argument. "I know it's not really ideal, but we think it's best that you not walk the entire airport in this condition."

Condition? I fucking tweaked my knee and will be back up in a couple days. I'm not in a condition.

"And we spoke with Samantha Lester, who coordinated all of this, and she let us know that you would most likely argue but that we shouldn't take no for an answer, so come on." Before I could say anything else, she reached over and took my duffel bag off my shoulder and pointed toward the chair. "Have a seat."

I took a deep breath in through my nose, fully aware that my nostrils were flaring and my jaw was tense. Without a word, I limped over and plopped down in the wheelchair, beyond pissed that I was being treated like a child.

"You hang on to this"—she dropped my bag in my lap—"and Carl here will have you down to your next stop in no time."

"Thanks." I looked up at her and tried to offer a smile, but I just couldn't do it. It had been a long, horrible day and if I couldn't have answers right away, I just wanted my bed.

Carl tried to make chitchat as we weaved through the halls of the mostly deserted airport.

"You play for the Wild, huh? That's cool. I used to play hockey back when I was younger. I was pretty good, too, but I never thought about playing professionally. How did you get into that anyway? Are there open tryouts or do you need to be invited? Do you have an agent? Can he maybe get me into a tryout?"

I pulled my Wild ball cap lower and ignored him. He seemed like a nice guy and all, but I could *not* have been less in the mood to hand out advice on how to make it big in the NHL. Not to mention he was about twenty years too late to make that dream a reality. He must have gotten the hint because eventually he stopped asking questions and started whistling instead. Just as annoying but at least I wasn't expected to respond.

BETH
EHEMANN

The air grew colder as we neared the door that lets out to the transportation area. It was only October but there was a familiar crispness to the late-night Minnesota air that comforted me, oddly enough.

Carl wheeled me over and parked the chair off to the side of the door. He pulled a pair of gloves out of his pockets and quickly put them on, his arms shivering.

I eyed him skeptically. "You're not from around here, are you?"

"No." He shook his head and cupped his hands over his mouth to blow warm air into them.

"I can tell."

"I'm from Florida. Moved up here this summer. I had no idea it got this cold so early." He bounced around on his toes to keep warm.

"This isn't even cold yet. Just wait." I let out a small chuckle. "Why did you move up here anyway?"

"For a girl."

I raised an eyebrow at him. "A girl?"

"Well, a woman. But yes. I got divorced a few years back and several months ago decided to try my hand at online dating. I found Sheila the first night and never looked further."

"Wow. And you moved all the way to Minnesota for her?"

"Yep," he said with a smile, nodding proudly. "Met her for the first time right here at this very airport."

"Wait a minute." I held a hand up in the air. "You never met her face-to-face but you moved across the whole damn country for her?"

"Yes, sir. Best decision I ever made, even with this weather. That woman makes my bad days good and my good days better."

"Holy shit. That's unreal," I exclaimed, shaking my head incredulously.

"What's unreal?" a voice called off to my right.

My eyes followed the familiar voice and saw a grinning Michelle walking toward us.

"Hey!" I immediately felt better just seeing her face. "What are *you* doing here? Sam said she'd arranged a ride for me." I dropped my duffel bag off to the side and grabbed my crutches to stand.

She held both hands up. "Freeze! Don't even try and get up." She bent down and wrapped her arms around my shoulders, squeezing tight. The smell of her perfume drifted into my nose and I closed my eyes, hugging her back with everything I had.

"And Samantha did have a ride for you, but I called her and told her I'd pick you up instead. I left the kids with Kacie and set my alarm. No way was I letting some weird car service come out here for you at this hour." She started to pull back but I tightened my arms again.

"Thanks," I uttered into her soft blond hair. "I didn't even see you sitting there. And I'm way happier to see you than some weird car service, too. That driver probably wasn't near as hot as you."

In one swift motion she pulled out of my hug and punched me in the shoulder. "Shut up. Let's go home."

Carl stepped behind my chair, but I stopped him.

"You know what, Carl . . . I think I got it from here," I said as I pushed myself up from the wheelchair and grabbed the crutches. "Can you just toss that bag in the backseat for me?"

"Are you sure, Mr. Finkle" Carl asked, picking up the bag quickly. "I'd feel better if you let me help."

"Seriously, what are you doing?" Michelle added.

"I'm fine, I swear."

She pressed her lips together and glared at me as I slowly made my way to her car, but she didn't argue.

Carl rushed past me carefully, opening the car door and setting the duffel bag on the seat. Then he shut the back door and opened the front one, stepping back and holding it open so

I could get in.

I smiled and nodded in acknowledgement as I lowered myself onto the seat.

"Hope you get better fast, Mr. Viper." With two hands, he gently closed the car door. I rolled the window down with one hand and reached into my pocket with the other.

"Thanks, Carl. Best of luck to you and Sheila." I held my hand out for him to shake.

He grasped it firmly as his eyes lit up. "Thank you, sir. Best of luck to you and this beautiful woman, too. She drove out here in the middle of the night for you. You're a lucky man."

Michelle slapped both hands over her heart and looked at Carl with glassy eyes.

My eyes slid from her back to Carl. "Best decision you ever made, huh?"

"Ever." His wide grin returned. "Have a great night, folks."

"Bye! Thank you!" Michelle called out as I rolled the window back up. "What a sweet man. I can't believe the nice things he said."

I let out a quick laugh. "I can. I had a hundred dollar bill in my hand when I shook his."

Her eyes widened and she punched me again. Then she slipped her hand in mine and drove me home.

Chapter
9

Michelle

JUST LIKE I FIGURED, I hardly slept at all that night. Except instead of worrying about Viper and waiting for his call, I was worrying about Viper and watching him sleep.

I felt a little better that he was in bed next to me and not several states away, but every little groan he made had me jumping out of my skin. Thankfully the meds seemed to be doing their job at keeping the pain away, but they didn't help with his restlessness.

"Are you okay? Do you need anything?" I asked quietly after he sighed for the fourth time in less than two minutes.

"No, I'm fine. Just uncomfortable." He let out another sigh. "I hate sleeping on my back. This sucks!"

"I know it does, but I don't think sleeping on your side or your stomach is a good idea with that big brace on your knee."

"Staying awake isn't a good idea, either," he grumbled as he shoved the covers off of him angrily.

"Is there anything I can do for you?"

He opened his eyes and stared at the ceiling for a minute. "Yeah, roll over."

"Huh?"

"Roll over."

I frowned and stared at him. "Why?"

"Please just do it."

"Fine." It was my turn to sigh as I rolled over and faced away from him. "But if you think this is some lame attempt to get yourself laid, that's *so* not happening. I'm exhausted and you're broken."

"I'm not broken. Hush." He grunted as he leaned on his elbow and turned on his side, scooting right up against my back and throwing an arm around my waist.

"What are you doing? Doesn't this hurt? Are you okay?" I rambled.

His scruffy chin scraped the back of my neck as he nuzzled in close. "I'm fine. I sleep better with my dick in between your butt cheeks. That's where it belongs."

I smiled to myself and laced my fingers with his, happy that he, and his penis, were home with me. Within a few seconds, his breathing evened out and his chest vibrated against my back as he snored softly. Thankfully I wasn't far behind.

A few hours later, the sun snuck around the curtains and filled my bedroom. I cracked an eye open and lifted my head off the pillow just enough to peek at the clock. It was a little past six and Viper had to be back at the rink by nine to meet with Dr. Jennings, the Wild's team doctor, to discuss his injury. We knew they would probably send him to the hospital for an MRI after that, but Dr. Jennings wanted to check him out first.

Viper still had his arm wrapped around me and was lying in the exact same position he'd fallen asleep in just a few hours before. Being up half the night wasn't fun at all, but I was thankful we'd both been able to grab a few hours of sleep, at least.

"Hey, you awake?" I ran my fingertips softly along the tattoos on his muscular forearm, tracing the dark lines back and forth.

He moaned a few garbled words that didn't make any sense and started snoring quietly again.

Since he obviously wasn't in the mood to wake up just yet, I figured I'd text Kacie and make sure the kids did okay overnight.

> Hey! I'm sure you're not up yet, but shoot me a text when you are. I just want to see how the kids slept. Hopefully they weren't too much trouble for you. Thanks so much for offering to keep them last night. xo

I tucked my phone under my pillow, surprised when it vibrated under my head just a minute later.

> Kacie: I'm up! How is he?

> He's okay. I have to have him at the rink in just a little bit, then I'll come and get the kids from you.

> Kacie: No, no! Don't worry about them. They're still sound asleep. I threw their outfits in the wash last night so they can wear them again today. As soon as they wake up and have breakfast, Mom and I are going to lather them up in sunscreen and take them back down to the lake to play. You do what you have to do and get them whenever. We're fine here.

> Thank you so much, Kacie. You've helped me more in the last 24 hours than anyone else my whole life.

> Kacie: Psh! Don't mention it. Go to the doc with him and keep me posted, okay? Brody is

a nervous wreck. I guess he texted Viper
a few times, but he hasn't answered.

He was pretty doped up on pain meds and crashed
right when we got home. I'll tell him to call after his
appointment.

Kacie: Okay, good luck! Love you guys!

Thanks. Love you, too.

I set the phone on my nightstand and scooted back into
Viper's warm arms for a few more minutes of snuggling before
we had to get up and face whatever the day was going to throw
at us.

"You okay?" I asked as we pulled into the players' parking
area of the rink. Viper had been in really good spirits all morning,
but I suspected it was an act.

"I am," he answered as he unbuckled his seatbelt.

I turned the car off but didn't make a move to open the door.
"No. I mean are you *really* okay?"

He turned in his seat to face me, his hard blue eyes softening
as they fixed on mine. "I am, I promise. I was freaking out last
night when it happened, but then the X-rays came back clean
and that was a huge relief. Plus, it hardly hurt at all last night. I
know they have to check me out, but I can tell it's nothing. I'll
probably even be able to fly out later tonight to make the last
two games of the road trip."

His voice was sincere, maybe even a little upbeat.

He reached over and squeezed my hand as he continued,
"Let's go in and get this over with, grab the kids, and go see
Gam, okay?"

I nodded. "We need to do that for sure. She was really
worried when I called her last night. She told me to let her know
when you were better so she can kick your ass."

He tilted his head to the side. "Kick my ass? For what? It's not my fault I got hurt."

"No, something about a nurse coming to the house? I didn't really catch it all because I was in the middle of a meltdown worrying about you."

His eyebrows shot up. "A nurse? Already? Wow. Ellie moves fast."

"Huh?"

"Ellie—Andy's assistant. I asked her to look into hiring a nurse to help Gam out around the house and stuff."

"Why would you do that?" I exclaimed. "I told you I could handle—"

"I know what you said," he interrupted, "but you have a lot going on with the kids and stuff, so I figured even someone just a couple days a week would help out and give you a break."

"It's not necessary, Viper. I am more than capable of handling the kids *and* Gam."

"I know you are, and me hiring someone to help out doesn't mean that you aren't. I'm just trying to make everyone's life a little easier." He flashed his cheesy, boyish smile that he knew I couldn't resist and my lips defiantly curled into a smile.

A million different thoughts started racing through my head. Part of me was disappointed that he didn't want to let me take care of Gam by myself, but another part of me felt a little . . . relieved. Taking care of Gam wasn't hard, it *was* time consuming. And while Viper may not have been worried about his injury, I was—not that I would ever tell him that. He was convinced he'd be flying out again that night, but I wasn't so sure. And if his injury turned out to be more than he thought it was, taking care of the kids, plus Gam, plus him would be really tough on me.

"Now come on." He lifted my hand to his lips and kissed the top of it. "Let's get this over with so Gam can kick my ass sooner. I'm hoping there'll be enough time after all the shit we need to do for a little quickie before I leave again." He dragged his tongue slowly along his top lip as he wiggled his eyebrows up and down.

"Ugh," I groaned playfully as I pulled my hand from his. "Do you ever *not* think about your penis?"

"Uh . . . no. He's my buddy and it's my job to take care of him. If he's not happy, I'm not happy. "

"Okay, okay. I get it. Now get your happy penis out of the car and let's go in before you're late."

"He's not happy right now. Actually,"—he paused and frowned, looking up in the air—"he's a little stoned from all the meds. I think he might code out! Hurry! Give him mouth-to-mouth resuscitation!"

"I'm going to give him fist-to-mouth resuscitation if you don't get out of this car right now." I giggled as I got out of the car before he could say any more.

Dr. Jennings was already sitting at a desk in the training room when we got there, looking at what I assumed were Viper's X-rays on the computer screen.

"Morning, Dr. J," Viper exclaimed as we walked through the door.

Dr. Jennings looked up and squinted at us before pulling his glasses down from his head. "Good morning, Mr. Finkle." He stood and crossed the room, offering Viper his hand.

Viper shook it and motioned toward me. "I think you've met Michelle before, right?"

I felt my face flush as I gave Dr. Jennings a tight smile. The last time I stood in this office, I was still Mike's wife, and now being there as Viper's girlfriend made me feel a little awkward.

"Yes, I have." He smiled warmly and cupped my hand in both of his. "Nice to see you again, Michelle." Dr. Jennings was a tall man with gray hair and years of wrinkles and laugh lines built into his face. His voice was low and comforting, his demeanor so gentle that he made my tension disappear instantly.

"Good to see you, too, Dr. Jennings."

"So, what do you think, doc?" Viper asked as he leaned his crutches against the wall and took a few slow steps without them. "It doesn't hurt too much and nothing is broken. So what . . . ice it today, maybe schedule some physical therapy for next week, and get on a plane tonight?"

Dr. Jennings let out a low laugh. "I know you're anxious, Viper, but I'd like to actually *see* your knee before I clear you, okay? Onto the table, please."

I sat down on a chair in the corner as Viper hopped up on the dark green leather-covered exam table. He shot me a quick wink before he lay down and lifted his legs up.

Dr. Jennings carefully removed Viper's leg brace and started examining his knee while rapid-firing question after question at him. He stepped down the side of Viper's leg a little bit, blocking me from seeing—or hearing—much else. As they exam went on, I chewed on my fingernails as my foot tapped nervously against the metal legs of the chair.

As quickly as we got there, we were right back out the door. Dr. Jennings wasted no time in sending Viper straight to the hospital for an MRI on his knee, just as we'd expected. Well, *I'd* expected.

In the car on the way over, I could feel how tense Viper was. Gone was the playful good mood he'd carried into the rink.

"Don't worry too much, okay? Everything will be fine. Whatever happens, it'll be fine." I said, trying to peek at him and the road at the same time.

His elbow rested on the window and his hand was near his mouth, picking at his lip like a scared little kid.

"Did you hear me?" I asked when he said nothing.

"I heard you. You're wrong, but I heard you."

"Wrong about what?"

"Everything being fine. If my knee is fucked up, *nothing* will be fine." His tone cut through me like a knife.

"Viper, don't talk like that, okay? I know you were hoping Dr.

71

Jennings was going to send you home with an ice pack and it would be fine, and maybe it still will be, but of course they are going to do an MRI to be safe. You knew this was probably going to happen last night. So let's not freak out until there's something to *actually* freak out about, okay?"

"Fine," he agreed dryly, looking down at his lap at his MRI script for the tenth time.

"Good," I said triumphantly, a little surprised that he'd agreed so fast. "Now hold my hand and take a deep breath. We're almost there."

Could the timing of all of this be any worse?

Chapter
10

Viper

"**F**OUR HOURS!" I SHOUTED ANGRILY. "Are you fucking kidding me?"

"Viper! Shhh!" Michelle scolded, grabbing my arm gently as the technician's eyes grew as big as the glasses on her face.

"I'm sorry, Mr. Finkle, but the results take a little while and then they need to be read," she said with an attitude. "Dr. Jennings asked that we send him the images as soon as we have them. He said that he'd contact you."

"I can't believe this can't be done sooner." I shook my head incredulously, beyond pissed that I wasn't getting answers. "This is seriously fucking ridiculous."

The technician rolled her tongue between her top lip and her teeth. "Sir—"

Michelle raised her hand, stopping her. "Let me talk to him. I'll handle this." She turned back to me and placed both hands flat against my chest. "Hey, look at me."

My eyes were fixated off to my right at a picture of a bunch of flowers on the wall, and it took all of my self-control not to rip that picture off the wall and throw it across the room.

"I said look at me," Michelle said as she took a hold of my chin and lowered my face to hers. "Calm down. It's four hours, not four years. Let's grab the kids, go have some lunch with Gam, and then when we hear from Dr. Jennings, we'll come back. Okay?"

I wiggled my twitching fingers, desperately trying to keep a lid on my temper before I punched a hole in the wall of the radiology waiting room.

"Viper, please. You're scaring me." Michelle blinked up at me, her eyes darting back and forth between mine.

Staring into her eyes brought me out of my rage as I took a deep breath and exhaled slowly. "Sorry," I grumbled quietly, feeling guilty that I'd scared her. I gripped the sides of her face with my hands and pulled her close, kissing her forehead. "Let's get outta here."

We walked to the car in silence, and then drove to Kacie's in silence. She ran in to grab the kids while I waited in the car, going over every possible outcome in my head for the hundredth time. My phone vibrated in my pocket and I fished it out. I had a bunch of texts from Brody that I hadn't opened yet, and a new one from Andy, my agent.

> Andy: Finkle. What's going on? I saw the game
> last night and talked to Brody today, but he
> said he hasn't heard from you. Are you okay?
> What did the doctors say? Answer me now so
> I can brag to Brody that you answered me
> before him.

I was lucky to have Andy as an agent. He wasn't stuffy and obnoxious like ninety-nine percent of sports agents out there. He was your best friend all the time and your pitbull agent when he needed to be.

> Hey, buddy. Sorry. Long night and an even longer day. I have no idea what the hell is going on. X-rays on my knee were negative, waiting on MRI results now. Apparently that takes all fucking day. I'll let you know as soon as I hear something.

Andy: Jesus. Hope it all turns out to be nothing. Yes, please keep me posted. And for the love of God, text Brody. He sounds like a depressed eight-year-old whose best friend can't come out and play.

> Thanks. I hope it's nothing, too. Stay tuned. And I'll text the Drama Queen, I mean Brody, right now.

I scrolled down my phone to Brody's texts.

Brody: Hey. Call me.

Brody: Yo! Where are you? What happened? Call me.

Brody: Coach Collins told us that the X-rays were negative. That's a good sign. I can't believe they still sent you home. Is it that bad? Call me, asshole.

Brody: Okay now you're pissing me off. They better have been wrong about your knee and it's really your hand that was hurt because if you're being a dick and just not answering me, I'm going to hunt you down, make sure you're okay, and kick the shit out of you.

Brody: Dude.

I rolled my eyes so hard I was surprised they didn't get caught in the back of my head as I hit the reply button.

Calm your little pink panties, Murphy. I've been kinda busy. Yes, X-rays were fine but no results on the MRI yet. Those are coming later today and hopefully, if all goes well, my ass will be on a plane tonight and back into your arms by morning, pumpkin. I'll let you know what happens.

As I shoved my phone back in my pocket, the back door swung open.

"Viper!" Matthew called out as he climbed into the seat behind me. He wrapped his short arms around me and the headrest, locking his hand underneath my chin and cutting off my air supply. He was so excited to see me that I didn't even care.

I reached up and squeezed his hands with mine.

"What's up, buddy?" I said when he finally let go and I could talk again.

He peeked around the seat and scanned my body from head to toe, pausing at my knee. "Mom said you got hurt. Is that where you got hurt?"

"Yep." I nodded, following his gaze to my leg. "I hurt my knee, but the doctors are checking me out and I'll be better fast."

"I have an owie on my knee, too, remember?" He lifted his leg up and pulled his shorts back, revealing a huge bandage. "That was from when I fell off my bike. They used glue. Maybe they can use glue on your knee, too?"

"That would be awesome, bud, but there's not really anything to glue on my knee. My owie is on the inside."

"Ooooh," he said as he nodded slowly.

"Matthew, hop up and buckle, please." Michelle said as she set Maura in her car seat. Maura craned her neck to the side to try and see me around Michelle's arm. "Hi! Hi! Hi!" she called out over and over.

"Hey, baby girl!" I reached my hand back and she wrapped her wet little fingers around it.

"Okay," Michelle sighed as she clicked the last buckle on Maura's car seat. "Everyone's buckled . . . we have all our stuff . . . I think we're ready to go."

She plopped down into the driver's seat and sat for a minute, rubbing her neck with her hand and moving her head in big circles. I'd been so focused on my knee that I didn't think for a second how exhausted *she* must have been, too.

"Sore?" I finally spoke for the first time since we left the hospital.

"Kinda. Everything's just tense." She pulled her shoulders back and lowered her chin to her chest, trying to stretch out her achy muscles. I lifted my left arm and put it behind her.

As I rubbed slow circles into her neck with my fingertips, she froze and let out a soft moan that lingered for several seconds.

"You like that?"

"Mmhmm," she answered without moving. "It feels really, really good."

I licked my lips and stared at her. She was beautiful all the time, but she was most gorgeous when she wasn't trying to be. Listening to the little groans and noises she was making as I rubbed her neck was torture . . . pure torture. They sounded a lot like the noises she made when I was moving in and out of her and suddenly, I wanted nothing more than that.

"Mooooooom, can we go now?" Matthew complained from the backseat.

Michelle's head snapped up and she turned toward me, her eyes traveling all over my face before connecting back with mine. No words came out of her mouth, but they didn't have to. I felt it. I felt her. I felt that moment.

She blinked a couple of times and sniffed, turning back to the steering wheel and pulling her seatbelt across her chest.

"What's wrong?" I asked.

"Nothing." She shook her head quickly. "Nothing at all. That was just . . . nice."

"It was more than nice."

Glancing at me out of the corner of her eye, she gave me a tiny smile. "It was."

"I'd like to do more of that later. A lot more." I stretched my hand across the center console and rested it on her thigh as she started the car. She didn't say any more, but she didn't need to. The last couple of weeks had been stressful for both of us, but we were in a good place. We were just fine.

We pulled up in front of Gam's house and parked in the street as usual. There was a car in the driveway that I didn't recognize, but Michelle had mentioned that lots of people were stopping by to visit Gam so I thought nothing of it.

Matthew hopped out of the car and was halfway across the yard before I even had my seatbelt off. Michelle shook her head and laughed. "You don't think he likes Gam or anything, do you?"

"Not at all," I joked.

As I climbed slowly out of the car, I noticed Gam was sitting on her porch, and Matthew was already sitting next to her on the wicker couch. Michelle set Maura down on the grass and she ran toward Gam's house as fast as her chubby little legs would take her.

"Go ahead." I motioned toward the stairs for Michelle. "You go first. It's gonna take me a few minutes."

Between the stupid brace I had to wear to keep me from bending my leg and the fucking crutches that had become my new best friend, everything took me longer. Especially stairs.

Michelle skipped up the stairs quickly and went right over to Gam, wrapping her arms around her shoulders. Gam leaned in and squeezed her right back.

"Sorry I didn't get up to give proper hugs," Gam said. "I'm

moving a little slow these days."

"Yeah, you and me both," I added as I finally got the top of the wooden steps.

She looked over at me and tilted her head to the side, shaking it slightly. "And my grandson. What in the world am I going to do with you?"

I shrugged my shoulders. "Take me out back and shoot me?"

"No!" Matthew cried, jumping up from the couch with wide eyes.

"I was just kidding, buddy. Sorry. Bad joke." I ruffled his blond hair as I stepped past him and leaned down to kiss the top of Gam's head.

"Look at us"—she waved her arm back and forth between the two of us—"you with your crutches and me with my walker. We're a mess. A hot mess."

I rested my armpits on the top of the crutches and arched an eyebrow at her. "Did you just say *hot mess?*"

"I did." She nodded proudly as Michelle giggled next to her. "I'm learning all sorts of new things from my nurse." She narrowed her eyes and glared at me. "You shouldn't have done that. I don't need help."

I looked over at her walker and back at her. "Oh, right. You're completely self-sufficient."

"Don't be a smartass," she snapped.

"Okay, Matthew and Maura, let's run inside and see if Gam has some apple juice in her fridge, okay?" Michelle said in an overly chirpy tone, clearly trying to distract the kids from the brawl that was about to go down between me and Gam, and our accompanying metal apparatuses.

"Do you have any cookies?" Matthew asked Gam.

"Do I have any cookies? Does a zebra have stripes? You bet your little rear end I have cookies. All kinds of cookies. Help yourself." She pulled him in for a quick hug before he stood up. "And Matthew," she lowered her voice to a loud whisper, "if

BETH
EHEMANN

your mom says you can only have two, tell her I said you can have three. Because . . ."

"Gam's in charge!" Matthew cheered as he jumped up and down, pumping his arms in the air.

Michelle rolled her eyes playfully and turned Matthew by the shoulders, leading him into the house with Maura following right along behind.

"Oh, Michelle!" Gam called out.

Michelle took a step back and peeked her head out the door.

"The nurse is in there. Introduce yourself. She's actually really great."

"Okay, I will." She smiled then disappeared.

"She's great, huh? Does that mean you're not going to kick my ass?" I said sarcastically as I sat on the chair next to her. Leaving my leg outstretched in front of me, I relaxed back into the chair and folded my hands on my stomach.

"Oh no." She raised her eyebrows. "I'm still going to kick your ass, but it's going to take me a few weeks to do it. This hip thing really slowed me down."

"Meh." I waved her off. "You're old as dirt, but you're also tough as hell. You'll be back to normal before you know it. Seriously though . . . you like the nurse? I'm really glad."

"I do. She's kinda sassy, and I love that."

"I was nervous because I had Ellie handle everything. I was going to take a look at the list she narrowed it down to, then this happened," I said, glancing down at my knee. "I haven't had a chance to talk to Ellie about it at all, so I'm glad she chose a good one."

"Ellie did a great job. I mean, she's only been here a couple days but I can tell we're gonna get a long."

The screen door creaked as it swung open, and we both turned.

"Oh, perfect timing. Here she is," Gam said with a big smile. "Kat, come over here. I want you to meet my grandson, Viper."

Kat froze in the doorway, our eyes locked on each other. There was no introduction necessary. Kat and I already knew each other.

We knew each other really, really well.

"Uh, nice to meet you, Viper." Kat smiled awkwardly as she walked across the porch and offered me her hand.

I tried to keep my shock to a minimum as I shook her hand. "Hi" is all that came out of my mouth.

"Have a seat." Gam patted the couch next to her.

Kat's dark red lips spread into a tight smile. "I really shouldn't. I just came out here to see if you needed anything."

"Oh, hush. Sit down. You work too damn hard." Gam grabbed Kat's hand and pulled her down next to her. She squeezed her shoulder and looked over at me with a big smile. "Isn't she the best?"

I nodded at Gam, trying not to make any more eye contact with Kat.

"You two actually have a lot in common. You'd never know she's covered in tattoos under this shirt." Gam laughed, tugging on her sleeve.

Except I did know she was covered in tattoos. I'd seen tattoos on Kat that Gam, and ninety-nine percent of the population, would never see. I'd been *with* Kat when she got some of her tattoos.

"That's awesome." I nodded, trying to figure out how the hell to get Kat out of Gam's house.

Fucking knee!

If this had never happened, I would have been able to go over Ellie's selections and Kat would have been a big, fat no. When the hell did she even become a nurse? Last time I saw her she'd been a fucking bartender.

My irritation was growing bigger by the second. I just wanted to throw Michelle and the kids and Gam in the car and drive away long enough for Kat to leave and never come back.

Michelle knew about my past. I'm sure Mike had told her about my antics when we were friends, but I also never kept secrets. I was an open book. If she asked a question, I gave her an answer. An honest answer that she sometimes wasn't expecting and didn't want to hear. So she stopped asking questions. She loves me for me and doesn't hold my past against me, but she doesn't like to think about it either. And here was a glaring part of my past, sitting on my grandmother's porch, holding her hand.

"Here you go, babe." Michelle handed me a glass of lemonade.

I was so lost in my own world that I didn't even hear her come back outside. She looked at me funny as I took the glass from her. "You okay?"

"Yeah, sorry." I lifted the glass to my lips and took a sip so that I didn't have to talk. The thoughts racing around my brain were moving so fast I couldn't keep up with them and I started to feel dizzy.

"You nervous about later?" Michelle asked as she sat down in the chair across from me.

"Later?" I frowned at her.

Her face fell into a deadpan expression and she stared at me. "Yes, later. Your knee?"

"Oh! Right!" I was losing my fucking mind. "Yeah, I'm a little nervous. I just want to get today over with."

"What happened to you?" Kat asked.

"I hurt my knee playing hockey," I answered, looking down at my glass.

"You play hockey?"

My eyes snapped up to hers. She knew damn well I played hockey. She practically lived with me for a year and knew *almost* everything there was to know about me. I chewed on my top lip as I debated what to say next.

"Yeah, I play hockey," I finally said, swallowing my anger for the sake of not upsetting Michelle.

My phone vibrated in my pocket—I'd never been more excited to get a phone call in my whole life. I pulled it out and stared at the screen. "Uh . . . I gotta take this. I'll be right back." I stood as quickly as I could and hobbled into the house, away from everyone.

"Dr. J! What's up?" My phone was at my ear but all I could hear was my heart thumping loudly. Nervous didn't even begin to cover it.

"Hi, Viper. I have the results of your MRI, and a couple of us have looked it over and talked about it. When can you come back in so we can go over it?"

I clenched my eyes tight and swallowed hard. "Is it really necessary to come back in? Can't you just tell me now?"

"Viper, this isn't a quick conversation. We need to talk about some things and make some decisions."

"Doc, I hardly slept last night and today has been the longest day. Can you please just give me the verdict and I'll come in tomorrow for the sentence?"

He let out a sigh and was quiet for a couple seconds. "Okay. Fine. You have a pretty significant tear in your anterior cruciate ligament—your ACL—and it's going to require surgery to repair before you can get back on the ice."

Fuck!

"Now this isn't a career-ending injury, it's not even season-ending, but it will keep you off the ice for about six months, depending on how quickly you heal."

He started going on and on about physical therapy and exercise, but I checked out. My stomach rolled as I sat down on the kitchen chair, my hands shaking so bad I could hardly hold on to the phone.

"Viper, did you hear me?" Dr. Jennings said loudly.

"Yeah, I'm here."

"I said don't let this discourage you. In the grand scheme of things, this is minor. You're young, you're healthy, and you'll be back on the ice before the year is over. Come in tomorrow morning and we'll discuss your surgery options."

"You're sure this can't wait and be repaired in the off-season?"

"I wouldn't recommend it, Viper. Not only will you not have full range of motion in that knee, you risk injuring it further and possibly doing permanent damage. Don't think about the next six months right now. Get a good night's sleep tonight and come in bright and early tomorrow so we can go over everything. Okay?

"Yep. Thanks, doc."

I didn't wait to see if he said anything else before I hung up. Frankly, I didn't want to hear any more. I put my head in my hands and sat stunned, staring at the wall. I really had convinced myself that it was nothing and the team was just being overly cautious. Dr. Jennings had his opinions on the injury and I had mine. It wasn't minor and it was a big deal. Not being on the ice for six months was devastating, especially this year when we were starting off the season so strong. Stronger than we *ever* had.

And now . . . I was no longer part of the team.

"Are you okay?" a familiar voice asked from the doorway, but not the familiar voice I wanted to hear.

I spun around in my chair and glared at Kat so hard my eyes were physically strained. "Why the fuck are you here?"

Her head jerked back in surprise. "I was assigned here, Viper. This is my job."

"It was your job. You're quitting . . . today," I hissed.

She shook her head vehemently. "No, I'm not. I love my job, and I really like Gam. I'm not going anywhere."

I bolted from my chair, ignoring the pain that spread from my knee like a lightning bolt, and took an intimidating step close to her. "Did you pick this job on purpose?"

"No," she barked incredulously, her jet-black hair falling around her face. "I can't believe you'd even think that."

I leaned to my left and stole a quick glance at the front door to make sure no one was coming before I turned back to her. "Well, it's pretty fucking coincidental that of all the jobs you could be sent to, you wind up at *my* grandmother's house, don't ya think?"

"I'm sorry. Perhaps you're remembering our past a little different than I am. You never even introduced me to one single family member, so how was I supposed to know she was your grandmother?"

"Gee, I don't know . . . the last name Finkle didn't ring a fucking bell?"

She sighed and crossed her arms over her chest, cocking a hip to the side. "When I was assigned, they told me what the case was and where it was. I didn't learn her name until the morning I was supposed to start. What was I supposed to do?"

"Quit!" I growled. "There was an easy fix. You march into whoever's office and say, 'Nope, sorry.'"

"I can't do that or I'd risk losing my job!" she snarled.

"I don't give a shit about your job!"

"I'm not surprised. You never really gave a shit about anything," she said in a cold tone. "I'd be surprised if you even really give a shit about that woman out there."

My jaw clenched and I curled my hands into fists as I lunged forward and glared down at her. "You know *nothing* about that woman out there, and if I ever hear you say one single thing about her, your job won't be the only thing you lose!"

She narrowed her eyes. "Did you just threaten me?"

I lowered my voice to a calm but intimidating tone. "Call it whatever you want, but I promise you . . . quitting this job is the best decision you'll ever make."

Before she could respond, I stepped to my right and limped

through the front door.

"All right, time to go." I clapped my hands loudly as I hobbled across the porch and picked up my crutches.

Michelle stopped talking to Gam mid-sentence and looked at me with bulging eyes. "What?"

"Yeah, you just got here," Gam added.

"I know, but I have stuff to do. I'll come back tomorrow, okay?" I bent down and kissed the top of her head again.

"Wait. You're serious?" Michelle asked, setting her drink on the table.

"Very. Get the kids together. I'll wait in the car." I turned and limped slowly down the steps as the front door creaked open. I didn't have to turn around to know who it was.

"Viper!" Gam called after me, but I didn't look back as I got in the car and stared straight ahead. I was so close to snapping already and seeing Kat on the front porch again might just push me over the edge.

Chapter
11

Michelle

WE WERE A COUPLE MILES from Gam's house and Viper was still breathing heavy, more agitated than I'd ever seen him.

"You wanna talk about it?" I asked, hoping he didn't blow up at my question.

He took a long, slow breath in and let it all out. "That was Dr. Jennings on the phone."

Oh crap.

"And?" I asked anxiously, quickly looking from the road to him and back again.

"And I have a torn ACL that needs to be surgically repaired."

"Oh, Viper! I'm so sorry." I wanted to pull over and wrap my arms around him, but I knew he'd recoil, so I just kept driving.

"Yeah. It pretty much blows. My whole season is shot."

"Not necessarily," I disagreed carefully. "It's only October.

You can be back before the end of the winter."

"That's practically the whole fucking season!" he shot back with a glare that I felt even though I wasn't look at him.

"Okay, don't snap at me, and please don't talk like that in front of the kids." I sighed and shook my head but didn't say another word. Talking to him when he was this upset was pointless. Obviously I felt horrible about his knee, and I wished more than anything it hadn't happened, but when he was lost within himself like this, no one could reach him.

Not even me.

As I pulled onto my street, I noticed someone standing at my front door.

"Who is that?" I said out loud to myself.

"Looks like Jodi," Viper answered dryly.

Jodi, and her much younger husband, Vince, lived right next door to me, and I could not have asked for more awesome neighbors. After Mike died, she helped me through some really dark days and weeks, until Viper came along and made those days and weeks bright again.

The headlights moved across the porch as I turned into the driveway. She turned and gave me a quick wave, following my car into the garage.

"Hey," I greeted her as I got out of the car.

"Hey, yourself. Long time no talk." She walked up the side of my car and gave me a quick hug.

"I know. Things have been a little crazy around here." I opened the back door and gently unbuckled Maura, who was sound asleep.

"I've heard. I mean I saw," Jodi said as Viper slammed his car door. "How are you feeling? Any verdict on that knee yet?"

"I have to have surgery," Viper mumbled without looking up at her. He opened the car door for Matthew and then sulked along behind him into the house.

Jodi's eyes widened and slid over to mine. "Wow. It's a little chilly in here."

"He just found out about the surgery a little while ago," I defended quietly with a shrug. "It's been a really bad day."

"Yikes. I can imagine. Maybe I should go."

"No." I shook my head. "I'm guessing he's going to go upstairs and want to be alone. It's fine."

Jodi followed me into the house. I dropped Maura's bag on the island and turned back to Jodi. "I'm gonna go lay her down. I'll be right back."

She nodded and opened the fridge, plucking herself a water bottle.

I quickly ran up the steps and changed Maura's diaper as quietly as I could. Thankfully, she didn't budge. It was barely even dinner time yet, but she was so wiped out from the last couple days, and probably didn't sleep as good at Kacie's as she would have in her own bed, so I decided just to let her nap. She'd eat when she was hungry.

I laid her in her crib, turned the music on, and went to check on Matthew in his room, but it was pitch-black.

I peeked my head in my bedroom. Viper was lying on the bed on his stomach and Matthew was sitting on his back, watching television.

"There you are," I said quietly as I walked over to the bed and put my hands on my hips. "Whatcha doing?"

"Watching *Ninja Turtles*," he answered in a squeaky little voice.

"Don't you think you should watch it in your room and let Viper rest?" I leaned down and kissed the side of his head.

"He's fine," Viper mumbled into the pillow.

"Okay. Are you gonna come downstairs at all?" I was pretty sure I already knew the answer.

"I don't know," he said with a shrug.

"Okay. Well, I'll check on you in a bit."

I grabbed the monitor from Maura's room and headed back to the kitchen. Jodi was sitting at the island, lazily flipping through a Pottery Barn catalog.

I let out a deep breath, puffing my cheeks out as I collapsed on the stool next to her.

Jodi glanced over at me. "You look exhausted."

"I feel exhausted. Between Gam's hip and now Viper's knee, it's been the longest couple of weeks." I lifted my head off the island and propped it up on my hand. "And I have a feeling it's going to get worse, not better."

"So what happened to his knee? I mean, I saw the game, but what does he have to have surgery on?" She flipped another page of the catalog.

"I wasn't kidding when I said that he just found out a little bit ago, and he hasn't told me a whole lot. All I know is that he tore his ACL and needs surgery." I got up from the stool and walked to the fridge, grabbing a bottle of water for myself. "And apparently he's going to be out for like six months."

Her eyebrows shot up. "Holy shit."

"I know. And I get that he's not happy about it, I *totally* get that. I just hope that maybe once surgery is over and he's on the mend, he snaps out of this a little bit."

She twisted the cap off her water and took several big gulps. "I hope so, too. How are you going to take care of both him and Gam?"

"Well, in an ironic twist of events, before he even got hurt, he hired a nurse for Gam. Not that she needs a ton of medical care, just someone to help out with whatever she needs." I grabbed a bag of Cheetos out of the pantry and tossed them on the counter. "Don't judge me, I'm starving."

Jodi pulled her bottom lip up and shook her head. "No judging here. I'll even open them." She pulled the top of the bag apart. "The nurse is a good thing though, right?"

"Oh, for sure!" I agreed. "We met her today . . . she seems

nice. And Gam seems to like her a *lot,* and that's what really matters."

"That's good. I guess it frees up some time for you to help take care of him." She pointed a finger toward the ceiling.

"It does. I'm just worried about the kids." I grabbed a handful of Cheetos from the bag and put them in front of me.

"The kids? Why?" She popped a Cheeto in her mouth and crunched it loudly.

"Well, the last couple of weeks we've been doing a lot of driving back and forth to Gam's house, and now we're driving Viper everywhere." I glanced down at the island and picked at the corner of a napkin that was sitting there. "A couple days ago we went to Kacie's and he was *so* excited to play with her kids. He still has preschool a couple days a week, and that's great, but he just wants to play."

"Oh! Oh!" Jodi perked up and held her hand over her mouth, chewing as fast as she could. "Sorry, I got excited. Get this! Vince has a buddy who just rented the house across the street from us . . . and he has a son!"

"Seriously? How old?"

She pinched one eye shut and looked up in the air. "I don't know, I have to ask, but I think he's around Matthew's age. He's not quite in school yet either."

"Really?" Excitement shot through me. "You have to find out details for me. That would be awesome!"

"I'll ask Vince tonight. I've never met the guy, but I think he works with him or something. Oh my God, take these away from me before I eat all of them." She pushed the bag across the island.

"You and me both. I swear I've become an emotional eater lately. That's *all* I've been doing." I grabbed a few more Cheetos and set them in front of me before I rolled the top of the bag down and put it back in the pantry.

Jodi and I chatted for a little while longer until Matthew came downstairs and complained that he was starving to death.

She went home and Matthew and I had a quiet dinner of macaroni and cheese. It was kind of nice spending some time alone together.

"Do you know what Miss Jodi told me today?" I asked.

He shook his head as he shoveled a huge spoonful of noodles into his mouth.

"She told me that Mr. Vince has a friend who is moving in across the street and he has a son who she thinks might be close to your age. How cool is that?"

His blue eyes lit up. "Does his son want to be my friend?" he said through a mouthful of food, sending a few noodles back into the bowl.

I couldn't help but giggle. "I bet he will. And maybe you guys can have campouts in the backyard and go sledding and do all sorts of fun stuff together."

"Will he be here tomorrow?"

"Mmm, I don't think tomorrow, but I'll ask Miss Jodi later if she knows when he's moving in, okay?"

He nodded excitedly. "I bet he likes *Ninja Turtles* like I do."

"You might be right, buddy. *Ninja Turtles are* the coolest." I reached over and smoothed his crazy blond hairs down.

Matthew told me all there was to know about *Ninja Turtles* as he finished eating. Then I gave him a quick bath and tucked him into bed. I peeked in on Maura one more time, who not only slept right through dinner, but hadn't moved a muscle since I put her in there.

"Sweet baby girl," I whispered to myself as I closed her door and tiptoed to my bedroom. The room was quiet and pretty dark except for the glow of the TV Matthew had left on when he went downstairs. I set the monitor on the nightstand and slipped off to the bathroom for a quick shower.

When I got out, Viper was sitting up in bed, looking down at his phone.

"Hey. How are you feeling? Do you feel better after getting some sleep?" I pulled the towel off my head and squeezed my hair with it.

Viper just shrugged without looking up.

"Are you hungry? Want me to make you something to eat?"

"No thanks," he muttered.

"Okay then." I turned and headed back toward the bathroom to brush my hair and put pajamas on.

The TV and all the lights were off when I came back. Viper had rolled over and was facing away from me.

I climbed into bed quietly and nudged him. "You still awake?"

"Mmhmm."

I picked my phone up from the nightstand. "I need to set my alarm. What time are you supposed to go see Dr. Jennings?"

"Andy's taking me," he said flatly.

"*What?*"

"I said Andy is going to take me," he repeated a little louder.

"I heard what you said, I'm just wondering why."

"Why not? We were talking a little while ago, and he said he had the morning free and offered to take me, so I said fine."

I was a little shocked and a little more hurt that Viper didn't want me to take him, but fighting with him about a ride was the last thing on my mind. "Okay." I set my phone down. "Will you at least call me and let me know what happens?"

"Sure."

He was being so cold and dry with me that tears stung my eyes. I'd done as much as I could have done for him the last couple days and he was keeping me at arm's length. I swallowed the pre-cry lump in my throat and lay down on my pillow, determined not to take any of Viper's actions too personally . . . and also praying that he'd be back to normal soon.

Chapter

12

Viper

"**L**OOK AT YOU! THAT'S QUITE a log you're dragging around there, huh?" Andy leaned against his car with his arms folded, harassing me as I slowly made my way over. "Could you hurry up, please? I'm hoping we can get there before dinnertime."

"Shut up, asshole," I joked as I opened the passenger side of his car.

As soon as we pulled out of the driveway, my cell phone buzzed and Michelle's smiling face popped up.

"Who's that?" Andy asked.

"A text from Michelle."

> Michelle: Hey . . . we didn't get to talk much this morning, but I just wanted to tell you good luck today. The kids and I are thinking about you and hoping for good news. Call me as soon as you can. Love you so, so much!

I knew she'd been trying so hard to keep my spirits up, and I appreciated it, but I just wasn't in the mood. I also didn't want to be a dick and completely leave her hanging, so I responded.

Thanks. I'll take all the good news I can right now.
Love you, too!

"You look like someone ran your dog over with a car, dude."

I set my phone on my knee and stared out the window. "I *feel* like someone ran my dog over with a car. Actually, scratch that. I feel like someone ran *me* over with a car."

"I know this sucks, but you gotta keep your head up. You're a boss. You'll have surgery, kick ass with physical therapy, and be back out there in no time." His phone rang through the speakers of the car and Blaire's name popped up on the screen.

"No way. Not today," he said, hitting a button to reject the call.

Blaire was Andy's crazy ex-wife, and I mean *crazy*. She sabotaged his friendships, treated their kids like shit, and was an all-around horrific human being. I had literally in my whole entire life never met a bigger bitch than Blaire—ever. "What's going on with her?" I asked.

"Who knows? She probably wants money. She always wants money." He clenched his jaw and shook his head. "I pay her more every month than most people make in six, and she still complains it's not enough."

"And she hardly sees the kids, right?"

"One weekend a month. It used to be two, but they were coming back so screwed up and weird for a couple days after that I offered her more money to go down to one weekend a month. She takes longer to figure out what she's having for dinner than she took to tell me yes."

"I don't know how you do it, man. She's such a bitch."

"I don't know how I did it for so long. I was so desperate to keep the family together for my kids' sake that I just didn't see it. And now they're happier than they ever were when we lived with her." He turned the car into Starbucks and looked over at me. "Want anything?"

I shook my head. "I'm good."

He ordered his drink and pulled around to the side. "So anyway, I don't know what to say about her. She's ruined me for all women, I think. I've never been so jaded in my whole life."

"That's bullshit. You'll get married again. That's who you are."

He laid his head against the back of the seat and turned toward me. "What do you mean by that?"

"I mean that's who you are. You're Andy Shaw, family man extraordinaire. You loved being married, even if it was to a heartless slab of concrete. And you really love being a dad."

"I do love being a dad, that's for sure," he said with a nod as he faced forward again. "We'll see. Who knows?"

I'd had enough of talking about Blaire. "Speaking of women and relationships . . . do you remember Kat?"

"Thank you," he said to the barista as he took his cup and drove forward. Setting it in the cup holder, he pulled his brows in tight. "Kat . . . Kat . . . I don't think I remember a Kat. Refresh me."

"She was probably the only other girl that I kind of dated. I mean, I wasn't ever faithful, but she hung around for a little over a year. Long black hair and tattoos all over. Killer body, too."

He rubbed his bottom lip with his fingers as he thought about it. "Okay. I think I remember her. She was a bartender, right?"

"Yep."

"And didn't you cheat on her once, with your maid or something?"

"Yep."

"And she got really pissed off. Like *really* pissed off."

"Yep, she launched a picture frame at me and cut my face. I have a little scar on the corner of my eye from her."

"Okay. I do remember. Why the hell are you asking about her?"

"So get this. Remember how I called and asked Ellie to help me find a nurse for Gam before we left for the road trip?"

Andy's face fell. "Shut up. No way."

"Yes way." I nodded. "She's Gam's fucking nurse."

"When the hell did she become a nurse?"

"I have no idea." I threw my hands up in the air. "But we went over there yesterday and Gam was sitting on her porch and we started talking. First she yelled at me for hiring a nurse at all, then she was telling me how much she liked this girl."

"I can't believe that." He shook his head incredulously as we pulled up to a stoplight. "What are the odds of that happening?"

"I know. I'm not happy about it."

"So what are you going to do?" he asked as he rolled his window down.

On cue, an older homeless man who was sitting on the ground against a building walked over. He had a long gray beard and long gray hair and his clothes were full of holes. He took something from Andy's hand and nodded. "Thank you so much, Mr. Shaw."

"You got it, Douglas. Do something good with that today." He rolled his window back up and repeated, "What are you gonna do about Kat?"

I stared at him in amazement. "Wait a minute. What just happened?"

Andy glanced at me quickly. "What? Douglas?" he asked nonchalantly. "He's a nice man. One day a few months back I was driving into work and there was an accident at this corner. I was stuck and couldn't move, so I rolled my windows down and turned my car off while I waited. Well, Douglas walked up and asked if I had change to spare, so I told him to get in and talk to me while I waited for the road to clear. We sat here for half an hour, and he told me all about his life and how he served three tours overseas. He was nice, and I liked him, so I offered him a job at my office."

"You offered him a job? How have I never heard this story?"

The light turned green and he shrugged and started driving again. "I don't know. I thought I told you guys. Maybe not. Anyway, he said thanks but no thanks. He likes it down here. He likes being free to go wherever he wants during the day and said for the most part, people leave him alone. He's not unhappy, just homeless. Well, later that day I ended up signing the huge Kenny Sparks shoe deal with Nike. Remember that deal?"

"Yeah, I remember that deal. That was massive. Why can't you hook me up with one of those, fucker?"

"'Cause you don't play football." He let out a quick laugh. "Anyway, I was convinced that Douglas was my good luck charm, so the next morning he was on the bench again and I gave him ten bucks. He was so thankful, and now it's become our thing. Douglas is my karma bank. I feel better helping him."

"So you drive this way every morning and give that dude ten dollars."

"Pretty much." Andy nodded. "Unless he's not here."

"Huh," I said, looking back out the window as we pulled into the rink parking lot. "You're either the nicest human alive or completely fucking insane. I haven't decided which yet."

Andy let out a hearty laugh that filled the whole car. "Trust me, I'm neither. I do it to counter all the horrible things I think about my ex-wife during the day."

The next hour flew by and my head spun with all of the medical terms and instructions thrown my way. Dr. Jennings asked Dr. Newell, the orthopedic surgeon, to come over and be there for our meeting, and I felt like my brain was the ball in their match of medical tennis. My surgery was scheduled for two days later and that's all I cared about. I just wanted to get it over with so I could get back on the ice as soon as possible.

BETH
EHEMANN

"Did you understand a fucking word of that?" I asked Andy as we walked to his car.

"For the most part. Why? You didn't?"

"Hell no. I'm gonna need the condensed, dumb man's version from you."

He kicked at a rock in the parking lot and laughed. "Why didn't you ask them to explain it again, bonehead?"

"I don't know. It was overwhelming."

We got to his car and both sat down, but he didn't move to start the engine. "Here's what I know for sure. Surgery is Friday morning, really fucking early so you're going to have to let Michelle handle that one. I'm out. But I do expect a call when it's over and you're done . . . and maybe a video if you're acting like an idiot from all the drugs."

"You want a video?" I challenged. "I'll give you a video, all right. One that has people calling you for a statement all weekend long."

He pressed his lips together and shook his head. "Unfortunately, that wouldn't be the first time I've had to deal with the media on your behalf, so scratch that. No video. But seriously, your recovery could take up to nine months if you don't take your physical therapy seriously and do everything you're supposed to do, got it?"

"Nine months? That's the whole season. Fuck that!"

"Then you have to be diligent. No blowing off appointments and do all the exercises at home that you're supposed to."

"Yes, Dad," I said sarcastically.

He rolled his eyes as he started the car. "So are you going to finish filling me in on this Kat situation?"

I totally forgot we hadn't finished talking about that. "It's not really a situation. Well, maybe it is? I don't know. I just want her gone and I don't know how to make that happen."

"So she's Gam's nurse. Does Gam know your history with her?"

"No."

"Does Michelle know your history?"

"Hell no."

"Were there . . . any . . . feelings when you saw her?" he asked carefully.

"*Fuck* no!"

"Okay, good. So basically you have no idea what the hell you're doing?"

"Basically."

"Good luck with that one, buddy. My only advice would be to not screw anything up that risks your relationship with Michelle." He glanced at me out of the corner of his eye for just a quick second. "That girl is good for you. You need her."

I turned and glanced out the window, unsure if he was talking to me, or warning me.

Chapter
13

Michelle

I T HAD BEEN EXACTLY FIVE days since Viper got hurt and they were five of the longest days of my life. I completely understood why he was grumpy and frustrated with what had happened, but I wasn't expecting him to take it out on me like he was. I was looking forward to putting his surgery behind us and hoping that once it was done, he would bounce back to normal.

Surprisingly, the morning of his surgery he was unusually peppy.

He stood at the bathroom mirror and I walked up behind him and wrapped my arms around his waist, resting my head against his back. "Are you nervous?"

"Not really," he said. "I'm more hungry than anything. Not eating and drinking after midnight is fucking torture."

I smiled to myself. "I think they do that so you don't get sick."

"Well, great. They don't have to worry about me getting sick, but they might have to worry about me scarfing down one of the nurses on the way into the operating room."

I giggled and let go of him, moving over to my sink to brush my teeth and put on a little mascara.

As I leaned forward and opened my eye wide, dabbing my lashes with the black wand, Viper stared at me in the mirror. "You don't need that shit, ya know."

I straightened up and blinked my eye a couple times, frowning at him. "Huh?"

"That." He motioned toward my mascara. "You don't need it. You don't need any of it."

"I totally do. My eyelashes look like a newborn's." I squinted into the mirror and inspected my stubby, thin little eyelashes.

"No way. I agree that a lot of women look better with makeup on, but not you." He shook his head. "You're perfect and you don't even realize it."

I stared in the mirror at my boyfriend—rough and tough hockey player, a body that looked like it was chiseled in stone, covered in tattoos and intimidating enough to scare the pants off of just about anyone—but when it came to me, and my kids, he was a softie. A gentle giant. *My* gentle giant.

I turned to the side and tucked my arms under his, listening to his heart beat against my ear. His arms came down around my back, squeezing me hard. This was the moment I'd been craving so desperately the last few days. Between the joke about food and the way he was acting with me, I *finally* felt like my old Viper was back. Hopefully he was sticking around for a while.

"Michelle Asher?" A nurse asked as she looked around the packed waiting room.

I jumped up. "That's me."

She gave me a warm smile and stepped back. "Follow me, please."

"How is he? Is everything okay? When can I see him?" I started rambling nervously as I walked past her. I hadn't realized how nervous I really was until that very moment.

"Everything is fine." She put her hand on my arm. "The surgery went great. He's in recovery now and should be back to his room in just a couple of minutes. The doctor is going to come in and talk to both of you real quick and then you're free to go."

My eyes widened. "That's it?"

"Yep." She nodded. "It was a pretty simple procedure, and there's no need for him to stay overnight, so he's all yours."

"Okay." I smiled nervously. I took a deep breath and gave myself a pep talk as I sat down in the chair in the corner.

You got this. You took care of Gam a couple weeks ago, you can take care of Viper today.

I texted Kacie, Brody, Andy, and Taylor, Mike's sister, who was babysitting the kids for me.

> He's out of surgery and the nurse said it went well. I haven't seen him yet, but I'll let everyone know when I do.

A few seconds later my phone lit up like a Christmas tree.

Brody: Ugh! A group text?! You're dead to me, Michelle.

Kacie: Glad everything went okay. Give him a hug for me. Brody, stop being an ass.

Andy: Don't forget to get me video of him all drugged up. One can never have too much blackmail when dealing with Lawrence Finkle.

Brody: I wasn't being an ass. Group texts SUCK! I'm glad he's okay though. Tell him I'll stop by tomorrow and see how he's doing. Hey, Kacie . . . can you send one of

105

> the kids up to our bathroom with a roll of
> TP?

Kacie: Really?

I pinched my lips to stifle a laugh.

Taylor: Matthew just pooped and when he came
out of the bathroom, he told me not to go
in there for twenty minutes or so. He's
turning more and more into Viper every
single day. Glad surgery went well. Keep
me posted.

The curtain sprung open and I quickly tucked my phone away, even though it was still buzzing.

Those should be fun to read later.

The nurse gave me a quick smile before she stepped back behind Viper's bed and wheeled him into the room. He was lying back and his eyes were closed, but he had a huge, goofy smile on his face.

"Good luck with this one," the nurse said playfully as she shook her head.

I looked down at Viper and back up at her. "Uh-oh, what does that mean?"

She shrugged as she dropped the metal sides of his bed and checked his IV. "Nothing bad. People normally come out of sedation really groggy and a little grumpy. Not this guy. He came out cracking jokes and asking for a peanut butter and jelly, then a minute later he was asleep again. He's a hoot."

A big smile spread across my lips. "That's Viper for ya."

Her eyebrows shot up. "You call him Viper?"

"Well, not just me . . . everyone does. His team started it years ago."

"What team?" she asked as she scribbled something on a clipboard.

"I play hockey. For the Wild," Viper shouted, scaring the hell out of both of us. His head turned my way and his eyes caught mine, but it took him a second to realize who I was. "Hey! That's my girlfriend!"

I let out a quick giggle as I walked over to kiss his cheek. "Hi, baby."

He titled his head toward me, leaning into my kiss. "You smell good," he said a I stood up, then he grabbed my hand. "Wait. Come back here. Lie down with me. Here, I'll scoot over."

"No, no!" I put my hand on his shoulder. "I can't lie down with you, just don't move."

"Why not?" He turned back to the nurse. "She can lie down with me, right? I mean, we're both consenting adults. And we've had sex before . . . a lot of sex."

"Viper!" I squealed as the nurse laughed. "Shut up."

"What? I'm just saying," he exclaimed defensively.

"Okay, honey. But maybe you just don't say for a while, okay?" I took a deep breath and exhaled through puffy cheeks.

The nurse hung the clipboard up and tilted her head to the side, giving me a sympathetic smile. "Like I said, good luck today. The doctor will be in in a minute." She shot me a quick wink and left the room.

"How does she do that?" Viper asked.

"Do what?"

"Close just one of her eyes like that?" He stared straight ahead, blinking both of his eyes hard.

Andy was right, I should have videoed this.

A little while later, we were back in the car heading home. His meds had worn off slightly, but not completely, and I learned that a drugged-up Viper was a lovable Viper!

"Do you have any idea how much I love you?" he asked for the thirtieth time when I pulled onto my street.

"I do know, but you can tell me again. I like hearing it." I chuckled.

"I don't tell you enough, do I? I'm an asshole."

"You aren't an asshole." I shook my head.

"I really want donuts. But not regular donuts. I want mini donuts, but I also want them to be crunchy." He sat forward quickly. "Ah! Cheerios. I want Cheerios. Do we have any?"

By this point my chuckle had grown into a full-blown laugh. "Maybe. I'll check the pantry when we get home."

"Pantry. Pantry. Pantry," he said slowly. "Pantry is a weird word. It's tricky. People think you're going to talk about pants and then you throw a 'ry' in there at the end and it's like . . . psych! Gotcha!"

"Let me get this straight . . . Cheerios are like mini-donuts?" I was glad that we were almost home because I don't know how much further I could have driven laughing as hard as I was.

"Yeah. Hey you know what else?" His voice grew louder and louder with each sentence. "We should take ski lessons this winter."

"Oh, honey." I shook my head as I turned into the driveway. "I'm pretty sure you aren't gonna be doing any skiing this winter."

"We'll see. I'm gonna bounce back and shock everyone." He lifted his hands and pumped them up and down, pretending to hold ski poles. "I'll be whooshing down hills and in and out of trees like a badass."

"Right now, let's just try to get in the house, okay?" I glanced over at him as I turned the car off. His face was still wearing the same goofy grin he'd left the recovery room with. When he beamed like that, with wide smiling lips and twinkling eyes, he looked so young and carefree. Those were the moments I fell in love with him all over again. "Stay right there. I'll come around and get you."

"You got it, babe." He pointed his finger at me and winked.

Once we got inside the door, Viper sobered up instantly. He pulled his eyebrows down low, grimacing.

"What's wrong? Does it hurt?" I panicked.

"No, but I feel like I'm gonna puke. I need to go lie down."

"Okay. It's probably the anesthesia. It makes some people sick." I gently rubbed his back. "Where do you want to go? You want to lie on the couch?"

"I think upstairs."

"Viper, I don't know if you should do stairs yet."

"I'm fine. I'll go up with my good leg first." He started toward the steps and moved up them slowly, one at a time. Matthew and Maura came running from the back of the house with Taylor right behind them.

"Viper!" Matthew called out, waving something in his hand. "I made you a card!"

Maura was right on his heels. "Me too! Me too!"

"You know what guys—" I stopped them before they ran up the stairs and knocked him over. "Viper doesn't feel so hot, so he's gonna go up and lie down. Maybe after he naps you can take the cards upstairs to him."

"Okay," they said in unison, a little sad.

I walked upstairs with Viper and tucked him into bed. He was sound asleep before I left the room, and I was thankful for that, hoping a good long nap would kick the rest of the meds out of his system and make him feel better.

What I didn't plan on was him not leaving that room for the next two days.

Chapter
14

Viper

"HEY, DID YOU HEAR ME?" Michelle's hand gently shook my shoulder.

"Hm?" I grumbled, drifting in and out of my narcotic induced sleepy haze.

"I said that your first therapy appointment is in a couple of hours. Do you want to get up and take a shower? I'll make you breakfast?"

My eyelids felt like lead as I struggled to pull them open. "What time is it?"

"Almost nine."

"Where are the kids?" I asked, surprised I hadn't heard them yet.

"I took Matthew to school and Maura is downstairs playing with her ponies. Want me to make you eggs or something?" She rested her hand on my bicep again.

"Nah. I'm just gonna shower and go." I sat up in bed slowly, trying to shake the clouds from my brain. I couldn't wait to be done with the pain meds. They made everything fuzzy and I felt like I moved in slow motion.

"Okay," she sounded disappointed. "Well, let me know when you're ready and we'll leave."

Her footsteps shuffled along the carpet and I turned just in time to see her walk out the door.

Grabbing my crutches from the floor, I stood and made my way to the bathroom, pausing at the sink. I reached up and rubbed the thick stubble across my face, thanks to not shaving for several days. For a brief moment I thought about shaving before therapy, but ultimately, I didn't give a shit. I turned the water on in the shower and put a waterproof medical bandage over my knee while it warmed up.

That's gonna feel good when I rip it off.

I stepped into the shower carefully and propped my arm up on the wall for support. Never in my whole life had I felt so incapable and weak. I couldn't walk without crutches, I couldn't drive until I was off my meds, I could barely even walk around the kitchen and make food for myself. I'd spent the last twenty plus years whizzing around the ice on skates, as part of a team where I was needed, and now I couldn't even take a shower without being worried.

"Knock, knock," Michelle said.

I turned as she walked into the bathroom with her hands folded across her chest and smiled at me from the other side of the glass.

"Hey," I acknowledged.

"Sooooooo . . . got room for one more?"

I glanced back at her. "Huh?"

Quickly dropping her eyes to the ground, she gave me a small shrug. "I went back downstairs and Maura was passed out on the couch, so I thought I'd come up here and maybe join you . . . in there? What do you think?" Her eyes lifted to mine and she chewed on the corner of her lip.

I poured shampoo into my palm and closed my eyes as I tilted my head back and scrubbed my hair. "Oh . . . uh . . . probably not. I just want to rinse off and get moving." I never closed my eyes when I took a shower, but I didn't want to see the disappointment on Michelle's face.

She didn't respond. A few seconds later, I opened my eyes and she was gone.

After I showered, I got dressed and carefully made my way down the stairs toward the kitchen. Maura was dancing in circles to some weird TV show and Michelle was loading the dishwasher.

"Hey," I said as I opened the fridge. I wasn't hungry or thirsty, but I knew she was probably upset with me and I didn't know what else to do with myself.

"Hey." Her tone was dry and she didn't turn around.

"We should probably leave in like fifteen minutes. Is that okay?"

"Yep," she answered shortly.

Those fifteen minutes felt more like an hour. Michelle and I didn't talk . . . she didn't even look at me. I sat on the couch, watching Maura wiggle and dance and sing her heart out, her blond curls bouncing up and down as she twirled around the room.

My phone buzzed on the coffee table.

> Brody: Yo! You gonna be around today? I was going to stop by but wanted to make sure you weren't going out for a jog or something.

> You're an asshole. I have physical therapy in a while but then I'll be home.

"Ready?" Michelle called from the kitchen.

Maura watched me get up from the couch. Her eyes scrolled

down the length of the crutches and back up at me, before she cracked a tiny smile and patted me on the butt.

"Come on," she said. I laughed out loud and scooped her up into my arms for a quick kiss before she led me to the front door.

On the day of my surgery, Mia texted over the information of the state of the art rehab center they wanted me to go to. We had an in-house rehab person at the stadium and I assumed I'd be going to her but apparently that wasn't the case.

We pulled up to the building and Michelle pulled into the first spot that was designated for the drop off and pick up of patients.

"You sure you don't want us to come in?" Michelle asked as I got out of the car.

"No, I'm good. There's nothing for you guys to do in there for an hour anyway."

"Okay. Well, we're gonna run some errands and we'll be back."

"See ya." I turned and hustled into the building as fast as my stupid metal appendages would allow me to go.

The heavy glass door made a loud thud as it closed behind me and a receptionist looked up and smiled. "Hi, can I help you?"

"Uh . . . yeah . . . I'm Vi—Lawrence Finkle. I have an appointment today."

"Hi, Mr. Finkle. Let me just look up here and see who you're scheduled with." She narrowed her eyes and leaned in close to her computer screen. "Okay, you're actually going to be with Sherman." Her head swooped up and she gave me another smile. "Lucky guy. He's our most requested therapist . . . has a wait list a couple months long."

"Wow. Sherman must be a beast." I knew nothing about this place or Sherman or wait lists, but clearly he knew what the hell he was doing if he was that popular.

"Just have a seat in one of those chairs and I'll let him know you're here." She motioned to a small waiting area off to the side.

"Okay, thanks," I said and turned to the chairs, feeling a little optimistic. Mia sent me to this place for a reason and somehow got me in with Sherman. He was probably ex-military or something and would kick my ass.

I sat in the chair closest to the door, so I could see around the desk and check out the facility a little bit. The walls were painted a light blue and other than one wall being lined with exam tables, it pretty much just looked like a big gym. A rack off to the left went floor to ceiling and had several giant balls on it, all different sizes and colors.

A man, who looked to be in his mid-fifties, came around the corner of the desk and walked right up to me. "Hi! Are you Mr. Finkle?"

"Yeah," I said hesitantly with a nod.

"I'm Sherman! Nice to meet you!" he pushed his hand into mine and we shook.

"You're Sherman?" I tried not to sound so surprised, but I'm pretty sure I failed. He had on a bright red button-down shirt with yellow suspenders that hooked to the top of his loose-fitting dress pants. His gray hair was cut short and he definitely wasn't as fit as I'd expected him to be.

"Yep, that's me," he said proudly as he waved for me to follow him. "Come on back and let's talk."

I followed him through the gym area and we walked to a small office in the back corner.

"I have all of your paperwork here and the plan your surgeon wants you to follow," Sherman said as he walked around the other side of the desk. "I understand you're a hockey player, is that right?"

"That's right." I nodded as I sat across from him.

"Okay." He sat down and leaned his elbows on the desk, folding his hands in front on him. "And I'm assuming they've explained everything about your recovery and the timeline we're looking at?"

I tilted my head back and forth. "More or less. We're looking at about six months, right?"

"Well, I hope so. It's all up to your knee, really. These injuries can take anywhere from six to twelve months to get your full range of motion back and obviously, as a hockey player, full range of motion is key."

"Wait, wait." My heart started racing as I held my hand up. "Twelve months? No one ever said anything to me about twelve months. I was told six months. I can't be out for twelve months."

He stared at me for a second and then gave me a big, tight-lipped smile. "Then we better get going. Hop up and follow me."

I stood and followed him out through the gym area and over to the opposite corner of the room. He spun to face me as he patted the seat of a stationary bike. "Every day when you come in, even if I'm still working with someone else, I want you to climb up here and spend ten minutes on it. Okay? It'll help with your strength, range of motion, and really get the heart pumping a little bit, and that's what we want."

My eyes glared down at the bike and drifted back up to him. "A bike? Seriously? Shouldn't we be doing harder stuff to move this along faster?"

Sherman pursed his lips. "Have I told you how to play hockey?"

I frowned. "No?"

"Then you don't tell me how to rehab you . . . now pedal!"

Sighing, I climbed up onto the bike and rode for ten minutes just like Sherman said. As my timer went off, he looked up and waved me over.

"Now hop on up here"—he smacked one of the exam tables—"and I'll show you what we're gonna do next."

I slid my butt onto the table and pulled my legs up carefully.

He rolled up a white towel and put it under my bad knee.

"Now, using your thigh muscles, slowly pull your toe toward you and lift your heel off the ground. Hold that for three seconds and put it back down. This is called a quad set. You're going to do three sets of fifteen reps."

I rolled my eyes. "Okay."

Sherman put his hands on his hips. "What now?"

"Nothing. This just seems very . . . simple. I'm a professional athlete. I need to be doing more than this," I rambled in frustration.

"Fine," Sherman said as he threw his hands in the air. "You wanna do more than this? Let's get out of here and go skate a few laps around the ice."

"I can't do that!"

"Why not?"

I gritted my teeth and let out a heavy sigh. "Because I can't put weight on this leg yet."

"Exactly!" Sherman said as he reached over and bumped my forehead with the heel of his palm. "Now stop questioning me and just do it."

I sat stunned, staring at him incredulously. "Did you just bump my forehead?"

"Yes, and I'm sorry I had to get violent, but you're being so difficult." He said as he flailed his arms around. I couldn't decide if he was gay or just dramatic.

"You weren't violent. It's just that no one has ever done that to me before," I said as I pulled my toes back and started doing his exercises.

"Really?" He pulled his top lip up and thought about it for a second as his eyes traveled the room. "Hm. I'm surprised by that, as stubborn as you are."

I couldn't help but laugh. Sherman was not at all what I'd been expecting in a therapist, but with any luck he knew what he was doing . . . and at the very least he made it interesting.

After therapy I was surprised by how exhausted I was. A couple of weeks ago, I could skate around the ice, chasing the puck and crashing into people, for three to four hours straight, and after just one therapy session all I could think about was a nap. As I was icing my knee at the end, Sherman told me I'd feel tired, but I argued and told him no way. I was more and more convinced that man knew everything, not that I would ever admit that he was right.

We picked Matthew up from preschool and headed home.

"You want some lunch?" Michelle asked as we all hustled into the house from the rain.

I set the paperwork Sherman gave me for my home exercises on the island and thought about it. "Um . . . nah. I actually think I'm gonna go lie down for a bit. Brody's supposed to come over later, but I want to take a nap first."

Her shoulders slumped as she pressed her lips together and gave me a small nod. "Matthew, Maura . . . you guys hungry."

"Y-E-S!" Matthew yelled out from the family room. "That spells yes!"

"S-S-S!" Maura tried to copy.

Michelle pulled a loaf of bread out of the pantry and giggled.

"All right." I cleared my throat. "I'm gonna go lie down. Let me know when Brody gets here, okay?"

"Yep," she said with a sigh as I left the room.

Chapter 15

Michelle

THE KIDS AND I SAT and had lunch . . . alone . . . again. Well, they had lunch. I didn't have much of an appetite.

"Why aren't you eating, Momma?" Matthew asked as he took another bite of his sandwich.

"Mommy had a big breakfast, buddy. I'm not hungry right now," I lied, taking a few grapes out of the bowl and popping them into my mouth, more for his benefit than mine.

Before he could respond, the doorbell rang.

Matthew gasped and hopped off the stool. "I'll get it!"

"Wait a minute, wait a minute," I called, hurrying after him. "We talked about this. You're not supposed to open the door without me."

He sprinted to the front door and stopped, lifting onto his tippy toes to see out the window. "It's Miss Jodi!"

"Okay, hang on. I think it's locked." I flipped the lock to the left and opened the door. "Hey! Oh—hi!" I said, realizing she wasn't alone.

"Hey, is this a bad time?" she asked reluctantly.

"No, no. We're just finishing up lunch. Come on in." I stepped back, putting my arm around Matthew's shoulders and pulling him with me.

Vince followed in right behind Jodi. "Hey, Michelle." He reached down and gave my cheek a quick kiss. "This is my buddy Joel. He's the one moving in across the street in a couple days."

Joel stepped into the house and held his hand out with a smile. "Hi, Michelle."

"Hi," I greeted, not expecting to have a houseful of people so suddenly.

Joel was tall with broad shoulders and had short dark—very dark—hair. His eyes were almost a startling turquoise blue that made you forget whatever it was you were saying when you looked at them.

"Sorry for dropping by like this, but I was signing the lease over at the new house and stopped by to say hi to Vince, and Jodi insisted we come over and meet you guys," he said nervously.

I waved my hand. "Oh, please. It's no problem at all. Who's this little guy?" I asked, leaning to my left and directing my attention at the small dark-haired boy hiding behind him.

"This is my son, Gavin. He's not normally shy, but apparently he thought now was a good time to try it out." Joel reached around and scooped Gavin out from behind him. "Gavin, be nice and say hello please."

Gavin chewed on his fingers nervously and stared up at me with his father's same beautiful eyes. "Hi."

"Hi, buddy. Nice to meet you. I'm Michelle, and this is my son, Matthew." I patted Matthew's shoulder and he giggled.

"Hi!" Matthew said excitedly.

I leaned down a little closer to him. "Matthew, these guys are moving in across the street from us soon. Won't that be fun to have someone *your* age in the neighborhood?"

He nodded but didn't say anything else.

"We're moving in this weekend, actually," Joel added, shoving his hands in his jeans pockets.

"Wanna go see my room?" Matthew blurted out, taking a step closer to Gavin. "I have Ninja Turtles in there."

Gavin's eyes shot up to his dad's but he didn't say a word.

"If you want to, buddy, go ahead." Joel shrugged, reading his son's mind.

Gavin looked back at Matthew and nodded, and with that, they both sprinted up the stairs.

"Hey, Matthew?" I called out. They stopped at the top of the stairs and turned to face me. "Remember that Viper is napping. Keep it quiet, please."

"Okay," he hollered back just before they both disappeared down the hall.

"So much for him being quiet." I sighed and rolled my eyes playfully as I bent down and picked Maura up in my arms. "You guys want something to drink?"

Jodi nodded and they all followed me to the kitchen.

"Sorry everything is kind of a mess. There just aren't enough hours in the day lately." I set Maura down and she ran over to play with her ponies that were still on the coffee table from earlier.

They sat at the island as I quickly cleared Matthew's and Maura's lunch plates. I grabbed the grapes and started to lift the bowl, but Jodi stopped me. "Leave those here. They look delicious."

"Okay." I laughed. "What do you guys want to drink? I have water, Gatorade, apple juice, beer—"

"Water for me," Jodi said before tossing a couple grapes in her mouth.

"Me, too," Vince added.

"I'll actually take some apple juice," Joel answered.

"Really?" Vince turned to him. "Apple juice? Are you five?"

He raised his hands defensively. "What? It sounded good."

I grabbed two water bottles from the fridge and two mason jars from the cabinet. "It actually does sound good. I'll have some apple juice with you." I handed Jodi and Vince their bottles and poured apple juice for Joel and me.

"To new neighbors." Vince raised his bottle and we all met in the middle.

I leaned on the other side of the island across from them and sighed, feeling a little guilty that Viper wasn't with us. "Hopefully Viper wakes up soon so you can meet him, too."

"I'm sorry, but who's Viper?" Joel cringed. "I should probably know this, sorry."

"Michelle's boyfriend," Jodi answered before I could. "He had knee surgery a couple days ago, so he's been napping a lot."

More like all the time.

"Oh, okay." He nodded. "Knee surgery. That's rough. What kind was it?"

I set my glass down and licked the apple juice from my lips. "He tore his ACL."

Joel hissed in through clenched teeth. "Ouch! I've heard that's rough. My brother had that done and was out of commission for a while."

"Yeah, well"—I looked at the ceiling—"don't say that too loud. He's been told he won't be back on the ice for six months and is already freaking out about *that*. Any longer and I'll probably have to institutionalize him."

"On the ice?" Joel's eyes moved to each one of us. "I missed something."

"Sorry." I shook my head quickly. "He's a hockey player . . . for the Wild."

His eyebrows shot up. "Oh! Like a *real* hockey player?"

Jodi laughed and threw a grape at him. "No, a fake hockey player."

"I didn't know," he said defensively. "I don't really follow hockey. I'm more of a football guy."

"Oh no, hockey is life in this house. Has been for a long time." I thought back and I couldn't remember a time where our lives didn't revolve around a hockey season or a road trip or playoffs.

The doorbell rang out. "Speaking of hockey . . . I think I know who that is. I'll be right back. Help yourselves to whatever," I said on the way out of the room.

As soon as I rounded the wall, Brody's smiling face was pressed up against the glass. I grinned and rolled my eyes as I pulled the door open. "Hey, crazy man!"

"Crazy? You put up with Viper voluntarily and you're calling *me* crazy?" He wrapped his arm around my shoulders and gave me a quick squeeze.

"Touché!"

"How's the patient doing anyway?" He leaned against the wall and crossed his arms over his chest.

I shrugged. "He's fine."

Brody narrowed his eyes and stared at me in silence.

"What?"

"I've been married a few years now, and if there's anything I've learned, it's that fine is never good. What's going on?"

"Nothing," I defended. "Really. Everything is great."

"You're a liar."

I pinched my bottom lip in between my teeth and stared out the front door, trying to decide if I should even say anything.

"Just tell me what it is," he said, as if he were reading my mind.

"This is just . . . hard. He's being very weird with me, very short. He won't let me in. He doesn't come downstairs . . . ever.

He doesn't eat. I just don't know how to bring him out of this."
My voice started to crack so I cleared my throat.

Brody nodded slowly, taking in all I'd just said. "Let me talk
to him. See if I can get him to open up at all. I know Viper is a
tough nut to crack—he always has been—but maybe I can big
brother some sense into him."

"Thanks." I sniffed and quickly blinked away the sting of
tears that I'd been holding in for over a week.

"You hang in there." He stood and cupped my head, pulling
it against his chest. "I'm gonna talk to him, but ultimately you're
the one he needs. Don't give up on him."

Brody let go and I gave him a tight smile. "Never."

"I'm assuming he's in your bedroom now?"

"Yep. He was sleeping, but he might be awake now. I don't
know."

"I don't care. I'll go wake his ass up." Brody wiggled his
eyebrows up and down and hustled up the stairs, taking them
two at a time.

I went back into the kitchen and Maura was sitting on Jodi's
lap, babbling on and on about Matthew and him taking her
favorite pony a couple days before.

Jodi chuckled and looked up at me. "I feel so bad. I don't
understand half of what she's saying."

"Me either," Vince added.

"I didn't get it all, but she said something about Matthew and
Rainbow Dash and the pantry . . . I think?" Joel's eyes slid from
Maura to me for confirmation.

"You got it. A couple days ago Matthew took her favorite
pony and hid it in the pantry. Clearly she's still not over it." I
reached over and took a grape out of Maura's closed fist. "Hang
on, let me cut this for you."

"How did you know that?" Jodi asked, looking at Joel
incredulously.

"I have a kid." He shrugged. "Granted, we all understand our own kids best, but sometimes we can get bits and pieces of other people's kids, too."

"That's true," I added with a laugh as I cut up a handful of grapes and put them in a plastic bowl for Maura.

We all sat and chatted for a little while longer and eventually, Brody and Viper appeared.

"There he is!" Jodi called out as she stood quickly and gave Viper a quick hug. "How ya feelin'?"

"Shitty," Viper replied in his new normal, grumpy tone.

"Well, perk up because we brought your new neighbor over for a visit." As soon as she acknowledged him, he stood and walked over.

"I'm Joel," he said as he extended his hand for Viper.

"Hi, Joel. Viper." He shook his hand with a nod.

"My son, Gavin, is the one upstairs playing with Matthew," Joel added, trying to avoid awkward silence.

"Thank God. I thought Matthew was in there talking to himself," Brody joked as he patted Viper's shoulder. "All right, I'm out. *You* call me if you need anything, and everyone else"—he turned to the room—"it was nice meeting you, seeing you, whatever. Bye!"

Brody left and shortly after Jodi, Vince, and Joel decided to go, too. I walked them to the front door as Joel called Gavin down from upstairs. As he trudged down the steps, with Matthew following, he whined that he didn't want to go.

"Guess that's a good sign that they got along, huh?" Joel laughed as he threw a mopey Gavin over his shoulder. "Gavin, can you please tell Matthew's mom thank you for having us over?" He turned halfway so Gavin faced me.

"Thank you for having us over." He giggled, his face turning beet red from being upside down.

"You're welcome, big guy. Once you guys are in and settled

you can come back and play, okay?" He nodded and Joel turned back toward me.

"Thanks again," he said. "I'm looking forward to finally being neighbors with some cool people, and not the weird guy who collects worms and old water bottles in the apartment next to me."

I laughed hard and touched his arm as he headed out the door.

"See ya," Vince said as he followed Joel out the door.

"Bye, babe!" Jodi pulled me in for a quick hug. "I'll call and check on you tomorrow. Remember, if you need anything, let me know."

Thankful for my friend, I squeezed her back. "I will. Thanks!"

I closed the door and skipped back to the kitchen, excited that Viper was actually downstairs for once.

He was sitting at the island, staring down at his phone.

"Well that was fun, huh?" I said cheerfully.

"Sure."

I sprayed the counter and wiped it with a paper towel. "I just mean . . . having a new neighbor, especially one with a son Matthew's age. I'm excited about it."

"I can tell," he said dryly.

I set the bottle down and turned slowly. "What's that supposed to mean?"

"What?" he finally looked up at me.

"I don't know. You said 'I can tell' with a tone."

"I don't know. I didn't really care for the guy. So he has a kid . . . great." He blurted out, then returned his attention to his phone.

"What is the *matter* with you?" I finally blurted out, feeling days and days of frustration well up inside of me.

"Nothing is the matter with me," he sputtered. "So I didn't

care for your new friend, big deal."

"First of all, he's not my new friend . . . he's our neighbor. Second, you talked to the guy for maybe five minutes and in that time you decided you don't like him?"

"Yeah, I did. Nowhere does it say I have to spend at least an hour with someone to determine if I like them or not." He shook his head, put his phone in his pocket, and grabbed his crutches. "I'm going upstairs."

I swallowed a huge lump in my throat and let him go.

Chapter
16

Viper

MICHELLE DIDN'T TALK TO ME when she came to bed that night. She changed into her pajamas, quietly brushed her teeth, and slipped under the covers . . . all without one single word. I almost reached out at one point and put my hand on her hip, but I could tell by how far away she was that she didn't want to be touched. Not that I blamed her.

In the morning, she got up before me and again . . . silence. She showered early, and then I heard her quietly talking to the kids as she got Matthew ready for school. Before she left, she popped her head into the room. "I'm gonna take Matthew to school and run to the pharmacy and fill your prescriptions. Do you need anything while I'm out?"

"No thanks," I answered without rolling over. I wasn't sure if I didn't want to look at *her* or if I didn't want her to see *me*. They sounded the same, but they were two entirely different things.

"Okay. I'll be back shortly."

I heard her footsteps head down the stairs, and a minute later, the front door shut.

Though I really wanted to take a shower, I decided to make something to eat while the house was empty, then do my exercises from Sherman, *then* shower. With the way things had been going, I'd probably be ready for a nap again after all that.

I left my crutches leaning against the island and cruised along the counter like a toddler, trying to find something that sounded even remotely decent to eat.

"Maybe I'll have her stop and get me some food," I said out loud to myself. Pulling my phone from my pocket, I leaned my hip against the counter and hit the button to call her. Her phone rang out loud in the kitchen and my eyes searched the room until I saw it . . . lying on the table.

"Shit! There goes that." I put my phone back in my pocket and limped over to the pantry. My eyes scanned the shelves of chips, soups, and cupcake mix, looking for anything that sounded edible.

I wandered back over to the fridge and decided that even though it was early, a turkey sandwich would be good enough. As I pulled the turkey and mayo out and set them on the island, Michelle's phone rang out again. Hobbling over, I glanced down at the screen. I didn't recognize the number, but I worried it might be Matthew's school or something important, so I picked it up.

"Hello?"

"Good morning. Is Michelle Asher available, please?" a woman asked in an annoyingly cheerful voice.

"No, she's not here right now. Can I take a message?"

"Can you please just let her know that Greentree OBGYN called to confirm her appointment for tomorrow morning at ten thirty with Dr. Brookes? And that if she needs to cancel or reschedule to please give us a call before six p.m. tonight."

"Uh . . . okay," I mumbled, hanging up the phone as she was saying good-bye.

Why does she have a doctor appointment?

Why didn't she tell me?

She would tell me if something was wrong, right?

Thoughts started pounding against my brain like punches to a punching bag, making my head hurt instantly. I got up and started to pace the kitchen, but that made my knee throb and I needed to sit again. Maybe she *had* told me in my sleepy drug haze and I just didn't remember?

Thankfully, I heard her key in the front door a few minutes later, so I didn't have to wait long to find out what was going on.

She walked into the room with Maura on her hip and dropped the bag from the pharmacy on the counter. "Hey! Surprised to see you down here. I forgot my phone. Did you need something?"

"No." I shook my head. "But it did ring."

"Oh, okay," she said, setting Maura on the island to take her jacket off. She hung the jacket on the back of the chair and put Maura down, laughing as she sprinted off like a rocket to find her toys. Looking back at me, she shivered. "It's actually a little chilly out there this morning."

"I answered your phone."

"Okay. Who was it?" She pulled the paper bag open and set my pills on the counter, reading through the paperwork that was attached.

"It was your OBGYN's office. They said you have an appointment tomorrow."

Her body froze and her eyes slid to mine. "Oh."

I turned in my chair to face her. "Why do you have an appointment? Is something wrong?"

"No, I'm fine." She set the paperwork down and walked to the table to pick up her phone.

"If you're fine, then why the appointment?"

She took a deep breath and let it out slowly, sitting down in the chair next to me. Her eyes danced around the table for a minute, avoiding mine, but finally she looked up at me with a strange look on her face. "I'm going for the OB part, not the GYN part."

"I have no idea what that means." I tossed my hands up in the air and let them land with a thud on the kitchen table.

She chewed on the inside of her cheek and stared up at me with big eyes. "An OB is an obstetrician, a doctor who delivers babies . . ."

"But why do *you* need to go see a—" Her words registered with my brain like a semi crashing into a gas pump. "Wait. *You're* pregnant?"

Her eyes softened and her lips spread into a tiny smile. She nodded.

"What? How? When?" I asked all at once.

"Well, the when part would probably be when we had sex. That pretty much covers the what and how, too." She giggled.

"But you're on the pill."

"Yeah, and remember a couple months back when I caught Maura's horrible chest cold and went on antibiotics, and I told you that we needed to be more careful while I was on meds? Well, apparently we weren't careful enough."

"I don't understand—how long have you known?" I leaned forward in my chair and rested my elbows on the table.

"A couple weeks. I didn't want to tell you until I was sure, and I for sure didn't want to tell you like this, but . . . surprise!" She lifted her shoulders and gave me a big grin, her eyes sparkling.

I tilted my head to the side and raised one eyebrow. "Until you were sure? So there's still a chance that you're not?"

"Well . . . no. I have my eight-week appointment tomorrow, but I've took like seven tests and they were all positive, so I'm pretty certain."

My head fell in my hands and I didn't say any more.

"I was going to tell you as soon as I took the first one," she continued, "then everything happened with Gam and your knee, and there just wasn't a good time. I didn't mean to keep it from you. Please talk to me." Her hand reached out and tugged at my fingers. "What are you thinking?"

"What am I thinking?" I dropped my hands against the table again, louder this time. "I think this is horrible! I think this is the worst timing ever!"

"What? Why?" Her voice rose in shock.

"I don't know if I want kids *period,* let alone right now!" I stood and started limping around the kitchen, ignoring the pain. "And now I don't have a choice. You're pregnant, and there's nothing I can do about it."

Tears filled Michelle's eyes as she jumped up from her chair and spun around to face me. "I can't believe you're saying all this. You didn't know if you wanted kids? What do you think Matthew and Maura are? You think we're just playing house for fun?"

"No, but they're *your* kids, not mine! I don't know if I wanted to father children of my own, but it's too fucking late now. The decision has been made for me!" I roared, trying to catch my breath as I set my hands on the island and tensed my arms.

"How do you think I feel, Viper?" Michelle blurted out as tears ran down her cheeks. "I find out I'm pregnant, but because of the timing of everything else, I can't even talk to you about it because all you do is hide out up in the bedroom! Even when you *do* finally come down here you're grumpy and barely talk to me."

"Yeah, I know exactly how you feel. Brody told me. Thanks for *that,* by the way," I snapped.

"Thanks for what?" she glared at me. "Talking to your best friend and telling him I was worried about you? If you think I'm going to apologize for that, you're dead wrong. I *am* worried about you. You don't eat, you don't talk to anyone, you barely get out of bed. I didn't know what else to do!" Her voice trailed off as more tears fell from her eyes.

"Well, this sure adds another layer of topping to the situation, doesn't it?" I hissed. "Did you tell Brody about this, too? Who else knows? Gam? Kacie? Jodi?"

"No one else knows," she said softly, dabbing her eyes again. "I wanted to tell you before anyone else."

"Well, now I know, so you might as well sing it from the rooftops." I stood up straight and threw my hands in the air. "Viper is getting screwed again!"

Michelle narrowed her eyes at me and took a couple steps closer, shaking her head. "I can't believe you're acting like this. I seriously can't. Ya know, if you don't want to stick around, don't. I can handle being a single mom. I've done it before."

"Yeah," I scoffed. "For all of five minutes."

Her hand landed hard against the side of my face. "How *dare you* say something to me like that? Get out! Get out right now!" Sobs fell from her mouth uncontrollably as she put her shaky hands over her eyes.

"Momma?" Maura walked up to her and pulled on her pants. "Momma okay?"

My face stung and my head throbbed.

I wanted to bend down and scoop Maura up and tell her that her mommy was fine. I wanted to put my arms around Michelle and tell her that everything would work out. I wanted to go back in time twenty minutes and not react the way I had. I wanted to go back in time even further and not answer her fucking phone in the first place.

But it happened. It had all happened, and there was no way to make it go away.

So instead I did the one thing I knew how to do best.

I left.

Chapter
17

Michelle

I SLUMPED DOWN INTO THE kitchen chair and pulled Maura onto my lap.

"Momma okay?" she asked for the third time, staring up at me with big eyes.

I sniffed and gave her my best fake smile as I tucked a wild curl behind her ear. "Yes, baby. Mommy's okay."

But I wasn't okay. I wasn't even a *little* okay. The last twenty minutes had gone so horrifically wrong that my head was spinning and I felt sick to my stomach. I swallowed the puke that was attempting to climb up my throat, determined to keep it together for Maura. She'd already seen, and heard, way more than I ever wanted her to, and having another meltdown was not an option. She put her head against my chest and we rocked back and forth slowly.

My hands shook as I picked up my phone and sent Taylor a text.

Hey, I'm not feeling great. Is there any way you can
grab Matthew from school for me and let him play
at your apartment for a bit?

My whole body tingled with adrenaline and fear. Adrenaline
from the confrontation with Viper. In the whole year we'd been
together, we'd never had a fight like that. Not even close. And
fear for my future. Fear for Matthew's and Maura's futures. Fear
for the future of the tiny baby inside of me who I already loved
just as much as the other two, even though he or she was only
about the size of a kidney bean.

Could I do it alone if I had to?

Yes.

Did I want to?

No.

When I'd first taken the pregnancy test a couple of weeks ago
and saw those two pink lines, I had a little freak-out of my own.
Sitting alone in the bathroom, on the edge of the tub, I panicked.

What would Viper think?

What would he say?

Am I ready for three kids under the age of six?

But . . . as quickly as the panic came, it left. Common sense
crashed over my anxiety like a wave over a match, and I started
to think about my life, but more importantly—my boyfriend. On
the outside, Viper was all tattoos, trucker mouth, and a razor-
sharp edge, but on the inside, he was caring and sweet and loved
harder than almost anyone I'd ever met. In that moment, I *knew*
everything would be just fine.

And now, just a couple weeks later, I wasn't sure about
anything anymore.

My phone beeped loudly, scaring me half to death.

Maura flinched, too, then immediately relaxed again, and I
could tell by the weight of her body that she was asleep. Holding

her head against me, I carefully stood and carried her over to the couch. I laid her down, pulled the blanket over her shoulders, and kissed her soft cheek.

I sat on the other end of the couch and checked my phone. I'd said a quick little prayer as I walked Maura over that hopefully it was Viper and he'd cooled down and was going to come home so we could talk . . . but it wasn't him.

> Taylor: Hey! Sorry, I was in the shower. Sure! I can totally grab him. I don't work until 6, so I can drop him off before then?

> That's perfect! Thanks so much!

> Taylor: No problem! Feel better!

Not likely.

Taylor had no idea I was pregnant, and to be honest, I was nervous to tell her. She'd been so helpful with Matthew and Maura since her big brother's death, and she supported my relationship with Viper completely, but having a baby with another man was an entirely different story. Unless I was going to be having a baby *without* that man.

My mind drifted back to Viper and my eyes welled up with tears at the thought of all the moments that wouldn't happen the way I thought they would. Viper and his goofy smile when he saw his baby on the monitor for the first time during an ultrasound. Him rubbing my protruding belly and pampering me in a way that only Viper knew how. The look on his face as he watched his son or daughter enter the world . . . then cut the cord. And the moment I was looking forward to probably more than any other: the first time he fell asleep with our baby sleeping on his chest. In my head, I already knew where I was going to put that picture in the house, and now that picture might never even be taken.

I curled up in a ball and lay down, letting the tears flow freely down my cheeks and drop onto the couch until I fell asleep.

The doorbell rang over and over and over, pulling me straight out of a deep sleep. I sat up in a hurry, not really sure where I was or what time it was. I blinked hard and looked around the room, waiting for my eyes to focus and relay the information to my brain. Maura was still asleep on the couch, but the loud doorbell made her roll over and moan.

Maybe it's Viper.

My heart sprang into my throat as I stood and hurried to the front door. I rounded the corner and tried not to look disappointed when I saw Matthew's grinning face looking back at me through the glass. I wasn't sad that it was him, but I was sad that it wasn't Viper.

"Hey!" I greeted as I pulled the door back.

Without even a hello, Matthew sprinted past me toward the back of the house. My eyes followed him until he disappeared around the corner. "Wow. Hello to you, too." I giggled and turned back to Taylor.

"I'm so sorry," she rambled, shaking her head. "I tried to call and text, but you didn't answer. I got called in to work early."

"Oh my God. Taylor, I'm so sorry." I rubbed my eyes with the heels of my palm. "I totally crashed on the couch with Maura and didn't even hear my phone ring."

"I called Viper, but he didn't answer either." She handed me Matthew's coat and backpack.

"You called him?"

She nodded.

"Did you leave a message?"

"Yeah." She shrugged.

"What did you say?"

Her eyes scanned the room quickly and then returned to mine. "I just said that I couldn't get a hold of you but that I needed to drop Matthew off early. Could he tell you to call me. Why?"

"I was just curious." I shoved my hands in my back pockets and tried to act normal.

Taylor knew better. She narrowed her eyes at me and slowly turned her head, just a little. "What's going on with you?"

"Nothing," I lied. "I'm fine."

"No, you're not. I can see it. Something's up. Are you okay?"

My chin started to quiver and I felt myself losing control again. Keeping my composure was next to impossible when I was already upset and someone asked if I was okay. It was permission to my brain to open the floodgates and let it all back out, no matter how hard I tried to keep it in.

"No, you're not okay," she continued, her expression softening as she stepped forward. "What's going on?"

"It's nothing." I waved, offering up another fake smile. "Really. I promise."

She put her hands on my shoulders and stared me straight in the eye. "*Nothing* doesn't make your chin quiver and *nothing* doesn't bring tears to your eyes. Tell me."

"Viper and I got into a fight—a *big* fight—and I told him to leave." I struggled to get the words out and keep my sob in.

"I don't understand." She dropped her hands and shook her head slowly as her eyes searched my face. "You two never fight. What was it about?"

I wrapped my arms around myself to hide my shaking hands. "Uh . . . well . . . he found out I'm pregnant, and the news didn't go as well as I was hoping."

Her mouth fell open. "You're pregnant?"

I swallowed hard and nodded.

"Congratulations!" she cheered and pulled me in for a hug. "I know you're sad right now and we'll get back to that, but I'm so happy for you and about this, so I just have to hug you first."

Her reaction made me feel a thousand times better, but also made my cry harder. We stood in the foyer, her arms wrapped around me, as I sobbed and sobbed against her shoulder. After what felt like an hour, I pulled back and turned toward the powder room. I pulled a handful of tissues from the box and blew my nose. Then I grabbed another handful and wiped my eyes before returning to Taylor.

"Sorry about that." I tried wiping my tears from her shirt but they'd already soaked in.

"Oh God, I don't care about my shirt. I'm worried about *you*."

She watched me like a hawk as I dabbed at my eyes again. It didn't seem to matter what I did, the tears would *not* stop coming.

"Hang on one second, okay?" she said as she pulled her phone from her back pocket and stepped into the living room.

I walked to the back of the house to check on Matthew, hoping my meltdown hadn't totally freaked him out. He was sitting on the couch, quietly playing a game on his Kindle as Maura leaned her head against his shoulder and watched him.

"Okay." Taylor walked up behind me. "I called in."

I spun to face her. "What? No! Don't do that. I'm fine . . . I promise."

"I'm sure you are," she agreed. "But I'm going to help you out around here tonight just in case. We're gonna feed these kiddos dinner in a while, tuck them into bed, and you're going to fill me in on everything, got it?"

I nodded. "Thanks, Tay."

"Anytime." She gave me a tight smile and sat with the kids on the couch.

I looked past her into the kitchen and my eyes focused on Viper's pill bottle on the island. As angry as I was at him for his reaction, I didn't want him to be in pain all night. I picked up the bottle and read the label closely. "Every four hours . . ." I mumbled to myself as I glanced at the clock on the stove. He'd already been gone for almost five.

I won't stop worrying all night if I don't make sure.

140

I took out my phone and sent him a quick text.

Do you need your pain meds tonight?

My heart raced as I stared at the screen, waiting for his reply. I was mad as hell for the way he'd treated me, but that didn't mean my feelings walked out the door with him. I still loved him a lot. More than anything, I wanted him to text and say that he needed the meds and would come back for them, then maybe stay and talk to me.

My phone lit up and I swiped the screen.

Viper: No

Gutted by his one-word text, I put my phone away and turned my attention back to Matthew and Maura. I'd spent most of the day crying and feeling sorry for myself, but I still had a few hours left before they went to bed to make up for it.

While Matthew and I played Candyland and Maura "helped," Taylor nosed around my mostly empty kitchen to try and find something to make for dinner. It was no secret that cooking was just not my thing, even after Viper spent a year trying to teach me, so when she offered to whip something up, I didn't argue.

Just as our third game was finishing, Taylor called us to the table.

"How did you do this?" My eyes took in everything she'd made in less than half an hour. There was a huge bowl of alfredo pasta with shredded chicken, a giant bowl of broccoli, and biscuits that were still steaming from the oven.

Taylor looked at the table and shrugged. "It really wasn't hard." Her eyes lifted to me and she giggled. "Close your mouth and sit down. You just need to practice. You'll get it."

I watched in awe as Matthew and Maura shoved bite after bite of noodles, chicken, and broccoli in their mouths without me begging them to eat. My appetite wasn't near as large as theirs, but I ate a little and pushed the rest around my plate while we all talked.

After dinner, I gave the kids each a quick bath and dressed them in clean, cozy pajamas. I tucked them into bed and went back to the kitchen, surprised and relieved to find Taylor already had the table cleared off and dishwasher running.

"Wow." I shook my head as I gawked at my sparkling kitchen. "I swear you were a mom of twelve in a past life."

She let out a loud laugh as she pulled her hair wavy blonde hair up into a ponytail. "Well, let's get this started. I'm probably going to want to stab him in the eye, but I want to hear what happened anyway. Let's pour some wine—wait—pour *me* some wine and lay it all out."

We sat on the couch for a long time, and I told her everything. About how Viper had been acting since his injury, the phone call and his reaction to the news—every single depressing word. I was able to hold it together just enough to get the story out, even though my voice shook. She sat stunned, her mouth hanging open and her blue eyes as wide as I'd ever seen them.

"I don't even know what to say," she finally responded.

I exhaled loudly. "So . . . that's why I called and asked you to get Matthew, because it had just happened and I was too upset to drive."

She scooted closer to me and took my hand in hers. "You should have just told me then. Not only would I never judge you, I would've been here hours earlier to help."

"I know that, but to be honest, I was nervous to tell you that I was pregnant, and I feel horrible about it now."

"Why were you nervous?" she asked softly.

I shrugged. "I was married to your brother, made a life with your brother, had babies with your brother."

"You were, but your relationship didn't end because you or him stopped loving each other and gave up. He died. It's horrible and sad, and I think about him every day, but he died. You didn't. Life goes on, and you're allowed to fall in love and make a new life that was just as great as the one you had with him." She gave me a tight-lipped smile, then added, "And even though I'm not going to be blood related to this baby, you bet your ass I'm still going to be cool Auntie Tay and spoil the crap out of him or her."

A small laugh broke through my sadness. "How is it that you're younger than me, never been married, yet you seem to have it all figured out?"

"Ah." She waved her hand and sat back against the couch. "My head is still in the clouds with Isaac, and I still want everyone to be in love all the time. I'm sure it'll wear off eventually."

"I sure hope not." I looked across the room at the bookshelf in the corner that held dozens of picture frames and memories. Some of me, Viper, and the kids. Some of me, Mike, and the kids. Some of Viper and Mike. Hopefully I would be adding to that shelf, not taking pictures off of it.

"So . . ." Taylor said after a minute. "What are you going to do about Viper?"

I picked my water bottle off of the coffee table and took a long drink, trying to think about my answer. "I don't know what *to* do," I finally said as I screwed the cap back on. "The things he said and they way he said them—totally not okay. But I *do* love him, and I do want him to be here with me. I don't know, Taylor. It feels like . . . he got on the plane for that road trip as one person but came back as someone totally different. And I miss that other guy, but I don't know how to find him again."

Taylor's eyebrows lifted quickly. "Wow. That was . . . wow. You know him better than anyone though, Michelle. If there's anyone that's going to bring him out of this, it's you."

Part of me hoped that she was right . . . but not only did I not know how to bring him back, I wasn't sure how much more rejection I could take.

Chapter *18*

Viper

DRIVING HOME FROM MICHELLE'S FELT weird. Not only was I on pain meds and not supposed to be driving, I hadn't been home to *my* house in a really long time. A couple of months, at least. When Michelle and I got serious, I'd started spending a night or two at her house a week, but over the last year that had gradually increased to every night. Since then, I only ran to the house to check on it maybe once every couple weeks or to grab something that I needed. All of my buddies gave me a hard time and told me to sell the house since I was never there, but for some reason I couldn't. I liked having an escape hatch if need be. But turning into the driveway, opening the garage, and pulling my car in felt foreign.

I didn't want to deal with my feelings or think about anything that had happened that day, so I went straight into my bedroom and never left.

The next morning I woke up to my knee throbbing. Michelle had texted to see if I wanted my pain meds, but like a stubborn douchebag, I'd said no. As I sat on the edge of my bed, I regretted not going to get them. I regretted a lot of things about the day before, actually. While I still wasn't sure how I felt about the whole baby thing, my response to Michelle, and the things I'd said to her, wasn't something I was proud of, nor could I take it back. I'd acted like a first-class asshole, and she'd had every right to tell me to leave . . . and slap me.

As I limped to my bathroom, I prayed that I had Advil or Tylenol in the cabinet; otherwise, I'd have to come up with plan B.

"Boom!" I called out when I pulled the mirror back and saw the bottle of pills. I tossed three in my mouth and swallowed them without any water, then went in search of food. I wandered aimlessly around my kitchen. It felt weird. Every piece of furniture, every appliance, every coaster in the house was mine, but I hadn't walked around and actually *looked* at everything in so long, it felt like I was in someone else's house.

I didn't even bother opening the fridge because anything in there wouldn't have been good anyway, and the pantry wasn't much better. Pulling my phone out of my pocket, I checked the time to see if I could run and grab something to eat before my therapy appointment. I would only have enough time for food or a shower, and I chose the shower.

"Morning," I said dryly as I walked past Gina, the receptionist at the physical therapy center. I propped my crutches up against the wall and climbed onto the exercise bike. I looked toward the ground and closed my eyes as I pedaled through the pain and stiffness in my knee.

"You're five minutes early!" Sherman bellowed from across the room, making my head snap up. With his signature jolly grin plastered to his face, he crossed the room toward me and I shook my head with a laugh. He had on a bright orange Hawaiian shirt and khaki shorts with white socks pulled up to his calves.

"Sherman, these outfits of yours. Let's just say you'd lose

terribly at hide and seek." I sat back and wiped the sweat from my brow.

He paused and put both hands on his hips, striking a pose. "I know, don't I look fabulous?"

A couple women a few stations over laughed. "You always look fabulous, Sherman!" one of them called out.

"Thanks, doll!" He waved as she blew him a kiss.

My eyes slid from Sherman to the women and back again. "You sure are popular around here."

"You have *no* idea. Everyone loves me, especially the ladies." He lifted a hand to the side of his mouth to block them from hearing and lowered his voice. "If you ever need pointers on how to get girls, you just let the Ole Sherm know and I'll teach you my ways."

I laughed out loud, so hard my shoulders shook. "Is that so? I'll remember that one."

"Okay, you ready to get started?" He clapped his hands enthusiastically. I'd barely had two sessions with Sherman and I could already tell that the man never ran out of energy. He was upbeat and energetic to the point where you couldn't help but smile when you were with him. It was contagious. And not only was he like that the whole hour with me, he was like with everyone in the center, even other people's clients. People were constantly coming up to him and giving him hugs or high-fiving him.

Sherman was hilarious to be around, but he was really good at what he did. If I gave him shit about an exercise, he pushed back harder. He explained everything he was doing and never treated me like a dumb jock.

After an hour of more quad sets, what felt like a million straight leg raises, and my new arch nemesis the prone hang, Sherman told me to follow him over to a table in the corner.

"Hop up!" He smacked the top of it loudly.

Confused by what we were doing next, I slowly lifted myself

onto the table.

"Lie down and put your leg up on this, please." He lifted a green plastic wedge up and gently put it under my knee to elevate it.

"What are you doing?" I asked, folding my hands and tucking them behind my head.

"We didn't do it the first day because you were being a bit of a drama queen, but we're going to do electronic stimulation of your knee today." He stuck four sticky things to my knee and attached them to the machine next to him. "What e-stim does is stimulate your quad muscles to contract, stimulate your nerves to decrease pain, and increases blood flow all over, which, as you know, speeds up recovery. Some therapists don't use it and think it's a waste of time. Personally, I say it doesn't hurt, and if it aids in the healing process and gets you back on the ice sooner, why not?"

"This is weird," I said, staring down at the sticky pads on my knee.

"You're weird," he mocked as he put one bag of ice under my knee and one on top of it. "Okay, here we go."

He pressed a few buttons and my leg instantly felt tingly.

"Whoa!" I sat up on my elbows. "That feels really weird. Is this gonna hurt?"

Sherman pressed his lips together and rolled his eyes. "Really? You're a professional hockey player *and* you go by the name "Viper," yet you're worried about a little electricity on your knee? Big baby."

I glared at him and opened my mouth to respond just as my quad muscles started contracting. "Holy shit!" I stared down at my leg, watching the muscles clench and relax, knowing that I had nothing to do with it.

"Trust me, you'll grow to love this."

"If you say so." I lay back against the table.

"You seem extra pissy today. What gives?" he asked after a

couple minutes.

I stared up at the ceiling and shrugged. "Nothing."

I glanced over at him as he arched one eyebrow at me. "We may have only had two sessions so far, but I'm dialed in to you. What gives?"

"I just did something I shouldn't have done yesterday, and it's on my mind."

"Ah," Sherman said with a small nod. "I'm not gonna ask you to tell me what it is, but I will say this . . . no man ever lay on his death bed pissed off that he apologized too many times throughout his life, but plenty wish they'd apologized more."

I swallowed hard and looked back up at the white ceiling tiles. "Look at you, Sherman. You're like a walking, talking fortune cookie."

"That's what they tell me!" he boasted loudly as he threw his arms in the air and walked away.

What he said played over and over and over in my mind. The way I'd acted was horrible and I needed to apologize about that, but I still wasn't sure that I wanted kids of my own . . . now, or ever.

After therapy, I was starving and knew exactly where I needed to go, even if it meant that I might see Kat. I drove straight to Gam's.

When I pulled up, the same car from the other day was in the driveway, but I did my best to ignore it.

"Hey!" I called out as I pulled the door open and walked into the house.

Gam looked up from her book and her face broke into a huge grin. "There's my boy!" She got up from her favorite chair in the family room and gave me a big hug. "I haven't seen you in almost a week. How are you feeling?"

"I'm hanging in there." I shrugged. "Still a little sore but getting better."

She frowned as she looked past me. "Where's everybody else?"

"Uh . . . home."

She straightened and looked at me. "How come?"

I gave her another shrug and slid past her to sit on the couch. "I just came from physical therapy, so they weren't with me."

Not a total lie.

She followed me with narrowed eyes. "Should you be driving already?"

"I don't know, but I am."

"Does it hurt?" she asked as she sat back down on her couch slowly.

"To drive? No, it's my left leg. It just kinda sits off to the side anyway. Now can we stop the interrogation, please? I'm starving to death." I pointed to the kitchen with my thumb.

"Oh, I can tell," she said sarcastically as she dragged her eyes down my body and back up again. "Come on."

I followed her into the kitchen and immediately tensed when I saw Kat standing at the sink with her back to us.

"What are you in the mood for?" Gam asked, making her way over to the fridge. Kat turned around and glanced at me before quickly going back to whatever she was doing.

I shrugged and pulled a kitchen chair out. "I'm not picky."

She lowered her head and peeked at all the shelves. "I have leftover spaghetti, grilled chicken, stuffed peppers . . . anything sound exciting yet?"

"All of the above," I said, half kidding, half not.

"Better in your belly than in the garbage." She leaned against the counter with one hand and started taking containers out of the fridge with the other.

Kat hurried over and took the food out of her hand. "Let me do that for you."

"No, I got it," Gam said stubbornly.

Kat tilted her head to the side and glared at Gam, who retreated like a little kid.

"How's therapy going?" she asked as she sat down next to me.

"Good. Really good, actually." I tore the corner off an envelope that was sitting on the table and rolled it in between my fingers. "My therapist is a dude named Sherman. I thought I was gonna hate him, but something about him is just . . . different."

"Different good?" Gam took a sip of the iced tea that she'd brought with her from the family room. At least I thought it was iced tea, but with Gam you never knew.

"Yeah. For sure. He's a fun guy."

"Fun is good."

"Fun *is* good," I agreed. "As long as he's kicking my ass back into shape so I can go be fun on the ice, that's all I care about."

"You'll be back out there in no time."

The microwave beeped, and Kat took out the hot plate and set it in front of me.

"Thanks," I mumbled without looking up at her.

"Want some root beer, too?" she asked nonchalantly.

Gam's head swooped up to Kat with a frown. "How did you know he likes root beer?"

Kat froze as her mouth dropped, her eyes darting back and forth between Gam and me. "Um . . . I . . ."

"She was in the kitchen the other day when I got one out of the fridge," I answered for her.

Idiot. Why did you do that? That was your chance to let the cat out of the bag so Kat could walk out the door.

"I see." Gam nodded, content with that answer. "I keep it in my fridge all the time for him. Nobody loves root beer like my Lawrence." She reached over and playfully pinched my cheek as I shoveled a forkful of spaghetti into my mouth.

151

As I chewed, my eyes followed Kat, who hurried to the fridge and returned with a bottle of cold root beer. She gave me a small smile and a quick wink as she set it down.

"I'm gonna go change your sheets," she said as she rested her hand on Gam's shoulder. "Unless you want me to do something else instead?"

"Nope. That's wonderful. Thank you!" Gam rested her hand on Kat's and beamed up at her.

I waited until Kat was out of earshot. "How are things going? With *her?*"

"With Kat? Oh, they're *so* great." There was a softness, a contentment, in her voice that I didn't hear often. "When I found out that you'd hired a nurse, I was irritated and so hesitant about this whole thing, but she's more than a nurse. She helps me pick up, she takes me places, she keeps me company. I'm so glad she's here, Lawrence."

As bad as I wanted Kat gone, it was obvious how happy Gam was to have her around, and Gam's happiness was the most important thing. That meant Kat was there to stay.

Chapter
19

Michelle

IT HAD BEEN THREE DAYS and not a word from Viper. I picked up my phone to text him at least a hundred times, but every time I pulled his name up, I got mad all over again and put my phone away.

I'd been to my first doctor appointment, and while it was too early to *hear* the heartbeat, I did *see* it on the ultrasound. Even though it was a tiny, grainy white blob, my baby's first picture hung proudly on the fridge. Thankfully Matthew hadn't noticed and asked about it yet, and I had no idea what I was going to tell him when he did, but I needed to figure it out fast. The one thing he had noticed was that Viper was gone.

"Momma, did Viper go on a plane to play hockey?" he asked as I sat on the couch folding tiny pairs of *Thomas the Tank Engine* underwear.

"No, buddy. Viper went to his house for a few days," I answered as nonspecifically as I could.

"Oh." His eyes dropped to the coffee table and thought about what I'd said. I braced myself for more questions but was grateful when he decided to run off to the playroom down the hall instead.

"Shhhh! Maura's taking her afternoon nap," I called after him.

Kacie had called a couple of times over the last few days, but I'd avoided her. I'd been avoiding everyone, really. I didn't know what to say or what to think, but as she called again, I knew I couldn't avoid her anymore.

"Hello?"

"Hey! What's going on? Where have you been?"

"Hey. I've been here, just busy. How about you?" Every nerve in my body was on high alert. I had no idea if Viper had talked to Brody and told him anything, but if Brody knew, Kacie knew.

"We've been busy, too, but we're hanging in there. How's Viper?"

Kacie wasn't the type to beat around the bush. If she knew something was up, she wouldn't have asked how he was.

"Honestly, I have no idea," I answered with a big sigh as I sat back against the couch.

"What does that mean?" she asked, her tone turning serious.

I turned and peeked over the couch to make sure Matthew wasn't anywhere near me. "We had a fight—a big fight—a couple days ago, and he left."

"Wait. He left? Left where?"

"I don't know. We haven't talked since."

"Holy shit! What did you fight about?"

I took a deep breath and closed my eyes, knowing I needed to just let it out. "I found out I'm pregnant, and the news didn't go over so well on his end."

"You're pregnant?" she asked softly. "Why didn't you tell me?"

"I don't know. I didn't tell anyone. I've been so preoccupied with Gam, then Viper, and everything just kinda ran together, and it was never a good time."

"Well . . . congratulations. I'm happy for you!" I could tell she was grinning by the tone in her voice. Kacie was a true friend who would always have my back, no matter what. "I can't wait to squeeze that little nugget. When are you due?"

"Not till June. I'm only eight weeks."

"So what happened when you told him?"

"Well, I didn't really tell him." I lifted my feet onto the coffee table and crossed my ankles. "I was running errands and forgot my phone. He intercepted the appointment reminder call from the doctor's office."

"Oh, shit," she said in a low tone.

"Yep. And when I got home, everything just kind of exploded." I spent the next several minutes filling her in on our fight and the last couple of days of radio silence.

"Michelle, you should have called me. I would have gone to the doctor with you."

"It really wasn't that big of a deal," I said, half lying. The appointment really wasn't a big deal, but I would have loved for someone to be at the ultrasound with me, sharing in my excitement—and my tears as I drove home alone.

"What can I do for you? You have to let me do something."

"Nothing. Really. I'm fine."

"When is your next doctor appointment?"

"In a month."

"Will you at least let me go with you to that?" she asked as if she had read my mind. "I don't want you going to your doctor appointments alone."

"Fine," I agreed. "But you have to promise to turn around during my weigh-ins."

She let out a loud chuckle. "Girl, you're talking to someone who delivered two five-pound babies at once. You don't even want to know how much weight I gained with that pregnancy."

We chatted for a few more minutes until Matthew came running back into the room. "Moooooom, you said we would go to the park today."

"Oh, crap," I mumbled.

"What?"

"I totally forgot that I told Matthew I'd take him to the park today. Think he'd go for a nap instead?"

"Good luck with that one. They never forget anything." She laughed again. "Call me later."

We hung up and I stared at Matthew, who had his hands clasped together and was giving me puppy dog eyes.

"The park, huh?" I sighed, already exhausted just thinking about it.

He nodded excitedly.

"Okay, let's go see if Maura is awake, and if she is, we'll go for a little while."

He threw his hands in the air in celebration and sprinted up the stairs.

"Good morning, Mrs. Klein!" Matthew waved to our neighbor as we made our way down the driveway. I gave her a wave, too, silently begging her not to come over. She was a wonderful lady, but her husband worked out of town during the week, and once she started chatting with you, any plans you had for the next hour would be canceled. I gave her a quick wave and hustled down the sidewalk toward the park.

A moving van was parked across the street, and Matthew's eyes lit up when he saw Gavin bouncing a basketball on the front porch.

"Mom! Can we go say hi?" he asked as he bounced up and down.

"Sure." I nodded.

He wrapped his hand around the edge of the stroller like he was supposed to and we crossed the street.

"Hi, Gavin!" he yelled before we even hit the driveway.

Gavin looked up and waved excitedly, running over to meet us. "Hi! We're moving in today. Wanna see my new room?"

Matthew's face swung up to mine with crinkled, begging eyebrows.

"Fine, but just for one minute." He turned and sprinted across the yard. "And take your shoes off in their house!" I called after him.

They barreled through the garage and into the house, almost knocking over Joel, who was on his way out. "Whoa!" he yelled and moved off to the side as they zoomed by. He looked out and saw me on the sidewalk. "Hey!"

I waved and he walked over.

"Move-in day, huh?" I asked.

"Yeah." He glanced at the truck and back at me, his clear blue eyes catching me off guard again. "I don't have too much left. Hopefully it doesn't take all night. You don't realize how much crap you've accumulated until you try and fit it all into one box truck."

I laughed and nodded. "Ain't that the truth."

Before we could get another word out, the front door swung open, smacking against the brick wall, and Matthew and Gavin came flying out on the lawn.

"Whoa, whoa, whoa!" Joel called out. "Let's not break the house before we've even finished moving in, okay?"

"Hey, Mom, can Gavin come to the park with us?" Matthew asked as he panted for air.

"Um . . ." I glanced from him to Joel. "It's okay with me if it's okay with his dad."

"Dad, can I? Pleeeeeeeease?" Gavin dropped to his knees and pressed his hands together.

Joel sighed and looked over at me. "You really want an extra kid?" he asked under his breath.

I shrugged. "It's totally fine. And honestly, he'll keep Matthew busy, which means I'm not spending my time running back and forth between two kids alone."

"Okay, well it's fine by me then." He turned toward Gavin, who was jumping up and down with Matthew. "Gavin, you behave, got it?"

Gavin's grinning face nodded up at his dad and the boys took off down the sidewalk.

"Ah, ah! Wait for me," I called out. "Guess I better go."

Joel gave me a small grin and a nod as I hurried after the boys.

The park by our house was one of my favorite things about our subdivision. It had a huge wood castle that spanned the entire side of the park, with a shaky chain drawbridge, hanging tire obstacle course, and tons more. It also had an area for littler kids where Maura loved to play. Having Gavin there to play with Matthew really was more of a treat for me. Not only did he have the best time ever, but he was so preoccupied with Gavin that it left me some time to focus on just Maura.

She laid her head back against the baby swing as I pulled it from the front and let go. Her eyes stared up at the blue sky, her blond curls peeking out from under her hat and blowing in the wind. Life had been so hectic lately that it seemed I'd just been going through the motions to get from the beginning of the day to the end, but while I stood there, watching my sweet girl on the swing, nothing else mattered.

As she swung toward me, I quickly reached out and squeezed her chubby thigh. It was her most ticklish spot, and she rewarded me with a deep, throaty giggle.

"Well that's the cutest sound I think I've ever heard."

I whipped around to see Joel walking toward us with a smile on his face.

"Isn't it?" I agreed, turning back to Maura.

"I haven't had a little one in a long time, but wow, I sure do miss those laughs." He walked up and leaned against the metal pole.

"I know. I swear they're what keeps me going most days," I said as I pushed her again. "Hey . . . aren't you supposed to be working?"

"I'm done!"

"What? No way!"

"Yes way!" He nodded with a laugh. "It's amazing how quickly you get things done when someone takes your crazy son to the park for an hour and a half."

"Have we been here that long already?"

"Yup." He nodded again, his bright, ice-blue eyes boring into mine. "Time flies when you're having fun."

"More like time flies when they're not asking for something every five seconds." I let out a quick laugh as I looked back at Maura. "We should probably head home and clean up for dinner soon. I'm hoping a long time at the park equals early to bed."

"You have to let me pay you back for this afternoon. How about I spring for pizza for dinner?"

"Oh, no, that's okay." I stopped the swing and took Maura out.

"Come on, you have to let me do something," he insisted.

I thought for a minute, staring down as I buckled Maura into the stroller. Dinner with a new friend was tempting, but I couldn't do it. Even though Viper and I were going through . . . something . . . it just felt disrespectful.

"No, really. Thank you, but I'm wiped. I'm probably just going to make them something quick and crash early right along with them."

"Okay." He stood and nodded, tucking his hands into his hoodie pocket. "I get it, but if you change your mind, I'm right across the street now, neighbor." He flashed me a big, playful grin that I couldn't help but return.

159

"Thanks. We'll be around all day tomorrow, too, if Gavin wants to come over again." I started walking toward where the boys were playing.

He stepped in right beside me. "Sounds good. They can probably hang for a bit in the morning, but I'll take Gavin back to his mom's after dinner."

"Matthew, Gavin, come on! Time to go home!" I hollered toward them before turning back to Joel. "Does she live around here?"

"Yeah, just a few miles away. I kinda followed her here, actually. We used to live in northern Iowa, but then she got remarried and moved here." He lifted two fingers between his lips and whistled loudly for the boys, who were running around in the field past the park. "Anyway, I couldn't stand to be that many hours away from Gavin, so I packed up and slept on a buddy's couch while I looked for a job and eventually, this house."

"Wow. That's awesome that you moved here to be with him."

"I don't know if it's that awesome." He shrugged, staring at the ground as he walked. "He's my buddy. The thought of missing out on the big stuff in his life was hard, but the thought of missing out on all the little everyday stuff was unacceptable."

Joel's feelings about being away from his son and needing to be part of his life overwhelmed me. I so desperately wanted Viper to feel that way about our baby, and I hoped that eventually he would. Though the longer we went without talking, the more nervous I became.

The boys hustled up next to us and whined for the next few minutes.

"It's not even dark yet," Matthew complained.

"Yeah," Gavin added. "We weren't done yet."

"Well,"—Joel reached over and pulled Gavin into a playful headlock—"the good news is that we live in this house now and that park is less than a block away, so you can play there any time you want."

Gavin squealed and flailed his arms. "Can we come back tomorrow?"

"Yes, probably for a little bit in the morning." Joel let Gavin go and he sprinted down the sidewalk ahead of us with Matthew right behind him.

"Those two are gonna run the world one day," I said with a quick laugh.

We said good-bye to Joel and Gavin when we got to their house and crossed back over to ours. "Did you guys have fun out there?" I asked Matthew.

He nodded excitedly. "He's so fun, Mom. We like all the same stuff."

My heart soared. He hadn't sounded that excited in a long time. "That's awesome, bud. I'm so happy for you."

Matthew grabbed the keys from me to open the front door like he always did, and I bent down and pulled Maura from her stroller. I stood and glanced over toward Joel's house, surprised to see him still standing out on his porch staring at us. He noticed me look that way and gave another small wave and a big grin that I could see clear across the street. I waved back quickly and turned toward the house, not at all comfortable with the pace my heart was beating.

Chapter
20

Viper

"I'M COMIN'! I'M COMIN'!" I yelled as I slowly made my way to the front door after the doorbell rang for a third time. I didn't need my crutches anymore, but I wasn't moving very quickly either.

Brody stood on the other side of the door with a smile on his face. "What's up, bud?" He held his hand out and gave me a quick hug.

"Hey! I didn't know you were coming by," I said as I shut the door.

He stuffed his hands in his front pockets and lifted his eyebrows. "I've texted you a few times, but you don't respond these days."

I rolled my eyes. "Sorry. Things have been a little crazy. Here, come with me."

He followed me into the garage, where I'd been when he rang the doorbell. I sat down on the bucket and looked over, noticing that he was frozen in the doorway with his mouth hanging open.

"What?"

His eyes moved back and forth around the garage. "What the hell are you doing?"

"I'm cleaning my bike." I motioned toward my motorcycle.

"Why?" He finally stepped down the wood steps into the garage.

I shrugged. "Why not? I haven't ridden it in almost a year. I figure once my knee is healed enough, I'm gonna get back on it."

"Okay," Brody said slowly as he took a couple of steps and leaned his shoulder against the wall. "Any particular reason?"

"Why own it if I'm not gonna ride it, ya know? There's a lot of things I don't do anymore that I want to start doing again." I picked the rag back up and gently rubbed circles into my once shiny chrome tailpipe. "And I've been thinking about it, since I'm going to be off for a while, what if I start the ball rolling on this bar thing? You said you'd be open."

"I did say I'd be open," Brody agreed with a nod.

"So I figure, instead of sitting on the couch doing nothing, I'll work on that. Then when you're home from road trips, I can fill you in. We can go to The Bumper and hang out like we used to."

"Sure. We can do that. But before you go off on your motorcycle opening bars, can we talk about something real quick?" He grabbed an empty five-gallon bucket from the corner, flipped it upside down, and sat down on it next to me. "Can we talk about what's going on with you and Michelle?"

I tried not to let it show that every muscle in my body tensed up. "How do you know about that?"

He tilted his head to the side and pursed his lips together. "Really?"

Duh. Kacie.

"There's nothing really to tell. She's pregnant. I'm not happy about it. We fought. End of story."

"Sounds like you did more than fought. You guys haven't

talked in over a week now."

"Yep. She told me to leave, so I did." I glared at him out of the corner of my eye. "What was I supposed to do?"

"I don't know . . . stay? Talk? Act like a grown-up for once?"

I turned my head toward him and narrowed my eyes. "I don't need this shit from you, Murphy. If you came here just to bitch at me, get the fuck out."

He let out a heavy sigh. "I didn't come here to bitch at you, Viper, but I am worried about you. This isn't you."

"Maybe it *is* me!" I exclaimed. "Maybe that nice, wholesome family man bullshit I was doing for the last year wasn't me."

"I don't believe that."

"Believe whatever the hell you want!" I stood up quickly, flipping the bucket over behind me. "Honestly, I don't really care who you think I am. I don't even know who the fuck I am. I am hockey. Hockey is me. That's gone, and now I have to find myself all over again, so I'm getting back to basics."

Brody stood up and gave me a hard glare. "You're more than hockey and we both know that, but if you're going to sit here and wallow around in some bullshit pity party, have at it. I'm out." He climbed the wood steps and opened the door, but turned back around. "I'm also gonna say this, since I have no idea when you're going to pull your head out of your ass and talk to me again. Last time you lost your mind, that doctor—Dr. Shawn—she helped you find it. Maybe it's time to give her another call."

The slam of the garage door shook the whole garage, followed by another slam from the front door a minute later.

Anger swirled around in my chest, gaining momentum with each rotation. I picked up the bottle of chrome polish that was next to me and hurled it against the wall as hard as I could. It exploded, sending streams of liquid down my wall and across my bike.

My chest heaved.

My nostrils flared.

My head throbbed.

Who the fuck did Brody think he was coming into *my* house, lecturing me on how to be a man? Maybe he was happy over there with Kacie and their house full of kids, mini van, and white picket fence, but that wasn't me. That would never fucking be me.

I spent the next few hours cussing out Brody, Michelle, my knee, Kat, and just about everything else as I lost myself in the bottom of a whiskey bottle. Unlike Gam, I hated whiskey. It tasted like shit, but it was what I deserved. My eyes felt like they were hopping all over the room. I couldn't control them no matter how hard I tried and suddenly, I remembered why I hated drinking.

Pulling my T-shirt over my head and kicking my shorts off, I crossed my room and sat down on the edge of my bed, setting my phone on my nightstand. I stared at it.

I stared at it like I was mad at it. Like I wanted to throw it.

Why did you have to answer her phone?

I grabbed *my* phone and squeezed it hard in my hand. When it didn't break like I was hoping, I took a deep breath and swiped at the screen.

A picture of me, Michelle, Matthew, and Maura standing by the lake at Brody's house was my wallpaper.

"No man ever lay on his death bed pissed off that he'd apologized too many times throughout his life, but plenty wish they'd apologized more." Sherman's words whirled around in my head for the ten millionth time. My head spun as I focused really hard to find Michelle's name in my text messages. Before I knew it, I started typing.

Hey. I should have called sooner and probably should have done this in person, but I'm sorry for the way I reacted in the kitchen. I was a dick and you were right to smack me. My head is in a weird place right now and this baby thing is making it worse. I need to figure some shit out. I'm sorry again. Kiss the kids for me.

I dropped my phone on my nightstand and crashed against my pillow, snoring before the text probably even reached her phone.

The next morning, I tried to sit up but my head weighed three hundred pounds. As I looked around the room, mentally clearing the cobwebs from my brain, everything from the night before came rushing back. My fight with Brody, the bottle of whiskey, the text I'd sent Michelle.

Holy shit!

I forgot that I'd texted Michelle. I rolled toward my nightstand too fast and my temples throbbed like my head was in a vice being tightened by King Kong. Pinching my eyes shut tight, I sat up slower and took a deep breath. Once the stars disappeared from my eyes and the puke in the back of my throat went away, I picked up my phone and saw that I had an unread text. I quickly re-read the text I'd sent Michelle and looked under it for a response.

Nothing.

I don't know what I wanted her to say back, but I would've rather had her tell me "fuck you" than not respond at all.

I hit the back button to go to my my main text screen and saw my unread text . . . from a number that was no longer stored in my phone, but that I recognized from a long time ago.

No. No. No. What the fuck? When did I text her?

I glanced at the time I'd sent Michelle the text. One o'clock in the morning. I switched back to the text I'd sent Kat. Two o'clock in the morning.

My head started throbbing again. I didn't even remember texting her. I thought I'd fallen right to sleep. My hand hovered over the screen, not sure I wanted to read what I'd said to her or what she'd said back. I swallowed puke again and pressed the tiny envelope on the screen. My text was above hers.

> Hey. So. Sorry I was such a dick the first day at Gam's. Seeing you was a shock, but she really likes you and I really like her, so I'm gonna stop being a dick.

She had responded half an hour later.

> Kat: Um . . . okay. I'm not really sure what to make of this. I'm assuming you're drunk, but I hope that you really mean this and you'll let me do my job in peace. There's no reason we can't be friends, Viper. We have a long history that wasn't always good, but I still care about you as a person. Anyway, I'm going back to bed. We can talk more about this later.

My heart started pounding. On one hand, I was relieved that I didn't say something way more fucking stupid, but on the other, I had no idea why I'd even texted her in the first place. Or how I remembered her phone number after all this time.

I flopped back on my bed and started thinking about what Brody said as he'd stormed out of my garage. Maybe calling Dr. Shawn wasn't such a bad idea after all . . . not that I would ever tell him that.

On my way to the kitchen, I stopped in my bathroom and downed four Advil, praying to everything that was holy that my head would feel better fast.

I didn't know how Gam drank that shit everyday.

I looked around my kitchen for Dr. Shawn's business card— it wasn't on any of the counters, on the front or side of the fridge, or on the cork board I had in the hallway to the laundry room.

Then it hit me.

I hurried over to the kitchen drawer I used to keep all the random women's phone numbers in and pulled it open so hard I practically pulled it out. Sitting right there in the middle of the drawer was her business card.

My hands shook as I dialed her cell number. I had no idea if things had changed in the year since I saw her last, but she'd never had an assistant. Her clients called her directly to schedule an appointment. The phone rang once and I thought about hanging up. I had no idea what I was going to say when she answered, but I didn't even have time to think about it because she picked up on the second ring.

"Viper?" her familiar, friendly voice said.

"Hey, Dr. Shawn. Long time no talk."

"Yeah! Really long time no talk. I'm surprised to hear from you. Is everything okay?"

"Not really. I mean . . . I don't know. My life has kinda gone into a shit spiral lately and a friend suggested I call you." The vulnerability of saying those words out loud weighed more than ten Zambonis. I didn't like letting my guard down, and I *hated* asking for help, but I didn't know what else to do.

"Well, I'm glad you called me, Viper, but—"

"So do you have any appointments open today? Maybe tomorrow?"

"Unfortunately, I don't." Her voice was soft and she sounded just as disappointed as I felt. "I'm guessing you don't know this, but I had a baby a couple of weeks ago. I'm actually going to be out on maternity leave for about four months."

I couldn't believe what she'd just said. "Baby? You had a baby? Oh, the fucking irony!" I was so annoyed that I started laughing like a maniac.

"Irony?"

"Never mind." I let out a heavy sigh, no longer in the mood to let my guard down. My walls went back up faster than they'd ever been built before.

"I have an associate who's seeing some of my clients while I'm out. Would you like his number?"

"No, thanks. I'll figure it out. Don't worry about it." Talking to Brody wouldn't fix me. Talking to Dr. Shawn's associate wouldn't fix me. Nothing would fix me.

"I'm so sorry about the timing, Viper," she said sincerely.

"You have no idea how laughable the timing is," I mumbled into the phone. "I gotta go."

Chapter
21

Michelle

VIPER'S TEXT CONFUSED AND INFURIATED me at the same time. What did *"I need to figure some shit out"* even mean?

Were we together?

Were we not together?

Did I even *want* to be with him after the way he'd acted?

I didn't even see the text until I woke up in the morning, but when I did, I took a deep breath and put my phone away. I was too hormonal and too angry to reply, and what I wanted to say wouldn't have been good. While I was happy that he finally made contact, after all we'd been through together and a year of him practically living with me, he owed me more than some lame apology by text.

A lot more.

Gam had called earlier that week and asked me to come by to

see her. I had no clue what Viper had or hadn't told her, but I was relieved that she obviously wasn't cutting off communication with me like I'd feared.

I dropped Matthew off at school and headed to Gam's with Maura.

She was waiting on her porch for me when we pulled up, and before I even had Maura out of the car seat, she was standing next to me with open arms.

"How are my favorite girls?" She hugged me and Maura together, so tight that I wanted to cry. Other than kisses and hugs from the kids, I'd had no affection for a few weeks and I was desperate for it. I squeezed her back and blinked away tears that had started to sting my eyes.

She pulled back and studied my face with a grin on her own. "God, I've missed you. Where have you been?"

"Well . . . busy," I said nonchalantly, still trying to gauge how much she knew.

"You're all busy. You're busy. Viper's busy. Everyone's busy. Meanwhile, I'm sitting here getting older by the minute, waiting for company." She let out a quick laugh as we walked up the steps of her porch.

"You're moving around really well," I said, looking down toward her hip.

"Thanks. The therapy is helping a lot, and of course, some days are better than others. But when I saw you pull up, it was like a jolt of energy shot through me. I practically ran across the yard." She sat down on the couch and held her arms out for Maura, who leaped right into them.

"Well that's good to hear." I sat down on the chair next to her and closed my eyes, taking a deep, cleansing breath. Gam's big ole covered porch was one of my favorite places in the whole world. It was full of brightly painted birdhouses and comfy wicker furniture that was just begging to be napped in. Bushes along the front and side provided privacy for you to see out but not many to see in. It was heaven.

"You look tired, honey."

I lifted my head and opened my eyes. "I *am* tired. Life has turned into a caveman and he's dragging me around by the hair."

"Well, why don't you fill me in since no one seems to want to." Gam reached under the couch and pulled out a small container of Maura's favorite toys. Her eyes lit up and she squirmed to get down, quickly spreading all of the little Disney figurines out on the coffee table.

"What do you mean?" I played dumb.

Gam shook her head. "I'm not dumb."

Busted.

She continued, "Viper has been weird and avoiding me. You haven't been around as much. Something is going on and I want to know what it is."

"I thought he would have told you by now."

"Told me what?" Her voice lowered and her eyes grew big.

"Well, I don't really know. I'm not sure what to tell. After his surgery he started acting really weird, pulling away from me and not talking to me. I knew that the injury was a lot for him to handle, so I just kinda dealt with it."

Gam's eyes softened in sadness and I had to look down at Maura as I told her the rest of the story.

When I was finished, she licked her lips and pinched them together, but she didn't say anything for at least a whole minute. That minute felt more like a year. She stared down at the coffee table and let her eyes drift over to Maura, but they never lifted to mine. I sat quietly, listening to the sound of blood rushing through my ears, and waited. Eventually, she swallowed and lifted her gaze to me.

She placed her hands over Maura's ears and shook her head. "I'm so mad at that fucking boy right now I could kick the shit out of him." Letting go of Maura, she patted the couch next to her for me to come over. Without saying anything, I slid next to her. She wrapped her arm around my shoulders and squeezed me tight as she pulled me close and kissed my temple. "Sweetheart, I'm so, so sorry he's done this to you."

Somewhere between the kiss on the head and her comforting words, tears filled my eyes and began to drip onto my pants.

She didn't let go of my shoulders, but she continued talking. "I'm so sorry you've had to deal with this alone for as long as you have. Please promise me you won't deal with it alone anymore."

I nodded and sniffed back more tears. "I promise, I've been okay. I talk to Kacie a lot, and she's going to go to all of my doctor appointments with me. I'll be fine."

"I know you will. Michelle,"—she turned to face me and took my hand in hers, looking me straight in the eye—"I'm not lying when I say this. I can't think of one woman on this planet who is stronger than you. You have been through so much already, and I know you can handle whatever life throws at you."

I pressed my lips into a tight smile and dropped my eyes. "Thanks. That means a lot coming from you."

"And I'm also going to add that even if that brat doesn't want to be part of this baby's life, his or her great-grandma sure does. I love my grandson like he's my own, but that doesn't mean I have to like his behavior."

Letting out a heavy sigh, I shook my head. "I don't want that, Gam. I don't want you guys to fight or not have a relationship because of this. I'm glad you want to be part of the baby's life and I'll gladly accept, but that doesn't mean you can't still have Viper in yours."

"We'll see about that," she said. It sounded more like a warning than a statement. "But I just want to say this one last thing—If you never want to speak to him again, I support that, but if there's even a teeny, tiny part of you that still loves him, give it a little more time. There are few human beings on this planet more stubborn than that boy, but when he loves, he loves hard. And he *loves* you. He loves you in a way that I've never seen him love anyone before. Love like that doesn't just go away in a couple of weeks."

Gam's words filled me with hope. She knew Viper better than anyone, and if she believed there might still be a chance, I owed it to myself, Viper, Matthew, Maura, and the bean in my belly to hang on just a little longer, too.

Maura swung her head up to Gam. "Juice box?"

"You want a juice box, Little Mo?"

Her head nodded excitedly and her eyes sparkled.

"Well, all right then. Let's get Maura a juice box and her momma some food." Gam smiled at me and took mine and Maura's hands in each of her own as we walked into the house.

Kat was in the kitchen sweeping the floor when we walked in. When she looked up and noticed us, her dark red lips spread into a wide, tight smile.

"Hi," I said cheerfully.

"Hi. Can I get you guys anything?" She looked back and forth from me to Gam.

"Nah, that's okay. I just want to make this sweet girl here some food. She's eating for two now," Gam said proudly as she pointed at me and made her way over to the fridge.

Kat's dark eyes opened wide and traveled down to my belly. "You're pregnant?"

I nodded. "I am."

"Wow, congratulations!" Kat said warmly.

"Thanks." It felt nice to be congratulated without having to explain to someone where Viper was or what was going on with us.

"Okay, what are you in the mood for? I have just about everything, literally." Gam turned from the fridge to face me.

"I don't know." I shrugged as I sat down in a kitchen chair and pulled Maura up onto my lap. "Anything. I'm starving."

Gam started pulling containers out of the fridge and dumping things on plates as I dropped my head toward Maura, who was babbling and chewing on my necklace. I brushed her thin little baby hairs off of her forehead and pressed my lips against it. She still smelled like her strawberry soap from the night before, and I closed my eyes and took a couple of deep breaths. My mind wandered to the thought of her being a big sister. Matthew was such an amazing big brother from day one and never jealous, but Maura was definitely a little more of a spitfire. It was still months away, but I couldn't *wait* to see her face when she saw the baby for the first time.

I opened my eyes and lifted them back to the room. Kat was standing with the broom still in her hand, staring right at me. My eyebrows shot up in surprise as our gazes connected, but she quickly lowered her head and went back to sweeping.

Gam turned from the counter and set a plate in front of me.

"How do you do this? You're magical," I said in awe, staring down at the chicken salad sandwich on a flaky croissant and the watermelon salad right next to it.

Gam laughed and sat down in the chair next to me. "I couldn't sleep this morning, so I got up and used my leftover chicken to make chicken salad."

I shook my head but didn't respond. I was too busy trying to fit as much of the sandwich in my mouth as I could.

"Mermelon?" Maura asked, clapping her hands together.

"You want some watermelon of your own, Little Mo?" Gam got up from the table and scooped a small pile of watermelon, cucumbers, and feta cheese into a plastic bowl and set it in front of her. Just as I suspected, Maura scrunched up her face as she picked the pieces of cheese out of the bowl and set them on the table.

Gam gazed at Maura with a smile and shook her head as I continued stuffing my face. I hadn't felt all that hungry when I got to Gam's, but suddenly I was ravenous.

Gam told me all about her lunch date with Phil a few days before and how she needed to get bird seed from the store since winter was on the way and she wanted her cardinals to be fed. I listened to her happily as I ate. We talked about everything and nothing . . . and it was amazing.

After I'd finished eating and it seemed like we'd covered just about everything we could cover for one day, I glanced down at my phone.

"Crap!" I yelled as I jumped up, startling Maura. "I totally forgot about Matthew. He gets out of school in a little bit. I gotta run." I carefully dropped my plate and Maura's bowl in the sink and hurried toward the front door with Gam following along behind me as best as she could. I zipped Maura's jacket as Gam let out a heavy sigh.

"What was that about?" I asked her as I stood and lifted Maura onto my hip.

She swallowed and stared at me for a second. "I'm just worried, that's all."

"I'm fine," I reassured her.

"I know you are. You're an amazing woman who will get through anything, but I'm worried for Viper, too. He's making a huge mistake, and I'm scared he's going to lose the best thing that's ever happened to him."

Taking a deep breath, I gathered my thoughts. I was furious with Viper, but that didn't mean I was done with him. I also didn't want to give Gam false hope that everything would be fine, because I had no idea what the future held. "I don't know what's going to happen with us. Right now, things are definitely strained, but I'll tell you this much . . . I haven't given up *yet.*"

A tight smiled grew across Gam's lips. "Good. Because as dumb as I think he is, I really think you two are meant to be together." She wrapped her arms around me and Maura, squeezing us both at the same time again. "Every pot has a lid, just remember that."

"Huh?" I said as she let go and pulled back.

"Every pot has a lid," she repeated in a firmer tone.

Gam had many quirky phrases and sayings that I'd heard

many times over the last year or so, but that one was new to me. "That's a new one."

"It's one of my favorites," she added as her eyes drifted out the front door and went somewhere deep in her mind. "My mom used to say it to me when I was younger, and when I met Don all those years ago, I just knew he was my lid."

"Every pot has a lid, huh?" I said with a sigh. "Well, hopefully my lid gets his head out of the dishwasher before he warps his brain." I lowered my head and planted a quick kiss on her cheek. "All right, off to get my little man. I'll call you soon."

"Please do!" she called out as she leaned against the door frame and waved.

I made it to Matthew's school just in time and we went straight home. Nap time had never sounded more appealing. Matthew hopped out of the car and ran to the front door as I took Maura out of the car and walked to the mailbox. As I pulled the tiny stack of envelopes out, something caught my eye. A folded up piece of paper was lying on top. I frowned as I switched the mail to my other hand and unfolded the paper.

> Just thought I'd give you my cell number in case you ever need help with anything, or a babysitter, or someone to come and drink your beer.
> Joel

I blinked a couple times and stared down at the piece of paper, reading the words and phone number over again. It was just a silly note from a helpful new neighbor, and I knew that, but then why had a teeny, tiny little butterfly started floating around in my stomach?

Chapter 22

Viper

"LAWRENCE FINKLE. THIS IS YOUR grandmother. I would like to have a word with you. Be at my house tomorrow morning at nine o'clock. If you have something else going on, cancel it."

Gam's voicemail from the night before played over and over and over in my mind as I drove to her house. She was pissed. She was pissed, and she knew. Her tone was cold and hard, something I rarely heard from her, and she didn't say good-bye. Gam always said good-bye. I pulled up to her house and my stomach twisted into the same knot I used to get as I made my way through the empty hallway toward the principal's office, usually with a teacher glaring at me from behind.

The porch was empty when I pulled up, but that damn car was in the driveway. Worst case scenario. While I'd finally made peace with Kat helping Gam, I still didn't want her hearing all the details of my personal life, and if I knew Gam, there was going to be nothing quiet about the next little while.

I crept quietly up the wooden steps of the porch, hoping to look through the door and see where she was before I went through . . . kind of like spotting my enemy before they could strike.

I held my hand up to the screen to shield my eyes as I peeked in and looked to the right.

Nothing.

My head turned to the left and my eyes connected with Gam's. She was standing in the kitchen doorway with her arms crossed over her chest, watching me like a hawk with narrow eyes.

"Oh! Hey!" I tried to sound casual as I pulled the screen door open and went in.

I walked straight over to Gam and opened my arms, but like a football player, she straight-armed my chest and stopped me dead in my tracks. "Don't 'Oh, hey' me," she said angrily. "I want to talk to you, and how you respond will determine whether or not you get a hug."

Wow.

"Uh . . . okay."

"Let's sit." She motioned for me to follow her into the kitchen.

I stopped in the doorway as soon as I saw Kat standing at the counter cutting something. "Why don't we go in the living room? I want to sit on the couch."

Gam turned and stared at me for a second. "Fine. Not that I give a rat's ass about you being comfortable right now, but fine."

We walked to the living room and she sat in her usual chair, me across from her on the couch.

My eyes darted around the room, avoiding hers. She wasn't talking or doing anything else, she just sat perfectly still, glaring at me.

After I minute, I took a deep breath, "So—"

"What the fuck is the matter with you?" she interrupted

immediately.

I exhaled heavily on the other side of her sentence. I knew damn well what she meant, but I needed every second I could buy. "What are you talking about?"

"Don't play dumb and stall with me," she said, shaking her head. "What the hell is going on in that puny little brain of yours?"

"You don't understand," I started to defend, but she cut me off again.

"Oh, I understand just fine. You had the best thing that ever happened to you tightly in your grasp, and you let her go."

"I didn't let her go—"

"You sure did. You walked out of that house."

"She told me to get out!"

"Because you were acting like an asshole. I would have told you to get out, too. Hell, I would have told you a lot more than that."

I didn't respond. There was no point. Gam was severely ticked off at me, not letting me get a full sentence out, and I needed a breather. "I'm gonna go get a drink. You take ten deep breaths while I'm gone and when I get back, we're going to talk like normal people, got it?"

I stood up and started my way to the kitchen.

"You sure you're coming back, right? You're not gonna just leave and then not call me for weeks on end?" she called out.

I gritted my teeth and kept on walking. My head throbbed and I just wanted to get in my car and go, but I knew that if I left, the next time I saw Gam it would be five hundred times worse. Pausing halfway across the kitchen, I gripped the back of the kitchen chair tightly and lowered my head, sighing loudly.

Michelle hated me.

Gam was mad at me.

Even Brody was pissed at me.

Every part of my life was a fucking mess, and I didn't even know where to begin cleaning it—or if I even wanted to.

"You okay?" Kat asked softly from somewhere behind me.

"Not really," I said quietly, shaking my head.

She took a step to the side of me. "Is there anything I can do to help?"

Without taking my hands off the chair, I turned my head and looked at her. Her jet-black hair was the same, her tattoos were the same, and her eyes were the same. Other than that, I hardly recognized her. She chewed nervously on the corner of her dark red lip as she waited for my answer. The old Kat would have told me to shut the fuck up and get over whatever it was that was pissing me off, but this Kat looked timid and sweet . . . softer.

"Uh . . . no. I'll be fine," I grumbled as I straightened up from the chair and went to the fridge.

"Congratulations, by the way."

"For what?" I bent down and reached way in the back of the fridge where Gam kept my bottles of root beer.

"Your baby."

Baby. Baby. *My* baby.

My hand closed around the bottle and froze. "How did you know about that?"

"Michelle was here yesterday, with Gam. They were talking in the kitchen, and there isn't exactly a lot of room in here, so I overheard."

I grabbed the bottle and shut the fridge. "Gotcha. Well, thanks."

"You're going to be a great dad," she added, peeking up at me from under her long, dark bangs.

I twisted the cap off of the root beer and took a long drink, the carbonation stinging the back of my throat.

As I lowered the bottle from my mouth, I leaned against the counter and stared at her. "Doubtful."

"No it's not." She shook her head.

"Sorry about my text the other night," I said, changing the subject. "I was really drunk and don't even really remember doing it."

She rolled her eyes and cracked a smile. "I figured. It *was* pretty random."

"Yeah . . . anyway, sorry about the text. Sorry about being a jerk."

She wrapped her arms around herself nervously. "Thanks. I appreciate the apology. I get it though. I'm sure it was weird for you to show up to your grandma's house and see *me* here, of all people. Then again, I know you've had a lot of . . . people . . . in your life, so I'm not trying to say I was memorable or anything."

I let out a quick laugh. "By people you mean women?"

She shrugged. "Kinda."

"I've definitely had my fair share of "people" but you weren't like all the others. It was different with you."

Her face flushed as she looked away shyly. "Thanks. That means a lot. I'm not the same girl I was back then, but I do have some really good memories of us . . . together."

"Lawrence! Quit being a chicken shit and get back out here!" Gam called from the living room.

I raised my eyebrows and gave her a tight smile without saying anything as I left the room.

I set my root beer on the coffee table.

"Okay. Where were we?" I said with a sigh as I sat back on the couch. "Let me have it."

Her shoulders dropped and her face relaxed. "I don't want to let you have it. That's not what I want at all. I *do* want to understand why you're acting like this though."

"Acting like what? Maybe I'm not acting like anything." I leaned forward and rested my elbows on my knees, looking her straight in the eye. "Just like I told Brody, maybe this *is* the real me. I've been the same guy all my life, then for the last year, I was someone else. Maybe *that* was the act."

"I don't believe that for a minute."

"Believe what you want. I don't know who I am anymore and I'm trying to figure it the fuck out the best way I know how."

Her head jerked back in surprise. "By ignoring your family? That's the best way?"

"I don't know what to do!" I yelled and threw my hands in the air as I stood and paced the room. "I don't know that I even want a kid. I wasn't even given the choice. What if I'm a bad dad? What if this kid doesn't like me? What if I never play hockey again and can't support it? What if I *can* play hockey again but my team doesn't need me anymore? These questions, plus a million others, buzz around my head all fucking day long until I can't see straight anymore, so I check out. I ignore everything and everyone until I figure out how to deal with all of this shit."

Gam took a slow, deep breath and tilted her head to the side. "I know there has been a lot of change for you in a very short period of time, but running away isn't going to fix it. It's only going to make it worse."

"I'm not running away, I'm just thinking," I defended.

"Same thing," she said in a gentle, but stern tone. "If you want to solve your problems, you need to turn toward them, not away."

Gam wasn't the first person who'd said something like that to me. "I know," I said with a sigh. "Look, I'll come back later if you want to yell at me more, but I have therapy at ten thirty and I gotta get going."

"I don't want to yell at you, Lawrence, but I do want to shake the hell out of you and wake you up. If you don't *think* fast, you're going to lose your lid."

I frowned at her. "My lid?"

"Yes, my mother used to say that every pot—"

"Has a lid," I finished the sentence for her with an eye roll. "I remember you saying that now. You used to say it all the time when I was little."

"I said it to Michelle yesterday, and she loved it."

My gaze dropped to the ground and I rubbed my cheek with my hand. "How is she anyway?" I asked nonchalantly. "Like, I mean, how did she look? Okay?"

"I should tell you that she was sad and heartbroken and had dark circles under her eyes and cried all morning, but you know what . . . she looked radiant. Her hair looked shiny, her eyes were sparkling, and her skin absolutely glowed. Pregnancy looks amazing on her. And of course, she has a little baby bump."

My eyes shot up to hers. "She does?"

Gam nodded with a small smile. "It's still pretty tiny, but it's there. Cutest little belly I've ever seen."

The thought of Michelle happily rubbing her pregnant belly popped into my head, and my heart started racing. My throat felt like it was closing and my fingers started to tingle again. "Okay, I gotta run. I'll call you later." My stomach twisted and turned as I walked to the front door an opened it, gulping in as much fresh air as I could all at once.

"Think about what I said," Gam called out.

I gave her a quick wave and hurried out the door to my car. Once I sat down, I gripped the steering wheel tight in my hands and tried to breathe slow so that I didn't pass out.

After a few seconds, everything calmed down and I felt like myself again, but instead of heading to therapy, I rescheduled my appointment with Sherman and headed back home.

Chapter 23

Michelle

THE THIRD WEEK OF NOVEMBER rolled around, officially marking one month since Viper and I had spoken face to face. With every day that passed, I lost a little more hope and anger grew in its place.

Gam and I talked regularly and every time we did, she asked me to keep holding on, but what was I holding on to?

Fantasies? Dreams? Fairytales?

Those didn't exist to me anymore.

Gam would tell me what Viper was up to and that he'd asked about me and the kids, but it only irritated me. I wasn't in junior high and I didn't like Gam being the middleman, so eventually, I asked her not to talk about him anymore. Until, and if ever, he grew up.

"This was so silly," I said to Kacie as we pulled out of the parking lot at my doctor's office.

"No it wasn't," Kacie disagreed as she buckled her seatbelt. "I haven't been to a baby doctor in a long time. I missed the smell."

"The *smell?*" I shot her a quick glance out of the corner of my eye and shook my head. "You're so weird."

"Shut up!" she squealed in a high-pitched voice. "I am not."

"Uh . . . if you miss the smell of the OB's office? Yes, that makes you weird. Do you miss peeing in a cup, too?"

"Ugh. I've peed in enough cups to last me a lifetime. Wait, where are you going?" she asked as I turned the car to the right.

"I'm celebrating the fact that I only gained four pounds this month with a milkshake." I let out a quick giggle. "Want one?"

"Hell yes! Chocolate, please. This might be the first milkshake in my whole life that I haven't had to share with any kids. No joke." She laughed as I pulled up to the window.

"In that case,"—I turned toward the speaker—"can I get two extra-large chocolate shakes, please? With extra whipped cream?"

Kacie let out an exaggerated sigh. "I just love you. Here, my treat."

"Get outta here." I pushed her hand away as she tried to hand me money. "Buying you a damn milkshake is the least I can do for you going with me today."

"Seriously, it's my pleasure. While I don't exactly miss being pregnant, I loved my baby appointments, looked forward to them all month long."

I looked over and gave her a tight smile. "They are kinda fun."

"And . . . in like eight weeks, you get to find out what you're having."

"Thank you," I said as I took the shakes from the worker and handed them to Kacie. "I totally forgot about that. I haven't even decided if I *want* to find out."

Kacie turned to me with wide eyes and a frozen expression.

"What?" I asked defensively. "Why are you looking at me like that?"

"Cause Auntie Kacie wants to find out so she can go shopping. If you don't want to know, look away, but I am all over that."

I let out a hearty laugh as she popped straws in both of our shakes and handed one to me. "Okay, fine. I'll find out."

"Ahem," she said dramatically. "I think you mean *we'll* find out."

Thanksgiving was just a few days away and Gam had insisted the kids and I come for dinner . . . about fifty times. As bad as my mouth watered every time she talked about turkey and stuffing and potatoes and cranberry sauce, I declined. Gam loved me and I loved her, but she was still *Viper's* grandmother. The thought of a quiet little Thanksgiving with just the three of us didn't sound all that bad anyway.

The night before Thanksgiving, my phone beeped and I frowned down at the strange number. I clicked on the little envelope.

Hey! I'm not sure if you kept my number, but it's Joel. Quick question, and no pressure, but I was chatting with Jodi and Vince the other day and they told me what happened with you. She also mentioned that it was just you, Matthew, and Maura for Thanksgiving. I was thinking . . . it's just me and Gavin for Thanksgiving, too. Do you guys want to maybe have dinner all together? If the answer is no, or this comes across as out of line, please forget I said anything.

I smiled down at my phone. Not only did I not think he was out of line, I thought he was really sweet. But . . . one big problem.

Hi! Dinner together sounds awesome, but there's

an issue. I can't cook. Is it weird to have grilled
cheese for Thanksgiving dinner?

I glanced over at Matthew who was sitting at the kitchen
table, trying to build a pirate ship with Legos. "Hey, bud?"

"Yeah?" he answered without looking up at me.

"Would you like Gavin to come over for dinner tomorrow?"

He gasped and his head shot up. "Yes!"

His excitement for his new friend made me excited. The
thought of having another adult around to chat with, especially
on a holiday, wasn't so bad either. My phone beeped again.

Joel: Grilled cheese is an acceptable meal 24
        hours a day, 7 days a week—holidays
        included. What time do you want us over?

Early Thanksgiving afternoon, I was rushing around like a
madwoman, picking up last-minute things around the house.

"Matthew, why do I keep finding your underwear in the
family room? You have a hamper!" I grumbled as I bent over
and picked another pair up.

Matthew looked up at me and shrugged. "Sorry."

I quickly picked up Maura's toys and put them in her basket,
stacked the books on the shelf, and took the bin of matchbox
cars to the playroom.

"Okay," I said with a sigh, looking around the family room.
"I think I got most of it. I'm gonna run upstairs and change. You
stay put, okay?"

Still staring down at his Kindle, he nodded.

I'd barely reached the bottom of the stairs when he called out,
"Don't forget to put your underwear in the hamper, Mom!" I let
out a hard laugh that didn't let up until I got to my room.

I stood in the center of my closet, studying each shelf and
rack of clothes.

"That doesn't fit. That doesn't fit. That *never* fit," I said out loud to myself with a sigh.

I had been so exhausted lately that going to the mall to buy new maternity clothes felt more like a chore than anything. Yoga pants and T-shirts were my main staple, and they would have to do for Thanksgiving, too. I pulled a clean pair of black pants from my drawer and barely squeezed my boobs into my too-small bra, praying to God it didn't pop back open. As I was picking out a T-shirt, my favorite Wild hoodie caught my eye.

Perfect!

Joel said that Jodi had told him what happened, but I had no idea exactly how much she had told him and whether he knew I was pregnant or not. Nor did I know if I wanted to talk about something like that on Thanksgiving if he didn't already know, so a big, baggy hoodie was just want I wanted. Not to mention it was worn-in and totally comfy.

I quickly threw some powder on my face and dabbed my eyes with mascara, trying to think back to the last time I'd actually put any makeup on at all. It had been . . . awhile.

Then why today?

I didn't have time to think about the answer to my own question. The doorbell rang and I sprinted from my room and down the steps as fast as I could, hoping to get there before it rang a second time.

"Hi!" I said breathlessly as I opened the door.

He pulled his brows in tight. "Hi. Everything okay?"

"Yeah." I puffed my cheeks out. "I was upstairs and Maura's napping. I didn't want the bell to wake her, so I ran. She'll be a monster if she doesn't get a good nap. What's that?" I pointed to the huge box in his arms.

"Oh! This . . . is a lot better than grilled cheese," he said with a wink as he walked past me into the kitchen. Gavin ran to find Matthew, and I followed Joel and his mystery box to the island.

"So I really wasn't kidding when I said I love grilled cheese. I do. But . . . I figured why not see if I could find something a *little* more special, so I made some calls and voila! Thanksgiving in a box."

"Thanksgiving in a box?" I lifted to my tippytoes to try and see over the edge.

Joel started pulling containers out and setting them on the island. My eyes grew wider, and my mouth salivated more as each amazing smelling box passed under my nose. Turkey and potatoes and corn and stuffing and cranberries and green bean casserole and gravy . . . it was never ending.

When he'd pulled the last box out, he looked back and forth from me to the food proudly. "What do ya think? Beats the hell outta grilled cheese, huh?"

I stared in awe at all of the food on the island and shook my head slowly. "Thanksgiving in a box. I had no idea that was even a thing."

"I've done it before, but back in Iowa. I wasn't sure anywhere around here did it, but we lucked out." He clapped his hands and rubbed them together. "So when do you want to eat? Couple hours?"

"Ooooor a couple minutes?" I said with a laugh. "I'm gonna set the dining room table, and the minute Maura wakes up, let's dig in."

"Sounds good to me," he agreed. "What can I help with?"

An hour and a half later, I was elated that I'd decided to wear yoga pants and a hoodie for the day. If my bump wasn't sticking out before, it sure was after dinner. I think I scared Joel when I went back for my third plateful of food.

Gavin, Matthew, and Maura ran off to the playroom and we both sat at the messy, empty table, too stuffed to move.

"That . . . was unbelievable," I said with a happy sigh.

He looked over and arched a brow at me. "We're not done."

"We're not?"

"Nope." His lips curled into a sexy grin and for the first time, I noticed a small dimple in his left cheek. "We still have pumpkin pie."

I lifted my arms on the table and groaned as I dropped my head on top of them. "I don't think I can."

"Come on, champ." He laughed and walked around behind me, massaging my shoulders like a boxing coach does to his fighter. "I have faith. You can do it."

"I think if I try, you'll have to wheel me to the hospital."

He let go of my shoulders and took a few steps toward the kitchen. "Okay, fine. More for me then. I'm gonna grab some wine. You want some?"

I didn't lift my head but my eyes shot open. "Uh . . . no. I'm good. Thanks."

"Okay, be right back."

As soon as I heard the fridge open, I sat up straight and my mind raced. Obviously Jodi hadn't told him that I was pregnant or he wouldn't have offered me wine. Should I tell him? Should I not? And why the hell was I so nervous and freaking out about it?

He set the glass down and sat back in his chair. "Boy, we have a mess to clean up, huh?"

"I'm pregnant," I blurted out, then cringed at how crazy he must have thought I was.

"Uh . . . okay," he said with wide eyes as he stared down at the table. "Well, I can clean the mess by myself then, that's fine."

"I'm sorry. I don't know why I blurted it out like that and I probably could've done it in a more tactful way but you asked if I wanted wine and I can't have wine and then you came back and out it flew," I rambled until I ran out of breath.

"Michelle . . ." He leaned forward on his elbows. "Slow down. I'm glad you told me, so please don't worry about the way you told me."

"Thanks," I said softly, staring down at my lap.

"At least that explains the twelve pounds of mashed potatoes you ate," he teased with a wink.

"Shut up!" I crumpled up my napkin and threw it at him.

We left the mess on the table and moved to the family room to talk, where I filled him in on *almost* everything that had happened with Viper. I told him about how he'd been acting weird after his surgery and how he was less than thrilled about my pregnancy, but I left out the really bad parts because, for some reason, I just didn't want anyone else thinking he was a horrible person, even if I did.

When I finished, he stared at me with raised eyebrows and a dazed look on his face. "Wow. So how long has it been since you've talked him?"

"Mmmm." I closed one eye and looked up at the ceiling, trying to figure out when he left. "It's been just about a month."

"And he hasn't contacted you *at all?*"

"Kinda. He sent a text once and apologized, and Gam says he asks her about me, but that's about it."

"I don't even know what to say."

"Don't say anything." I shook my head quickly. "That's my story. It's out there now. It's over. I don't want to talk about it anymore."

"Okay." He nodded. "I just want to say one thing and then I promise I won't bring it up again, okay?"

"Okay," I agreed reluctantly.

"You have my number now. If you need anything, and I mean anything, I want you to use it. I'm right across the street and can be here in ten seconds if I need to be, fifteen if I have to put pants on first."

I giggled. "Well, it's about to be winter in Minnesota, so pants would probably be a good idea if you're going outside."

"True. Freezing cold air and naked dudes don't go well together, and I certainly don't want anyone spreading *that* rumor."

My shoulders shook as I laughed again . . . hard. It felt good to laugh.

Joel kept his promise and didn't bring up my situation, or Viper, again. We small-talked for a few more hours, then pried the boys apart after they'd fallen asleep in Matthew's bed together. He slung Gavin over his shoulder and made his way to the front door.

"Thanks for having us," he turned and said.

"Are you kidding? Thank *you* for the amazing dinner. To think we almost ended up with grilled cheese sandwiches instead of all that." I laughed.

He tilted his head to the side and gave a little shrug as his eyes locked on mine. "It still would have been worth it."

My pulse sped up and suddenly I wanted him to leave. Fast. I put my hand up on the edge of the door and pulled it a couple of inches toward me, hoping he'd get the hint. "Okay, well I'm gonna call it a night. I'm pooped."

"Me, too. Thanks again." Moving quickly, he reached down with his free arm and wrapped it around my waist, pulling me in for a tight hug against him. I rested my hand on his shoulders and squeezed back as I forced air in and out of my lungs. After a few seconds, he let go and walked out the door.

"Happy Thanksgiving!" he called out as he stepped off the front porch, totally unaware that he'd just made my heart skip thirty-seven beats.

"Happy Thanksgiving to you, too."

Chapter 24

Viper

FOR THE FIRST TIME IN my whole life, I spent Thanksgiving alone. In the past, if I wasn't out on the road with the team, I was at Gam's, but this year was just . . . different. Gam had invited me over, and I'd initially said yes, but I changed my mind at the last minute. I didn't want to get out of bed. I didn't want to leave my house. I didn't want to lie and say I was thankful for anything because I wasn't.

I was miserable.

I missed Michelle and the kids so bad that my chest ached when I thought about them. I wondered what they were doing every second of every day. On Thanksgiving morning, I couldn't stand it anymore, so I got in my car and drove to her house, where I parked a couple houses down while I thought of what the fuck I was going to say when I knocked on the door. I sat there for over an hour, playing scenario after scenario over in my head and nothing I came up with saying even came close to how I was actually feeling. All that popped into my head was that she didn't answer my last text. I didn't blame her for ignoring me,

God knows I deserved it, but maybe it was too late. The thought of never being able to hold Michelle again, make love to her again, lie in bed and have her put her cold feet on me again . . . it was crushing.

Fucking crushing.

Add to that not being able to build Legos with Matthew or read books to Maura or a million other little things I'd taken for granted and I had to leave. Sitting on that street, staring at that house, knowing they were inside was gut-wrenching. They were less than a hundred yards from me. I could have been at the door within one minute, but I didn't know what to say. I also didn't want to make Michelle mad and totally ruin her Thanksgiving.

Instead, I started my car and left, drove straight to McDonald's, and ate alone in my car before heading home and not leaving my bed the whole night.

Frankly, other than to go to therapy, I didn't really leave my house—or my bed—for the next week. Then I got a text from Andy.

> Andy: Hey! I'm gonna pick you up at about 4 p.m.
> Be ready.

I quickly tried to remember if we had plans but came up with nothing.

> For what?

> Andy: You haven't been to a game since you got hurt. It's been long enough and you're going to make an appearance there tonight. You still need to cheer on your team.

> I do cheer them on. I watch every fucking game!

> Andy: That doesn't mean shit. They need to see you there. With them. Be ready at 4, and that's an order.

Andy *was* my agent, but I hated when he acted like it. I also knew that when he told us to do something, we didn't have a choice. At all.

Fine.

It wasn't that I didn't want to go to the game—those guys were my brothers—but I didn't really know what to say to them either. Most of them had called and texted after my surgery, but I'd ignored them. Brody had come by my house, but we got into a fight. These guys were all hockey players, but I didn't feel like one anymore, so what the hell did I even talk to them about?

Four o'clock snuck up on me pretty fast. I threw on a Wild hoodie and jeans and walked out the front door. As I walked down the sidewalk toward his car, Andy rolled his window down.

"What the hell are you wearing?"

I looked down at myself and back up at him. "What?"

"Get back in the house and put your damn jersey on!"

I rolled my eyes and turned back to the house without saying a word. My closet was a total disaster and I couldn't find anything in there. After five minutes of kicking dirty clothes around and snapping hangers in frustration, it dawned on me. My jersey was still at Michelle's house.

I prepared myself for a fight with Andy and left my room.

"Dude. What the fuck?" Andy's words startled me. I hadn't even heard him come in.

"What now?"

He was standing in the kitchen, his eyes slowly scanning the piles of pizza boxes and empty Chinese food containers that were stacked high and covering most of my counters.

"This." He motioned toward the garbage with horrified eyes. "Is this all you've been doing for the last month? Eating crap and letting your life waste away?"

"Listen, if your plan is to lecture me all night, then you can just go by yourself. I'm in no mood for this shit."

"I don't want to lecture you, Viper, but look at this. You're out of control," he exclaimed.

"I'm not out of control!"

He glared at me. "Have you even been going to therapy?"

"Yes!" I yelled back. "I go all the fucking time! It's practically all I do."

Andy put one hand on his hip and sighed as he ran the other one through his hair and looked down toward the ground. "I'm worried about you, Viper." His head raised and he stared back at me. "You're not just my client, you're one of my best friends. And you're acting so erratic that I'm worried about you. Not just your career. Fuck your career at this point. I'm worried about *you*."

"Don't worry about me," I grumbled. "I'll be fine."

"I have serious doubts about that, but we'll have to talk about it later because we're gonna be late. Grab your jersey and let's go."

"I don't have it." I shook my head. "It's at Michelle's."

He pulled his lips in and pinched them tight as he inhaled deeply through his nose, making sure I heard his annoyance. "Fine. Whatever. Let's go."

We didn't talk much on the way there. It was awkward and quiet—a lot like the rest of my life at the moment.

As soon as we pulled into the players' lot at the stadium, my pulse quickened. My body knew where we were and it was responding.

"You excited?" Andy asked as we made our way down the concourse toward the locker room.

I put my hands in my pocket and shrugged. "I don't know what I am. Nervous. Excited. I feel like I'm gonna barf, so that's something."

He let out a loud laugh and punched my shoulder. "You got

this. I know it's probably weird to be back here, but you have to know these guys are dying to see you."

"I hope so." I nodded.

The closer we got to the locker room, the louder the music from inside grew. My heart slammed against my chest as we got to the door.

Andy looked over at me. "You want to go in first?"

"Uh . . ." I stammered and took a deep breath, puffing my cheeks out.

He put his hand on my shoulder. "I got this."

He walked through the door ahead of me and I lowered my head, staring at the back of his feet as I followed.

"Holy shit!" a familiar voice called out. "It's Viper!"

I looked up to see Louie, wearing only a T-shirt and nothing else, walking toward me with his arms open. Several other guys called my name and cheered and followed Louie my direction. The next several minutes were spent giving high-fives and hugs and filling all the guys in on the latest with my knee.

"I'm so glad to see you here, man." Louie slammed his hands on my shoulders.

I leaned back and glanced down at his junk. "Not *that* excited though, huh? Tiny Louie is still pretty tiny."

"Fuck you!" he said with a laugh.

The crowd dispersed and everyone went back to suiting up for the game. Over in the corner, I noticed Brody sitting on the bench, putting new tape on his stick. I walked over and nudged him in the shoulder from behind.

"Hey."

"Hey," he answered without looking up at me.

"How's it going?"

"Fine."

It was obvious that he didn't want to talk to me and the last thing I wanted was to fight with him before a game, so I just walked away. Andy shot me a shrug and patted my shoulder as I walked past him out to the ice. The game didn't start for a little while, so the stadium was still fairly empty except for the guys skating around and the vendors starting to set up. I stood in the doorway that led from the bench out to the ice and took a deep breath, inhaling the smell of the rink that I missed so much.

"Excuse me," Brody said gruffly as he brushed past me. I stepped far to my right and tried to stay out of the way. A minute later, Coach Collins came out from the tunnel, too. His eyes scanned the ice as he took mental stock of everyone who was there. He was just about to walk back into the tunnel when he noticed me.

"Finkle!" A big smile grew across his face and he hurried over. "Good to see you upright without crutches!"

"Thanks," I answered as he pulled me in for a big hug.

"How's it feeling?"

I shrugged. "Feels great. No pain except for soreness after therapy. I'm making pretty good progress, too, and it's only been a little over a month."

"I'm glad to hear it." He nodded and pushed his glasses back up his nose. "Keep working hard, because we miss you out there. We've got some good guys, but it's just not the same. You give this team an energy when you're out there that no one else can replace."

"Thanks, Coach."

Damn, that was nice to hear.

"All right, I've got some stuff to do still before the game." He started to walk away but turned back to me after a few steps. "You're sticking around, right? We've lost three games in a row. We could use a shake up on the bench."

"I'm sticking around," I answered, trying to keep my smile in check. It felt good to hear Coach say he missed me, on both the ice and the bench.

Once the game started, I struggled to keep up with all the excitement. Who knew that spending a whole month lying in bed would zap your stamina and turn you into a sloth?

Thankfully, the adrenaline kicked in when the energy ran out. Before the first period was over, I was bouncing up and down the bench, slapping guys on the helmet and turning toward the crowd, waving my arms for them to stand on their feet. I knew my knee would hurt like hell the next day, but I didn't care.

During a time-out in the second period, I was listening to Coach Collins rile the guys up when all of a sudden, the crowd started cheering loudly. I lifted my head and looked to see if someone had launched something down to the ice. Louie elbowed me and nodded up toward the big screen above the ice. My face was on the screen. The fans were cheering for *me!* I raised my hands above my head, pumped them in the air, and the cheers roared to a deafening level. Being in that building, being with my team, being with those fans pumped some life back into my dead heart. I felt a small piece of myself returning.

The Wild's losing streak came to an end that night. The Wild Anthem belted from the speakers as I high-fived all the guys on their way into the tunnel, and then the celebration continued for another hour in the locker room.

As Andy drove me home, I couldn't stop my mind from racing or my legs and hands from twitching. A bright blue current of electricity coursed through my veins, and I couldn't sit still, no matter how hard I tried.

I got home and decided to scrub my kitchen top to bottom, throwing out four huge bags of garbage. I also began making a mental list of all the shit I needed to do to put my life back together.

It was no secret that the number one thing on my list was also going to be the toughest. As bad as I wanted to, I couldn't just march in and demand my family back. Michelle was a lot of things. She was strong, she was caring, and she was forgiving . . .

but I might have pushed her too far.

Even so, I knew one thing for sure. If I was going down, it wouldn't be without the fight of a lifetime.

Chapter 25

Michelle

"MOMMA! MOMMA!" MATTHEW SPRINTED DOWN the hall and flew onto my bed.

I blinked several times, trying to get my eyes to adjust after being startled awake. "What's wrong, buddy?"

"Come with me." He tugged on my arm and tried to pull me to a sitting position.

"Come with you? Where?" I glanced at my phone. "Matthew! It's not even six o'clock yet."

"To the window!" he said excitedly, ignoring my complaint.

While I climbed out of bed slowly, he bounced around in front of me, clapping his hands. I reached out and took his hands in mine. "No clapping. If Maura wakes up, I'll cry. Okay?"

He gave me a huge grin and nodded as he dragged me to the window and pulled back the curtain. "Look!" he exclaimed.

"Whoa," I said in a whisper as my eyebrows shot up and I

leaned toward the glass. We'd had an unusually mild November and I knew the winter weather would be coming eventually, but apparently I'd missed the memo. A fresh blanket of snow covered the whole world outside my window. It was calm and glistening and absolutely beautiful. I'd always loved the way the snow looked first thing in the morning before the cars started driving over it and people walked through it.

"Can we go play in it?" Matthew asked.

"We can . . . in a little while. It's still early." I cupped his head and pulled him against me. "Hey, I have an idea."

He pulled back and looked up at me with big blue eyes that had the power to get anything they wanted out of me.

"How about we snuggle in my bed until Maura wakes up, then we'll have pancakes, then we'll play in the snow?"

He knitted his brows together. "But momma, Viper makes the pancakes."

"I know he does, honey, but he's not here. I'll make them for you."

"When's Viper coming home? He's been gone forever." He walked over and climbed up onto my bed, flopping down dramatically on the pillow.

Oh God. What do I say?

I took a deep breath and lay on the bed next to him. "Sweetheart, I don't know what's going to happen with Viper. He's going through some really hard grown-up things right now."

His eyes searched my face. "What are grown-up things?"

"It's hard to explain . . . just stuff that adults have to deal with sometimes. I don't want you to worry about that though, okay? You just keep being the great kid that you are and everything will be fine." I leaned forward and gently kissed his forehead, letting my lips linger for a second.

His eyes fluttered open as I pulled back and I knew that he was tired. I ran my finger back and forth along both of his eyebrows and swirled it across his forehead. Within a couple of minutes, his breathing evened out and he was sound asleep. I kissed his soft cheek a couple times and nuzzled into him until our foreheads touched. Then I went back to sleep.

After I made mediocre pancakes, and Matthew complained that he wanted Viper's *again,* I bundled the kids up and we headed outside. My energy level was still pretty wiped out, but thankfully Matthew and Maura were content making snow angels and throwing the snow up in the air while I sat on the big bench on my porch.

My cell phone rang from somewhere deep in my jacket pocket. It was Kacie.

"Hey!" I answered cheerfully.

"Hey yourself! How are ya?"

"I'm good. Well, at the moment I'm sitting outside while the kids play, trying not to freeze to death, but other than that I'm good. How about you?"

"Ugh. I'm good. It's been one of those days though. Is it frowned upon to have wine at ten o'clock in the morning?"

I laughed out loud. "What happened?"

"What didn't happen? Piper took one of Lucy's shirts and tried to wear it to school, so I had them screaming at each other. Then Emma dumped her plate full of French toast and syrup *on* Diesel's back." She paused and let out a heavy sigh. "I'm just waiting for Grace's head to spin in a circle or something."

"Holy crap. Syrup on the dog? I would have given up right there."

"Right? I was tempted. Anyway, how was your Thanksgiving? I wish you would've come over and spent it with us."

"I know you do, and I love you for asking, but it actually turned out really nice. My neighbor ended up coming over and brought this whole feast with him."

"*Him?*" Her tone raised in curiosity. "I thought we were

talking about Jodi, but I'm pretty sure she doesn't have a penis."

"No," I said through a small giggle. "Remember I mentioned Joel before? The one with the son who moved in across the street?"

"Yeah?"

"Well, it was just him and Gavin for Thanksgiving, so we decided we might as well spend it together. I was planning on making grilled cheese, but he showed up with this huge Thanksgiving feast in a box. It was amazing."

"Wow!" Kacie said incredulously. "That's awesome. So . . . what's the deal with this guy?"

I shrugged even though she couldn't see me. "He's just a neighbor. Nice guy."

"Michelle. It's me. Don't lie."

"I'm not lying!" I defended with a laugh. "I swear."

"Is he cute?"

"I don't know. Sure."

The line was silent.

"Hello?" I asked slowly.

"I'm here. Just waiting for you to tell the truth."

"You're such a brat," I grumbled. "Yes, he's good-looking. Tall, broad shoulders, really dark hair, the craziest light blue eyes you've ever seen."

"Hmm . . . interesting. Any feelings?"

"Feelings? I have nothing but feelings, Kacie. I'm heartbroken, I'm furious, I'm confused, I'm lonely. I have feelings coming out of every pore in my body, but none of those are for Joel. Tiny butterflies, maybe, but all of my feelings are stuck on someone else right now. And all of these hormones raging through my body aren't helping." I took a deep breath and stared at my babies running happily around the front yard as they threw snow at each other.

"I'm so sorry, Michelle," Kacie said sadly. "I'm so fucking

mad at him. I swear if I ever see him again, I might just kill him."

"I might be okay with that." I laughed. "All right, I'm gonna run and try and get these kids in the house. I'm not feeling so hot and I want to lie down."

"What's going on?" Her voice turned concerned.

"Nothing. I think I'm just dehydrated. I didn't drink a lot yesterday, and now today I've been a little crampy."

Kacie let out a heavy sigh. "Listen, I want you to call your doctor if anything doesn't feel right, okay?"

"Okay."

"Promise me," she demanded.

"I promise," I agreed.

"And if you call them and they want you to come in, you call me. Got it?"

"Yes, Mom," I joked.

"I can't help it. It's the nurse in me."

"Yeah, yeah. I love you for it. I'll check in with you later, okay?"

"You won't have a choice." She laughed.

We got off the phone and I called Matthew and Maura into the house. They whined at first, but I promised hot chocolate with extra marshmallows and they came running.

A couple hours later, after a nap with the kids, my hands shook as I called Kacie back. "Hey, uh . . . can you come over? I'm gonna head in to the doctor."

"Yes! Of course. What happened?" Her words were rigid and nervous.

"I took a nap with the kids and when I woke up and went to the bathroom, there was a little blood."

"Oh, shit," she mumbled under her breath. "Yes, I'm on the way. Be there in a while."

Thankfully Taylor had the night off and rushed over to sit

with the kids when I'd called.

"Keep me posted, okay?" She gave me a quick hug as I slipped my feet into my boots.

"I will. Thanks, Tay." I squeezed her hand and was out the door.

On the way to my doctor's office, I could tell Kacie was trying to keep my mind busy by talking about everything she could think of, but I barely listened as I stared out the window. If something was wrong, I had no idea how I would feel. Devastated about the baby, but that was a given. I would also never, ever be able to look at Viper again. Ever.

When we got to the doctor's office and checked in, I didn't even have time to sit. A nurse took me right into the ultrasound room and had me hop up on the table.

"Do I need to take my pants off?" I asked.

"Uh . . ." She looked down at my chart. "Nope. You're fourteen weeks, so they won't be doing an internal ultrasound at this point. Everything will be outside. She'll be in shortly." She flashed me a quick smile and closed the door behind her.

Kacie sat on the chair in the opposite corner of the room, her legs bouncing up and down.

"Knock it off," I said as I lay back on the table. "You're making my nervousness nervous."

Her face fell. "Sorry, I'm just so—"

The door opened and in walked Sandy, the tech who had done most of my ultrasounds.

"Hey, honey!" she said cheerfully, squeezing my arm as she walked around me to her machine.

I wasn't so upbeat. "Hey."

"Okay, I know you must be a wreck, so let's skip the small talk and see what you have going on."

I nodded and turned my head to the TV hanging on the wall, praying that I would see a little blinking white light any second. Sandy spread warm jelly on my stomach and put the wand on top of it. She moved it just a couple of times, and there it was in plain view: a cloudy little figure with two arms, two legs, a big round belly . . . and a blinking heart. Relief washed over me and my eyes teared up.

"There it is," Sandy said, sounding almost as relieved as I felt.

"And everything's okay?" My voice cracked.

"Baby looks great so far. I'm going to take a bunch of pictures and see if I can find out what's going on, so if you hear me snapping away, don't get nervous, okay? It's just me being thorough for the doctor."

I nodded as a tear dripped from the corner of my left eye. Kacie stood and walked over behind me a little bit, taking my hand in hers.

Sandy clicked several pictures and then froze in one spot. "Hmmm," she hummed.

My head whipped around to her. "What? Is something wrong?"

"Wrong? No. But I know what you're having," she said as a big smile spread across her face. "Do you want to know?"

"Yes!" Kacie blurted out before I could answer.

"Wait. I don't know. Do I?" I looked over at Kacie. "He's not here. Should I wait and see if he wants to find out, too?"

Kacie cocked her hip to the side and crossed her arms over her chest. "You want me to answer that honestly, because there will be a lot of four-letter words involved."

"You're right. Don't answer that." I turned back to Sandy. "Spill it."

"Well,"—she grinned and shook her head as she stared down at her screen—"look up there and you can probably see it for yourself."

I looked back at the TV.

"Let's just say your baby isn't very shy and is opening nice and wide for us." Sandy let out a quick laugh. "See that little bulge right in the middle there? It's a boy!"

My eyes welled up again as I squeezed Kacie's hand hard.
"Are you sure?"

"Yep. If it were a girl there would be three little lines.
Definitely a boy . . . and from what I can tell he likes to show it
off."

"Like father, like son." I laughed. In the back of my mind, a
pang of sadness reared its ugly head. I had no idea how or when
to tell Viper this news, nor did I know how he would react to it,
but I chose to put that sadness in a box for later and just be
ecstatic about my son. *My* son.

As it turned out, I had a small bleed—a subchorionic
hematoma—that the doctors would have to keep a close eye on,
but they reassured me that it typically fixes itself and told me just
to take it easy for a couple of weeks. I was on cloud nine as we
left the office and walked back to the car, unable to take the smile
off my face.

Kacie stared down at the ultrasound pictures she was
carrying, the extra set she'd asked Sandy to print for her.

"I can't believe you did that." I nudged her. "What are you
going to do with ultrasound pictures of my baby, anyway?"

"Who knows?" She shrugged. "I might wait until bedtime and
casually hand them to Brody. He'll probably crap his pants, but
it would make me laugh, so it's all worth it in the end, right?"

"If you do that, you better video it and send it to me." I
laughed as I shook my head. "Seriously though, thank you for
coming with me today. I was really scared."

"I know you were," Kacie said sincerely. "I was, too. I'm so
happy he's fine."

I exhaled loudly. "Me, too. And I can't believe we found out
so early!"

"I know!" she exclaimed. "Now Auntie Kacie can start
shopping!"

Chapter
26

Viper

A COUPLE DAYS AFTER THE GAME, I was still high on adrenaline. I'd gone to two more home games, but that part was about to end because the Wild was heading out of town for a road trip . . . which might have been a blessing after all. Coach Collins asked if I wanted to go with, but I told him no. There were things at home I needed to deal with, and I *knew* I needed to deal with them, I just needed to figure out how.

In the afternoon, I headed off to therapy with a lot on my mind, hoping that Sherman would kick my ass and make me sweat it all out.

Sherman was leaning against the front counter when I walked in.

I froze in the doorway. "Are you kidding me with that?"

"With what?" He raised his hand defensively.

My eyes traveled up and down his outfit. He had on bright blue shorts, yellow socks that went up to his calves, a SpongeBob T-shirt and heart-shaped sunglasses that sat on top of his head. "That!"

He looked down at himself and back up at me. "You don't like my outfit?"

"Is that what we're calling it?" I answered with a laugh.

"You're just jealous that you can't pull something like this off. Now, shut up and get your ass on the bike!" He pointed.

I went over and did my ten minutes, just like I had done at the beginning of every therapy session for the last six weeks. My time on the bike had become both a blessing and a curse. I was forced to sit in one spot with no distractions. If Sherman saw me on my phone, he'd walk over and take it away, so I didn't even bother pulling it out anymore. I sat on the uncomfortable bike seat and rode while I stared out the window and took stock of my life, or what was left of it.

"What's your deal today, grumpy pants?" Sherman asked, interrupting my thoughts.

I turned toward him. "Grumpy pants? Who says I'm grumpy?"

He arched one eyebrow at me. "With you . . . it's obvious."

I rolled my eyes and hopped off the bike. "I'm fine. Come on, kick my ass today."

"Gladly," he mumbled and walked with me to the mat in the corner.

My face flushed and sweat beaded on my forehead as I worked my way through leg presses and lateral lunges.

"Let's head over to the stair machine for a bit," Sherman said once my sets were done.

"The stair machine? Really?" I complained.

He took my hand and pulled me up from the floor before he turned me and gave me a gentle shove toward the stair machine. "Quit your bitching and move it."

The stair machine kicked my ass. Within three minutes the sweat that had previously been on my forehead was now dripping onto my T-shirt and I was panting like a fool.

I watched in the mirror as Sherman took the hands of Emily,

one of the other therapists, and danced around the room to Stevie Wonder. He spun and twirled her as she threw her head back, laughing wildly.

After a few minutes, he huffed and puffed his way back over to me. "How's it going?" he asked breathlessly as he looked at my screen.

"Sherman." I shook my head slowly. "What is your deal?"

He tilted his head to the side. "My deal?"

"Yeah. The crazy outfits . . . your ridiculously happy mood all the time . . . what's your deal?"

He stared at my reflection in the mirror and took a deep breath. His voice lowered. "I wasn't always a happy man, Viper. I was actually a very miserable man for over half of my life."

I frowned back at him. "You? Miserable? I don't buy it."

He pressed his lips together and nodded, his face serious. "It's true. Very true. Here, come with me." Reaching across me, he stopped the stair machine and nodded his head toward the e-stim table.

"We're done already?" I asked as I hopped up.

"You asked a question, and now I'm gonna answer it." He put the sticky things on my knee, connected the wires, wrapped me in ice, and turned it on. "So. I was married right outta high school."

I lifted my head and looked at him incredulously. "To a *woman?*"

"Shut up and lie down." He pushed my forehead down until I was lying flat against the table again. "Yes, to a woman! Anyway, we married young and I went off to work. That's what I was supposed to do, take care of her and our two kids."

"You have kids?"

He sighed and put his hands on his hips. "Did you go to kindergarten?"

"Kindergarten? Yeah."

"Were you absent the day they taught kids that it isn't polite to interrupt? Hush!"

I rolled my eyes and shut my mouth.

"So I went off to work, but I was resentful. Angry. I wasn't even ready to be a husband, but before I knew it, I was also a father. So I started drinking . . . a lot. The more I drank, the more I retreated from real life. Eventually I started missing work, and then I lost my job. She took the kids and went to live with her parents while I rotted in our house until the bank eventually took it."

My heart sank. I wanted to tell him to stop talking but my mouth wouldn't open. I needed to hear the rest.

"She divorced me and I couch surfed at friends' houses for several more months. One day, I woke up and decided that I was done. I was lonely and missed my family, so I went to get them back." He paused and stared down at the table, pulling his brows down low. "But I was too late . . . she'd already moved on. I went to see her and she had a new ring on her finger. My daughters looked at me like I was a stranger, and my wife looked at me with hate in her eyes. I walked away from that house and never went back."

"Never?"

He shook his head. "I went back to school and got my dream job, and eventually I started smiling again. Then I smiled a little more, then a little more. But it took a *long* time. And now, I wake up every day and decide to be happy."

"What about the days you feel like shit and just don't care?"

"Those are the days I pick out the wackiest outfits," he said with a wink. "Because everyone around me laughs, and ultimately, that lifts my mood." I was so invested in his story, I'd forgotten all about my knee. He lifted the ice and started peeling the tabs off. "Okay. You know my story, now tell me yours."

I wasn't as open as Sherman, but after all that, I couldn't not tell him anything. "There's a girl in my life, and we're having some problems. I'm kinda shutting her out at the moment because I don't know how to handle my problems."

He stood up and crossed his arms. "Is she worth fighting for?"

I didn't even have to think about that answer. "Yes."

He raised his eyebrows quickly. "Then you better fight fast. Or else one day, you'll go back and some other man will be holding your girl's hand and carrying your kids through the park."

I had no idea I could learn so much from a man who wore heart-shaped sunglasses.

After therapy, I drove straight to Brody's. I didn't care that it was almost dinnertime and I might be interrupting. I needed to talk to him.

Brody and I had never gone two days without talking, let alone more than two weeks. I took a deep breath and climbed the front steps of his porch.

As soon as I rang the bell, I heard kids squealing and screaming as they sprinted toward the front door. "Quiet down or I'm giving you to whoever is on the other side!" Brody hollered. He pulled the door open and stared at me. "Never mind."

I let out a nervous laugh. "Probably not a good idea to give them to me, huh?"

"What are you doing here?" he asked with a stone face.

"You got a minute? I want to talk to you."

"Uh . . ." His eyes darted around. "Yeah. Kacie's actually out with some friends. Come on in." He pushed the door open and let me in.

I carefully stepped over dolls and books and princess crowns as I followed him through the house. "Whoa. What happened in here?" I surveyed the disaster in his normally spotless kitchen.

"Dinner happened." Brody ran a hand through his hair. He walked to the pantry and pulled a garbage bag out, quickly filling it with paper plates and crumpled napkins. "So what's up?"

I pulled out a stool and sat down at the island. "I know you're going out on the road again tomorrow, and I just wanted to talk to you before you left again."

"Okay."

"I feel bad about our conversation at my house. I know you were trying to help and I was a dick about it."

Brody nodded. "You were definitely a dick."

"Yeah. So I just wanted to apologize." I looked down at the island and pulled a bunch of crumbs into a small pile.

He leaned against the counter and crossed his arms over his chest. "I appreciate your apology, but I don't really need it. I'm just worried about you."

"I know." I nodded. "I've been a little out of it."

"A little?"

I shrugged. "A lot."

"And now?"

"Better . . . I think. Being at the games helped."

He tilted his head to the side and narrowed his eyes. "Why did that help?"

I dropped my eyes to the island again. Talking about my feelings with anyone wasn't easy for me, and holding eye contact while talking about my feelings was impossible. "I felt like I was still part of the team. It made me feel important again."

"Is that what you've been thinking this whole time?" His voice raised in surprise. "That you weren't part of the team?"

I shrugged again. "It wasn't just that. I don't know. I felt . . . lost."

"Lost?"

"Yeah. Hockey is my life, Brody. That's all I have. If I don't play hockey, I don't know who I am."

"Viper, hockey is a *part* of your life. A small part, and that's it." He shook his head vehemently. "That's what you don't get. You have Michelle and Matthew and Maura."

I scoffed at his response. "I *did* have them. I royally fucked that whole thing up, too."

"You absolutely fucked that up . . . royally," he agreed.

"I don't even know where to begin trying to fix it."

"Well, here's my question. And for once, just answer me honestly. Don't dick me around." He walked over and leaned on the island across from me, staring me straight in the eye. "Do you want to fix it? And I mean that. Do you want to be there with her and the kids . . . and the new baby?"

I stood up from the stool and paced the room. "Yes. No. I don't know."

"Bro, you have to figure that part out first. What's your holdup? Is it Michelle?"

"No."

"The kids?"

"No. I love those kids. I miss them like crazy."

"The baby?"

I stopped pacing and glance back at him. "Maybe?"

"Okay. Why does that freak out you?"

"Are you kidding?" I threw my hands up. "Look at me. I'm a fucking mess. I can't even handle myself. How the hell am I supposed to be a father? What am I gonna teach this kid . . . do everything the exact opposite of the way *I* do it?"

"Viper." Brody straightened and put his hands on his hips, looking me square in the eye. "You already *are* a father. Don't you see that? Everything you've been doing with the kids for a year now . . . You've cleaned up barf, you've put Band-Aids on skinned knees, you've read bedtime stories. That's all being a dad. You're already doing it, and you're amazing at it."

I stared at him but didn't respond.

"Listen," he continued, "you seem to have this victim mentality right now that you need to get rid of. You feel like everything is happening *to* you, but have you taken the time to look at the bigger picture?"

I shook my head.

"Fate doesn't ask permission and it doesn't give warnings," he said. "I know that sounds cheesy, but it's true. Maybe you're *meant* to have this baby. Maybe it's going to be the best thing that ever happened to you. When I met Kacie, I had no idea she would lead me to all *this*." He held his hands out wide. "And I wouldn't trade it for the world."

A big thud from above our head, followed by a loud cry, made Brody take a deep breath and exhale through his nose. "A little bit of peace and quiet maybe, but not the world. I'll be right back."

His words bounced around in my head as he ran upstairs to check on the girls. I walked over and sat down at the kitchen table, trying to soak everything in and think about it one step at a time. Brody had been one of my best friends since he joined the team, but he was more than a friend. We were each other's brother. We'd been through just about everything together, and I respected him more than almost anyone else on the planet. For him to tell me I was *already* an amazing dad really hit home.

Brody was back within a couple minutes. Just as he crossed into the kitchen, I heard the front door close. He turned back and looked toward it. "What are you doing home already?"

I couldn't make out what she said, but I could tell by the voice he was talking to Kacie.

Brody walked farther into the kitchen, staring at me with wide eyes. "Play dead," he mumbled.

I frowned at him. "Huh?"

Kacie was saying something about cars as she walked into the room and froze when she saw me. Her eyes narrowed. "What are *you* doing here?"

Play dead. I get it now. Too late.

Kacie was five foot nothing and about as threatening as a ladybug, but the look in her eyes made my stomach drop.

"I just came by to talk to Brody," I answered.

"Oh, you wanna talk? Good, 'cause I wanna talk, too." She marched over and slammed her purse down on the table before plopping down on the chair next to me.

"Babe, are you drunk?" Brody asked.

"Shush," she snapped at him before turning back to me. "You're a piece of shit, you know that?"

Brody sighed and rolled his eyes. "Definitely drunk."

"What makes you think you can just up and leave and not call her for this long?"

I looked to Brody for help, but he just shrugged.

"It wasn't intentional," I said.

"Oh." She nodded and tilted her head to the side. "It was accidental? What, did you just *forget* her phone number and address? I hate when that happens." Her tone was sarcastic and condescending, and I deserved every bit of it.

"I know you're mad at me—"

"I'm not mad at you," she interrupted. "I actually want to thank you."

"Thank me?" I said skeptically.

"Yeah, for showing her what a true asshole you are *now* instead of five years from now," she snarled coldly. "But don't worry about her. She doesn't need you anymore."

I dropped my eyes to the table and didn't respond. Everything she said was true and I deserved to hear it.

"I've been taking care of her. Joel's been taking care of her. *You're* not needed anymore," she said one more time.

"Kacie, that's enough," Brody warned, taking a couple steps toward the table.

"Joel?" I kept my head down toward the table but peered up at her.

"Yeah. The neighbor across the street. He's shoveled her driveway, taken Matthew when she needed a break. They even spent Thanksgiving together."

My stomach rolled and I thought I might puke. I licked my lips and tried to take a slow, steady breath in through my nose.

"Some other man will be holding your girl's hand and carrying your kids through the park . . ." Sherman's words from earlier that day suddenly had a very different meaning.

"Do you know where I was yesterday?" Kacie came back again.

I shook my head.

Kacie raised one eyebrow. "I was at the doctor, with her. She was bleeding, so they told her to come in."

I had many emotions running throughout my whole body, but when Kacie said that Michelle had been bleeding, ice ran through my veins and froze out everything else. "Is she okay?"

"Yep, she's fine . . . thank God." Kacie opened her purse and slid a black and white picture across the table so angrily it bounced off my chest. "So is your *son.*"

Brody marched over to the table. "Okay, that's enough. You clearly need to go up to bed and sleep this off." He gently took Kacie by the arm and lifted her.

"I'm not going to bed, it's not even eight o'clock yet," she argued.

"I know, but let's just close our eyes and sleep all this anger off, okay?" Brody said. "I'll be back, Viper."

I heard their muffled voices arguing all the way up the stairs, but I didn't give two shits what they were saying. I stared down at the grainy black and white photo of a silhouette . . . of my son. *My* son. My hand shook as I brought the picture closer to my face, desperately wanting to see it better. Suddenly, in that moment, sitting at Brody and Kacie's kitchen table . . . I was furious.

Furious at myself for acting like a selfish prick after I'd gotten hurt.

Furious at myself for blowing up at Michelle when I'd found out she was pregnant.

Furious at myself for not telling her about Kat.

Furious at myself for not calling her sooner.

Furious at myself for not going up to her door Thanksgiving morning.

Furious at myself for not being there when she'd been bleeding and scared.

But most of all, furious at myself for not being in that room with her when she'd heard the news that we were having a son.

I stared down at that picture of my son. "I'm so sorry," I said as my eyes stung. "I'm so sorry I wasn't there for your mom and your brother and sister. I'm so sorry I wasn't there for you." I blinked back a tear, got up, and left Brody's house without saying a word . . . and I took the picture of my son with me.

Chapter 27

Michelle

"BUT, MOMMA, I DON'T UNDERSTAND. We just had turkey and now we're singing Christmas songs," Matthew complained as I stuck the comb under water and brushed it through his hair, trying to calm his crazy bedhead.

"I know, buddy. It's hard to explain. Your school goes on break for a month, so they have to have your show kinda early, but Christmas still isn't for a couple of weeks. And they're holiday songs, not Christmas songs, remember?" I kissed the side of his head as I took him off the counter and set him on the floor. "Go find somewhere to sit completely still, please. I'll be ready in just a minute."

I threw on my stretchy jeans, boots, and oversized red sweater and looked at myself in the mirror. "How is it that my belly seems to have doubled in size overnight?" I said out loud with a sigh.

"Your tummy *is* big, Momma!"

I jumped and turned around. Matthew stood in the doorway with a big smile on his face. "You scared me, you little monster!" I reached out and pulled him to my side.

He raised his hand and set it on my stomach. "What's in there anyway?"

Matthew was a smart kid. He'd asked a couple of times about my growing tummy and I'd been able to change the subject and avoid his answer, but with Maura down for her morning nap and him and I alone, it just felt like the right time.

"Come with me, honey." I took his hand and we walked out to my room. I sat on the chair in the corner and pulled him onto my lap. "Okay, you wanna know why mommy's tummy is getting big?"

He looked up at me and nodded.

"It's because there's a baby growing in there."

His eyes bulged and he leaned back and stared down at my stomach. "There is?"

"Mmhmm." I nodded. "And do you know what else? That baby is a little boy. You're going to have a baby brother."

He let out a tiny gasp. "I was gonna ask Santa for a brother!"

My heart overflowed. I knew that he'd probably just made that up, but I didn't even care. "You were?"

He nodded. "When does he come out?"

"Not for a while yet. He's gotta grow big and healthy first."

"Okay," he said, sounding a little sad.

"I know it's hard to wait, but it'll be worth it. I promise. Now, go sit and wait for me. I just have to brush my teeth, grab Maura, and we'll leave for your party."

He hopped off my lap and headed toward the door as I walked to the bathroom.

"Hey, Momma?" he called back.

"Yes, buddy?" I stopped in the bathroom doorway and leaned back.

"How did that baby get *in* your tummy?"

"Uh . . ." I stammered. "You know what? I'm worried that we're gonna be late, so let's talk about that part later, okay?"

"Okay." He turned and walked down the hall, and I breathed a sigh of relief.

His classroom was decorated so perfectly with blue, glittery snowflakes hanging from the ceiling and construction paper mittens taped to the walls.

Miss Lori, Matthew's teacher, asked all the parents to sit in the chairs and face the small riser that was along the far wall. I sat in the front row, down at the end, just in case I needed to get up and deal with an unpredictable toddler.

As the parents took their seats, Miss Lori took her spot at the piano. Matthew and all of his classmates giggled nervously and waved at their parents. Miss Lori turned and whispered something to them, then counted to three. When she got to three, they all began singing "Frosty the Snowman" as she played the tune on the piano. At first Matthew was shy and stared at the ground, but by the second verse, he was belting the song out as loud and proud as he could.

"Five Little Snowflakes" was up next, and Maura was happily clapping along and wiggling her little booty as much as she could from my lap as I tried to video with my phone. They were on the third little snowflake when Matthew looked toward the classroom door and his face lit up.

"Viper!" he called out above all the other kids singing.

I dropped my phone in my lap and followed him with my eyes as he sprinted to the door and leaped into Viper's arms. Viper scooped him up and closed his eyes as they squeezed each other. Miss Lori kept playing the song, but the other kids were so distracted by what was going on that they eventually trailed off. The piano stopped as Viper set Matthew down.

"Go finish singing, bud. I'll talk to you after, okay?" he said.

Matthew nodded and excitedly bounced back to his spot on the step. Viper stood and scanned the group of parents until our eyes met. "Sorry about that," he apologized to the parents with a wave as he walked past them and sat in the chair next to me.

My throat felt like it was going to close up and my whole body
tingled with anxiety. Never in a million years did I expect Viper
to show up at Matthew's school program. I didn't look at him as
he sat down, but the minute Maura saw him, she reached her
arms out for him.

"Hey, sweet baby!" he said as he shifted her onto his lap and
kissed her cheek at least a dozen times.

I didn't know what to say. I didn't know what to do. Part of
me wanted to get up and leave, but I couldn't pull Matthew from
his performance, nor did I want to make a huge scene. Matthew
kept looking over at Viper with a big grin on his face to make
sure he was watching him sing, and I just tried to breathe
normally. My hands were shaking so bad I rolled them into fists
so that no one else would see. But someone did see. Viper saw.
He reached over and wrapped his hand around mine. I still
refused to look over at him, but I didn't pull back. Not only was
Matthew watching us like a hawk, as much as I didn't want to
admit it, it felt amazing to have his warm hand covering mine.
I'd had zero contact with him in over a month, but my body
craved his touch, which was something I couldn't turn off, no
matter how hard I tried.

As tears stung my eyes, I tried to focus on Matthew and the
absolute joy that was on his face as he belted out song after song.

The singing part ended and the food part began. Parents
stood around and made small talk as the kids feasted on cheese
and crackers, cookies, fruit, and popcorn. Maura wanted nothing
to do with me and I had yet to make eye contact with Viper
again. As the party wrapped up, I led the way as Matthew skipped
to the coatroom and grabbed his jacked from his cubby. Viper
and Maura followed us.

"Viper, are you coming home with us?" Matthew asked
innocently.

My heart climbed into my throat and clung to the side of it
for dear life. No matter how many times I swallowed, I couldn't
get it to go back down. I was terrified he was going to say yes,
but even more terrified he was going to say no.

"Yeah, buddy. I am," Viper answered. Matthew threw his little hands in the air and spun in a circle, nearly falling over. Viper lifted his eyes to mine and spoke softly. "Is that okay with you?"

"It's fine. They miss you," I answered dryly, refusing to admit that I missed him, too.

The whole way home I kept checking my rearview mirror, half-expecting that he would change his mind and bolt again. But he didn't. I pulled my car into the garage and he pulled his into the driveway right behind me.

He followed us into the house and I had no idea what I was going to say. I wanted to yell. I wanted to cry. I wanted to punch him in the face. I wanted him to hold me. I was a fucking mess, and I had no idea which Michelle was going to take over.

As soon as we were in the house, Matthew started talking to Viper a mile a minute and didn't stop for at least an hour. Maura also refused to leave Viper's arms, even fussing when he put her down for one minute to use the bathroom. As soon as he was out, she clung to him again. I mostly stayed in the kitchen, folding laundry and avoiding Viper's stare every time he looked over at me. After a little while, I noticed the family room was quiet. Matthew and Maura had both fallen asleep with their heads lying on Viper's shoulders. He shot me a small smile as I walked over and picked Maura up to carry her to her room. He carefully held Matthew's head as he slid out from under him.

"Want me to take her up?" he offered, holding his hands out.

"Nope, I got her."

"You sure?"

I gave him a quick glare. "Yeah. They're *my* kids, remember?" Before he could answer I turned and hustled up to Maura's room. I expected him to be gone when I went back downstairs, but he was sitting at the kitchen island.

"Are you leaving or what?" I asked, leaning my back against the kitchen counter.

"I was kinda hoping I could stay and we could talk?" His eyes were soft and pained. It was hard to be mad at him when he looked like that.

"Fine. Talk."

"Michelle . . . I've thought over and over about what I was going to say to you when I saw you, but now that you're in front of me, I just want to hug you. Can I hug you?"

"No."

He nodded slowly. "I know that my apology doesn't mean shit to you right now, but I want you to know from the bottom of my heart how sorry I am about everything. The way I acted when you told me about the baby, for not checking in this whole time, for the way I acted before all of this even started. I'm sorry for all of it, Michelle."

I pinched my lips together and watched him as he spoke. I waited for him to break eye contact and look away, but he never did. He delivered his apology and was more sincere than I'd probably ever heard him, but that wasn't enough to make over a month's worth of anger disappear.

I took a long, deep breath through my nose, trying to choose my words carefully. "You've been gone for weeks, Viper. Weeks. Not a couple hours, not a couple days. *Weeks.* And now you stroll into Matthew's school and my house like nothing ever happened?"

He shook his head. "It's not like nothing ever happened. I know I fucked up. Trust me, I know that. But I want to make it better."

I tilted my head to the side. "Really? How do you plan to make that better? How exactly do you plan to erase all of the memories from my head about what an asshole you were when I told you I was pregnant and the following weeks when you completely ignored me and the kids?" I said through clenched teeth. I wanted to scream at him, but Matthew was sleeping on the couch in the next room. "You weren't here when I needed you most. You rejected me—and my kids. How are you gonna fix *that?*"

"I don't know how to fix it, Michelle, but I wish I could. I wish more than anything I could go back and do everything differently. Everything!" His voice sounded desperate, frantic even. "When I found out I couldn't play hockey, I went to a bad place. That darkness spread like poison through every part of my life. It's not an excuse, but it is the truth. Hockey has been all I've known since I was eight years old. It was like someone ripped my foundation from under me and everything else just fell right along with it."

I listened intently but didn't respond.

"And now," he continued, "I'm trying to rebuild. I *want* to rebuild, but I'm putting my house back up in a different order. You and the kids are all the foundation that I need. If I've learned anything being away from you, it's that. I need you guys way more than I need hockey. Hockey is still an important part of my life, but it's just a couple of bricks."

I cleared my throat and tried to make my voice strong. "I appreciate your apology, but I think it's best that you leave."

His shoulders fell. "Leave?"

I nodded. "I don't know what to say to you. Right now I'm angry and I'm upset. I wasn't planning on seeing you today. And let's both be honest, once you walk out that door, I have no idea when I'll see you again."

"That's what I mean," he said as he stood and walked over to me. "I get it. I get now what an ass I am and how I run away from the things I should be running toward. I don't want to leave, Michelle. I don't want to leave ever again. I want to stay here and make things better again. I want to prove to you and the kids and to *him*"—he put his hand on my belly—"that I can be a good dad again. I promise. I can do it. Please let me."

The corners of my eyes stung as I gently pushed his hand away. "Go."

"No. I'm not," he said adamantly as he took my hands in his. "I want to stay and talk to you. I'm not running any more, from this or from anything else. Ever again. Let me fix this."

One single tear dripped down my cheek and I shook my head. "Viper, I can't do this with you right now. I'm supposed to be taking it easy and this is *not* easy." My whole body strained as I tried to keep the rest of the tears in.

"Okay, okay. Please don't cry. The last thing I want to do is upset you." He took a deep breath. "I'm gonna go and let you calm down. You let me know when you're ready and we'll talk, okay? No fighting. Just talking." His eyes moved back and forth between mine, hopeful as he waited for my answer. "Okay?" he repeated when I didn't respond.

"Fine," I resigned, pulling my hands back from his.

"Okay," he said with a relieved nod. "I'll be on the porch."

"Wait. What?" I frowned as he grabbed his hoodie from the back of the kitchen chair and threw it over his head.

"I meant what I said. I'm not running and I'm not leaving. You just let me know when you're ready for me and we'll talk." He gave me a tight smile and headed out the front door without another word.

I stood in the kitchen with my arms wrapped around myself, convinced that I'd been abducted by aliens and dropped into *The Twilight Zone*. I rubbed my forehead with my fingertips and waited to see if I heard his car start in the driveway, but I never did. Tiptoeing quietly to the front of the house, I peeked out the dining room window. Sure enough, Viper was sitting on the bench on my porch with his arms folded over his chest.

What a stubborn, stubborn man.

Fine. If he wanted stubborn, I was going to give him stubborn. I was in a warm, cozy house and he was sitting on a front porch in Minnesota in December wearing nothing but a hoodie. We'd just see who caved faster.

Over the next hour, I caught up on all the laundry, scrubbed my powder room top to bottom, and found any excuse to walk near the front of the house, just to see if he was still out there. So far, absolutely no movement from him.

When Matthew and Maura woke up from their naps, they asked where Viper was. I had to think fast, so I told them he was on the front porch having a time-out. They spent the next several hours going back and forth from their playroom to the front window to make funny faces at him.

It was getting late and I was running out of steam.

"Hey, guys, we're gonna go up and do your baths early tonight, okay? Then we'll do dinner after."

Used to their baths being the last thing of the night, they both started to complain.

"If you guys go upstairs without a fight, I'll let you take your bath together just this one time." I dangled an elusive carrot in front of them to get them to listen to me.

They both turned and hustled up the stairs without another word.

I ran the warm bath and poured an extra capful of bubbles into the tub. They each grabbed a couple of toys from their room and sprinted to the bathroom. I let them splash and play, basically washing themselves, for a long while as I sat on the floor next to the tub, trying to avoid their splashes. After I dried them off and put them in toasty jammies, we all headed downstairs to find one dinner.

Matthew ran ahead of me and looked out the window. "He's gone!" he cried out.

"He is?" My heart sank, but I wasn't surprised. I knew he wouldn't last. I walked over and stood above him, peeking out the window, too. Sure enough, no Viper. He'd seemed so sincere when he was talking to me that I really thought he meant what he said, but old habits die hard. "Maybe he'll be back later," I said unconvincingly to Matthew. "Come on. Let's go in the kitchen."

His shoulders slumped, but he turned around and followed me anyway. Maura climbed up to the kitchen table and started coloring furiously as I scanned my pantry for something to make them for dinner. I let out a heavy sigh. "Guys, we need to go to the grocery store tomorrow." My stomach growled as I thought back to the Thanksgiving feast in a box and wondered how long it would take them to get that together if I called now.

As I walked back into the kitchen, the doorbell rang.

Matthew's face shot up to mine with wide eyes. "Maybe Viper's back!" He sprinted toward the front door and I followed. On the other side was a man in a royal blue polo shirt with a wide smile, holding two pizza boxes.

"Hi?" I said as I pulled the door open.

"Hi there. I have your pizzas." He held the boxes out toward me.

"Uh . . ." I looked down at them and back up at him. "I didn't order any pizzas."

He pulled them back and looked at the receipt stapled to the top of the box. "You didn't?"

I heard a car door slam. "Wait! Those are for me." Viper popped out from around the corner of the garage.

"Oh, sorry about that." The pizza guy turned back and walked down the sidewalk a little bit. They exchanged the pizzas and money and he headed toward his car.

"You're still here?" I said to Viper as Matthew wrapped his arms around my thigh.

Viper looked up at me and nodded. "I told you I wasn't leaving until you talked to me. It was cold, so I got in my car." He grinned and nodded toward the garage. "Hope you don't have to go anywhere. I'm parked behind you."

I fought back a tiny smile that threatened my lips.

"Oh, and wait." He lifted the lid to the top pizza box and walked over. "This one is for you guys."

"It is?"

"Yeah." He shrugged. "I wasn't gonna get dinner for me but not for you. It's your favorite . . . extra pepperoni."

234

I took the box from him and we stood there and stared at each other for a few seconds. It was freezing outside, but the air between us was warm and intense. It was clear we both had so much to say but neither of us knew where to begin.

"Okay, well, I'll be in my car." He smiled and disappeared around the side of the garage . . . and I didn't stop him.

As the kids ate their pizza and blueberries, Matthew chattered happily about the snow that continued to fall outside and Maura nodded, probably only half listening to him. I, on the other hand, couldn't get my mind off the stubborn man currently eating pizza alone in his car in my driveway. My brain was exhausted from swinging back and forth like a pendulum. One side was angry and felt like he deserved to sleep in a cold car by himself, but the other side wanted to go out and bring him into my warm house, at least to the couch.

After we finished eating and cleaned up, we headed upstairs. I tucked the kids in and peeked out my bedroom window, just barely able to see the back of his car sticking out behind the garage. Clouds of white smoke billowed from the back of it and I knew that he must have been really cold and started his car. I climbed into my warm bed, feeling a little guilty that I was letting him sleep in the car, but also hopeful that he'd finally reached out.

I'd known the moment I met Viper years ago that he was a complex, stubborn man. Mike had told me stories about him that made my head spin. When Viper and I had finally gotten together, I knew he would never be typical with me either. His whole life was on his own terms and he never did things the way they *should* be done, but this last several weeks had shown me just how complicated he *really* was. Nothing about him was cut and dry, black and white.

He was one big gray area. But . . . that gray area is what I loved most about him. It's what kept me on my toes and feeling alive. I just needed to sort out how much gray was too much.

Chapter
28

Viper

MY PAST WAS . . . COLORFUL . . . AND I'd definitely spent a night or two in my car, but never for such an important reason. My refusal to leave was dramatic, but so was my need to be with Michelle and the kids. I meant every single word that I'd said and I needed her to see that. I was *done* running. I was *done* turning my head when shit got too serious. Things had spiraled too fucking out of control over the last several weeks and I'd let my pride get in the way of my heart. I could never get back the time I'd missed with her and the kids, but I would never, ever be away from them like that again . . . if she'd let me back in.

I ran my car on and off all night, both to charge my phone and warm the inside up a bit. Thankfully I had a couple extra hoodies and a blanket in the backseat so it wasn't too bad, but the next night was supposed to get really, really cold. But I meant what I'd said to her. I was in it for the long haul.

As I sat in my car, replaying my conversation with Michelle from the day before over and over and over in my head, one thing she'd said kept coming back to me.

"How are you going to fix that?"

They were just seven little words from her mouth that she probably didn't think twice about after she'd said them, yet I couldn't stop thinking about them. That was it. I needed to show her, not tell her. I needed to do something drastic, something totally un-Viper like to prove to her that I was serious about being here and never leaving her and *our* kids again. I made two quick phone calls, and just like that, my plan was set in motion. In a few shorts hours, I would be able to show her just how serious I was.

In the meantime, I needed something to keep my mind busy. Sitting in the same position for hours on end was not only hurting my knee, it was driving me insane. I got out of the car and bent over, picking up a pile of snow in my hand. I formed it into a ball and tossed it in the air a few times.

Hmm. Good packing snow today.

I put it on the ground and rolled it across Michelle's front yard, making a huge snowball . . . or the perfect base for a snowman.

I quickly pulled my phone out and sent Michelle a text.

Can the kids come outside for a while?

She didn't respond, but a couple minutes later, Matthew came running out the front door dressed in black snow pants, his navy blue winter coat, winter hat, and gloves. He ran over and threw his arms around me as Michelle closed the door.

"Where's Maura?" I asked as I picked him up.

"Maura didn't want to come out. She's watching *My Little Pony* or something." He shrugged.

"She passed up snowman building for ponies?"

Matthew pulled one corner of his mouth up and nodded. "She's crazy."

I laughed out loud. "She is, but let's build the biggest

snowman anyway."

"Yes!"

I set him down and we got to work. "Let's make this bottom a little bigger, okay? Can you help me push it?"

He nodded and leaned his hands against the huge snowball I'd already started, grunting and groaning out loud as we pushed it together to make it as big as we could. Then we started on the middle section, rolling and rolling it together until Matthew said it was the perfect size. I lifted it on top of the bottom part and we stepped back to look at it.

"What do you think?" I asked.

"I think it's perfect!" he cheered.

"Ready for the head?"

He turned and looked up at me. "I want to do that one by myself."

I motioned toward the ground. "Have at it, big guy."

Standing there with my arms crossed over my chest, I watched Matthew make a tiny snowball, no bigger than a golf ball, and hold it in his hand. I almost jumped in and told him to start with a bigger one, but then I remembered how my asshole father had never let me do things on my own. I always had to do them *his* way. So I shut my mouth and let Matthew build the head just the way he wanted. Getting snow to attach to the little snowball was hard, and he threw it down in frustration.

"Just keep rolling it. It'll stick. You got it," I called out.

He picked it up again and started spinning the ball through the snow as he crawled on his knees behind it. The bigger the snowball grew, the bigger his smile grew.

"Viper! Look!" he yelled proudly as he tried to lift the basketball-sized snowball in the air above his head.

"Good job, bud! Whoa! Careful!" I rushed over and put my hand on it before he dropped it and lost his mind. "Here. Hold on tight." I lifted him with one arm and put my other hand under the snowball so that he thought he was doing it himself, and we put the head on the top of the snowman together.

"What do you think?" I asked as Matthew beamed at our snowman.

"I think it's awesome."

"I think it needs some decorations," Michelle called from behind us.

We turned around and she was standing on the porch holding a few things. Matthew squirmed out of my arms and ran over to grab them from her. We tied an old red scarf around the snowman's neck, used a carrot and grapes for his face, and found rocks and sticks for his arms and buttons.

"I think he's done," I said as we put an old sun hat on his head.

"Not yet." Matthew shook his head. "He needs a name."

"He does need a name. You're right. Any ideas?"

Matthew pulled his top lip in and thought hard about it. "How about Earl?"

"Earl?" I repeated with a loud laugh.

He nodded.

"Whatever you want. If you want Earl, Earl it is."

The front door opened again and Michelle called Matthew's name.

"Do I have to come in?" he whined.

She nodded. "It's lunchtime."

"Can I come back after lunch?" He pulled his hat off and slinked toward the house sadly.

"We'll see. Come on." Matthew walked past her into the house and she looked out at me. It took all I had not to run up to the porch and wrap my arms around her, but instead I gave her a tight smile and quick wave before I walked back to my car. I started the engine and plugged my phone back in, noticing that I had a text.

Brody: Just checking in on you. I talked to Andy

and he said you slept in your car last night. Have you completely lost your fucking mind?

I laughed out loud.

Yes, I did and yes, I have. I'm not leaving here until I win her back.

Brody: And what if that never happens?

Not an option.

Brody: Well, I'm crossing everything for ya, buddy. I hope it works out. I really do.

Thanks. Can you also do me a favor?

Brody: Sure

Can you thank your wife for me?

Brody: Kacie? Sure. For what?

For giving me the kick in the balls I needed. I knew that I needed to talk to Michelle, but I was too scared to come over here without a plan. After Kacie ripped me a new one, I thought about it a lot and decided it wasn't so much the words I used, but the feeling behind them.

Brody: Look at you. My little Viper is all grown up. I'll let her know. Good luck, brother. Keep me posted and let me know if you need anything.

Actually, I do need one thing. Have you left for the airport yet?

Brody: Not for a couple hours. Why?

Half an hour later, Brody's black pick-up truck pulled up behind mine and I hopped out.

"You're the best!" I rubbed my hands together as he walked around the back of his truck and pulled two big red plastic gas cans out. I took them from him and walked back to my car.

"Nice snowman." He nodded toward the yard as he followed me.

"Thanks. That's Earl."

"Earl?" He laughed out loud.

"Yep. Matthew named him," I added. I unscrewed the gas cap and lifted the first gas can, pouring it into my tank.

Brody leaned against the back of my car and shook his head. "You're really going to sleep out here again?"

My eyes lifted to his and I spoke in a low, steady voice. "Yes, I am."

"In that case . . ." He turned and walked back to his truck and pulled a large bag out of the front seat. "Here. This is for you."

I frowned down at the bag. "What is it?"

"Baby wipes, antibacterial hand cleanser, a couple bottles of water, a large quilt, and a thermos of soup."

"Huh?"

He shrugged. "I told Kacie what you said. Then I told her what you were doing. She said she's glad she kicked your ass, too, and that she hopes this all works out. Then she packed you a bag and heated you some soup, further proving that I will never, ever, ever understand women as long as I live."

I laughed and started pouring the gas from the second can into the car. "You have a good wife, Brody Murphy. A very good wife."

He nodded slowly. "You will, too, Lawrence Finkle. I can feel it."

I took a deep breath and exhaled loudly. "At this point, I just want to hug her and make the kids pancakes. Anything extra would be icing on the cake."

"Keep up the good fight, brother. Kacie was so fucking mad at you the other night. I thought she might actually kill you. If you can get her to make you soup after that, I'm convinced anything is possible."

"Thanks. And thanks for bringing this by." I tilted my head toward the gas can. "It would have been a long, cold night without it."

"Yeah, well I head out on the road in a few hours. If you run out again, you'll have to call Andy, and we both know how that will go."

I rolled my eyes. "Lecture city."

"You know it!" He patted me on the shoulder and picked up the empty gas can. We both carried one back to his truck and set them in the back.

"All right, well . . . good luck. Hopefully you see the inside of a house again real soon. And maybe access to a shower. You smell bad as it is on a regular day. I can't imagine how that car is gonna smell after a few more days." He laughed and gave me a quick hug.

"Too bad Kacie didn't pack deodorant, huh?"

"Amen to that." He got into his truck and waved as he pulled away. I walked back to my car and put the blue duffel bag in the backseat.

As soon as I shut the back door, another car pulled up. I squinted my eyes and lowered my head to see who was in it. Vivian put her car in park and waved at me.

Go time!

Chapter
29

Michelle

I CIRCLED THE FRONT WINDOW like a hungry shark stalking a
school of fish. The thud of a car door caught my attention
and the beautiful woman talking to Viper at the back of his
car kept me from moving. She was doing most of the talking and
waving her hands around as he leaned his elbow on the trunk of
his car and listened. They talked for a good five minutes as I hid,
peeking out from behind the curtain. After a few more minutes,
the woman pulled some papers out of a bag and set them on the
back of the car. Viper hovered and looked at them as she kept
talking. Eventually she handed him a pen and he signed whatever
the papers were. Then she got back in her car and drove away.

Pacing across the front of the house, I went back and forth
about whether or not to go out there. The jealous fourteen-year-
old in me wanted to fly out the door, stomp my feet, and demand
to know everything. The adult in me glared at that kid and told
her to sit down and shut up. Ultimately, the fourteen-year-old

won.

He was leaning against his car, staring down at the papers when I walked down the sidewalk toward him. The sounds of my feet crunching over the ice made him look up.

"Hey." He stood up from the car and gave me a big, genuine grin.

"Hey. Who was that?" I tried to sound nonchalant but failed miserably.

"That was Vivian."

"Oh. Who's Vivian?"

He stared at me and took a deep breath. Then his eyes fell to the ground for a couple of seconds before reconnecting with mine. "Can I come in and talk to you?"

I was taken aback. "Huh?"

He shrugged. "Can I come in and can we talk? Please? No fighting. No yelling. Just talking, like this."

"Viper, who's that woman?"

"That's part of what I want to talk to you about."

I shook my head, frustrated that he wasn't giving me any real answers. "Ugh. Fine," I groaned and turned back to the house.

We walked in and I knew the kids—especially Maura—would want a few minutes to crawl all over him, so I didn't stop it when it happened. He picked them both up, one in each arm, and covered their faces in dozens of kisses. After a few minutes of his attention, they scampered back to the playroom and he sat on the stool at the island. My heart was thumping fast. I didn't know who that woman was or what he was about to say.

"Okay. Go," I finally said, preparing myself for anything.

He folded his hands in front of his mouth and looked at me. His face was expressionless, but his eyes stared at me so intensely that every nerve in my body awoke and stood on end.

"I love you, Michelle," he finally said.

I pulled my brows in tight. "What?"

"I love you. I really, really love you. Like . . . from-the-bottom-of-my-heart-don't-know-how-to-live-without-you kind of love."

My heart urged me to tell him that I loved him back, but I bit my lip so the words couldn't come out.

"I have been horrible to you," he continued. "The way I acted after surgery, the things I said when you told me about our baby, calling the kids *your* kids and not *ours* . . . I was horrible. I wouldn't blame you if you told me to leave and never come back again, but don't think for a second that's going to make me stop loving you, because nothing will."

"You were horrible," I agreed softly.

"And I wish I could go back in time and take it all back, but I can't. All I can do is vow never to do it again and move forward. But I want to do more than that. I need to prove to you that not only will I never treat you like that again, I'm never going to leave again."

My head swirled as I tried to think of what to say back, but he wasn't done.

He swallowed and looked down at the island. "Walking out that door that day was the single worst mistake I've ever made, and I see that now. I should have stayed. I should have taken a time-out. I should have done anything other than walk out that door. The longer I was gone, the harder it was to come back, but when Kacie showed me this"—he put an ultrasound picture on the island in front of him—"and told me about our son, I couldn't stay away one more day." His eyes lifted back to mine. "But . . . I'm an idiot. I'm not good with words and presents like Brody. I'm not in control and focused like Andy. I'm a big dumb idiot who is impulsive and pretty damn stupid."

"You're not stupid." I sniffed.

"I am stupid. Walking away from you guys for all that time was stupid. But I want to make it better. I want to make it right. I want to make you feel secure again and show you that I'm not looking for the door ever again. So"—he laid the other papers on the counter—"I listed my house this morning. That house was my bachelor pad, my old life. Everything I want is here, in this house . . . all of my physical belongings and my people. I don't ever have to go back to that house again."

My eyebrows shot up. "You're selling your *house?*" I exclaimed.

He nodded.

"Viper, I haven't even let you back in yet."

His shoulders shrugged. "I know, but I don't want to go back there. I want to be *here*. Plus, that house reminds me of the worst time in my whole life, a time away from you and the kids, and I don't want to go back there. *Ever.*"

Several weeks' worth of feelings and emotions welled up inside of me and came bubbling quickly to the surface. I rubbed my forehead with my fingers as tears started falling from my eyes as fast as my eyes could make them. I believed him. I believed every word he said. I believed that he missed us. I believed that he wanted to be here. I dropped my hands and looked at him. He was staring back at me with tears in his eyes, too.

He tilted his head to the side. "Please, baby? Please let me come home. Please let me be a dad to the kids again. Please let me love *you* again. I can't be without you guys for one more day."

My breath hitched as I put my head in my hands and started to sob. Shoulder-shaking, stomach-clenching, couldn't-breathe sobs. Viper rushed around the island and wrapped me in his arms. As soon as I felt them cover me, I cried even harder. He didn't say any more, he just held me and let me cry until there was nothing else to let out. After several minutes, I pushed his stomach back gently and reached for a napkin to blow my nose. After I tossed the napkin in the garbage, before I could say anything, he pulled me against him for another hug.

There was a point, a month before, where I wasn't sure if I'd ever feel his arms around me again, and now that they were, they felt so good that I didn't ever want to move. I closed my eyes and leaned into him, inhaling the smell of him and feeling his chest muscles flex against the side of my head every time his arms moved up and down as he rubbed my back.

"There is one more thing that I need to tell you," he said.

My eyes shot open and I froze. "What?"

His arms tightened around me. "The nurse at Gam's . . . Kat—"

"Oh God! Viper." I pulled back quickly and glared at him. "You did not!"

His mouth fell open and he raised his hands defensively. "No! No! Nothing happened. God no!"

My chest rose and fell heavily as I waited for him to explain himself.

"Years ago—*several* years ago—we dated. I had no idea she was going to be at Gam's. I didn't even know she was a nurse now. I asked Ellie to make all the arrangements, and before I got a chance to look over who she picked, I got hurt and it kind of took my attention off of that."

I eyed him skeptically as my blood pressure slowly came back down. "So are there feelings there?"

He shook his head vigorously. "Absolutely not. Not even a little. Nothing."

"Why didn't you tell me sooner?" I asked.

He shrugged. "Same reason you didn't tell me about the baby right away. There wasn't really a good time. After I got hurt and we went to Gam's—the day I got the call that I'd torn my ACL—that was the first time I saw her. I was going to fire her, but then she'd bonded with Gam and everything happened between you and me, and I just didn't care about her anymore. I still don't."

I let out a heavy sigh as he took a step toward me and bent his head down to catch my eyes with his. "I want a fresh start with us, Michelle. Clean slate, starting today, so I don't want anything that could be viewed as a secret hanging out there between us."

"You're sure there's nothing there?"

"Michelle, I promise. There's less than nothing."

"Well, I have something to tell you, too." I looked up at him and his head jerked back in surprise. "I spent Thanksgiving with Joel and Gavin."

"Oh." He waved his hand. "I already knew that."

"You did?" My voice rose.

"Yeah, Kacie told me that, too."

Blabbermouth.

"Are you mad?" I asked cautiously, not wanting to ruin all the progress we'd just made.

"Yes." He nodded. "Mad at myself for not being here to spend the holiday with you guys, but not mad at you for having dinner with a friend. As much as it pains me to think about it, I'm glad he was here for you."

"Wow!" I said in amazement. "I didn't expect that to come out of you."

"I didn't expect it to come out of me either, but I mean it. I'm done playing games and having temper tantrums. That's not who I am anymore. I want this. I want us." He moved his hand back and forth between the two of us, then motioned down the hall toward the playroom. "I want them. I want *our* kids . . . Matthew, Maura, this little guy who has yet to be named . . . maybe even a couple more after him."

My eyes flashed open and I let out a quick giggle through the tears. "Whoa! Slow down. You were living in your car up until an hour ago. Let's not get ahead of ourselves with more babies, okay?"

He grabbed my shoulders and pulled me against him, squeezing me as hard as he ever had. "I love you, Michelle. And I'm so, so incredibly sorry. I can't say that enough."

"Yes, you can." I hooked my arms under his and hugged him back. "That was your one and only get-out-of-jail-free card."

"I won't need another. I promise."

We stood in the kitchen, hugging and swaying back and forth, until the kids came in and interrupted us several minutes later.

"I'm hungry!" Matthew whined. "I want lunch."

"I have some soup in the car," Viper joked.

I pulled back and looked up at him. "What? Soup?"

He let out a quick laugh. "Kacie made Brody bring me soup. It's in my car."

Matthew turned up his nose. "I don't want soup."

"I'll make you something, bud." I took a deep, cleansing breath and started toward the pantry, but Viper caught my arm.

"You sit. How about I make pancakes?" His eyes slid from me to Matthew, whose face lit up as he threw his hands in the air.

"Yes! Yes! I want pancakes!"

"Pancakes it is." He grinned with a nod and kissed the side of my head.

Chapter
30

Viper

CHRISTMAS HAD ALWAYS BEEN MY favorite holiday, but I couldn't remember a time in my entire life where I'd been more excited for that morning. Michelle said she was already done with all of the Santa shopping for Matthew and Maura, but I only saw that as a challenge. After therapy sessions, I'd stopped and gotten a few more things but hadn't told her. I couldn't wait to see the kids' faces on Christmas morning.

The morning of Christmas Eve, I went to pick up Gam. Michelle and I had invited her to the house to spend the day with us, then sleepover and spend Christmas with us, too, but Gam was a homebody, so she turned us down initially. That's when we'd handed the phone to Little Mo and told *her* to ask. Needless to say, I was picking Gam up to come home with me for a few days.

"Seriously. How long do you plan on staying?" I said playfully as I picked her bag up off the couch.

"Shut up, you little asshole," Gam spat as she walked into the kitchen.

I ignored her and continued teasing. "This thing is *so* heavy!"

"Of course it is. My whiskey is in there," she called out.

"You brought whiskey? We *have* whiskey."

"Probably not enough." She shut the kitchen light off with a laugh and headed to the front door.

"You ready, you old bat?"

"Ready as I'll ever be!" She grinned up at me excitedly.

"Everything locked up?"

"Except your mouth." She punched my arm and laughed so hard I thought she was going to fall over.

I rolled my eyes and hooked my arm under hers, holding her tight as we walked to my car together, both of us still with slight limps . . . like two mangled peas in a broken little pod.

When I pulled into the driveway at mine and Michelle's house, Maura and Matthew were jumping up and down at the front door. Typically when we saw Gam, we went to her house because it was just easier. She rarely came to ours for a visit, let alone a sleepover, and the kids were bouncing off the walls excited.

"Look at that." Gam motioned to the door as we walked up. "You should have been as excited as they are when you rang my doorbell."

I laughed out loud and helped her up the porch steps.

Gam slid out of her coat and I hung it in the closet as she pulled the kids against her and wrapped them in a huge hug.

"Boy, you guys sure know how to make an old lady feel good!" she said as she kissed the tops of their heads.

The house smelled amazing. Michelle had been working so hard all day, desperately wanting to impress Gam with making a big dinner all by herself. She wouldn't even let me help. The whole thing had her so frazzled, I didn't even have the heart to tell her that her apron was on inside out.

"Ooooh, it smells fantastic in here!" Gam lifted her nose in the air and closed her eyes.

Michelle's eyes lit up. "Really? It does?"

"It does. If it tastes even *half* as good as it smells, we're all in for a real treat."

Michelle looked over at me and took a deep breath as a tiny grin crept across her lips. Her pleased blue eyes sparkled and the little bit of chocolate I noticed on the end of her nose only made her cuter.

"Were you baking, too?" I asked with a laugh.

She squished her eyebrows together and blinked up at me. "Yeah. I made fudge. Why?" Before I could answer, her eyes crossed and she looked down at her nose, finally noticing the chocolate. "Oh! Oops!" She giggled as she grabbed a paper towel and wiped it off.

Gam clapped her hands once and looked around the kitchen like a woman on a mission. "Okay, what can I help with?"

"Nothing." Michelle shook her head. "I just want you to sit and relax while I do everything."

Gam eyed Michelle skeptically for just a second before she shrugged. "In that case, I'll make myself a drink."

Michelle bent over and pulled the sweet potatoes from the oven just as the doorbell rang. She stood and stared at me with wide eyes and a hot dish in her hand.

I held my hand up. "You do that, I got this."

A tiny body, all bundled up in a coat and hat, stood with its back to me on the other side of the glass door. As I walked up, Joel stepped onto the front porch and waved.

"Hey!" I opened the door and motioned them in.

"Hey!" Joel said, turning Gavin around and pushing him gently into the foyer. "We're not staying. We're heading out of town to my aunt's for the evening, but then Gavin goes back to his mom's house, and he just threw a royal fit because apparently he made Matthew something for Christmas and *had* to give it to him before we left."

I glanced down at Gavin, who was grinning up at me anxiously. "Hang on, bud. I'll get him." I stepped back toward the hallway that led to the kitchen. "Matthew!"

Within seconds, he came sliding around the corner, holding onto the counter for stability, and ran toward us. "Hi!" he said as he ran up to Gavin.

"Here. I made this for you." Gavin held out a small box.

I lifted my head to Joel who shrugged. "He made it at his mom's. I have no idea what it is."

Matthew opened the box and his mouth fell open. "This is *awesome!*" He pulled a rock that was painted to look like a Ninja Turtle out of the box and stared down at it in amazement.

Gavin smiled shyly and took a step back toward Joel.

Matthew's face swept up to mine. "Can Gavin come and help me put it in my room?"

"Uh . . . fine by me, but it's up to his dad."

Joel gave Gavin a warning with his eyes. "You have two minutes, got it? We're already late."

Gavin nodded and he and Matthew shot up the stairs together.

Joel and I stood in the doorway like a couple of awkward teenage boys. I wasn't sure what to say to him. Do you thank the man who spent Thanksgiving with your girlfriend? The old Viper would have probably punched him right in the mouth, but I didn't feel like doing that anymore.

"I had dinner with Jodi and Vince the other night," Joel said. "She told me that you're home and you guys are doing really good again."

I nodded slowly. "I don't know that we're *really* good, but we will be. I was a fucking moron and I realized it before it was too late . . . thank God."

"I've been a fucking moron a time or two in my life." He let

256

out a quick laugh. "I'm glad it worked out though. She seems like a pretty awesome woman."

"She's the love of my life," I said humbly.

"And you're obviously the love of hers, too."

"No." I shook my head. "I'm lucky enough to share that title with my best friend."

Joel's face pinched together and he narrowed his eyes but didn't say anything.

"Oh! You don't know *that* story?" I exclaimed, shaking my head again. "Bro, we'll have to talk one day when we have time. That's a story that requires at least three beers and is way too emotional for a day like Christmas."

Joel grinned and held his hand out to me. "Noted. Another time, man."

I shook his hand just as the boys came flying down the stairs again.

"Dad! Dad! Look what Matthew gave *me* for Christmas!" Gavin held out the box that the rock was in.

Joel leaned over and stared at the box closely. "Wait. Are those—"

Gavin interrupted him. "His dead roly poly collection! He's been saving them for almost a whole year."

"Wow." Joel tried to sound excited, but his face looked horrified as he turned to Matthew. "You sure you want to part with all those, buddy?"

"Yeah." Matthew nodded. "He's my best friend!"

Joel took a deep breath and let it out on a loud sigh. "Well, okay then. You can take those home and keep them at mom's house." He shot me a quick wink as he opened the door. "You guys have a good Christmas."

"You, too. Thanks for coming by and taking all those corpses off our hands." I laughed and he rolled his eyes and went back across the street.

"Who was that?" Michelle asked as Matthew and I walked

back into the kitchen together.

"It was Gavin," Matthew said excitedly. "He painted me a rock for Christmas, so I gave him my roly poly collection."

Her face flashed to mine, and it was obvious the roly poly collection wasn't her concern.

I walked over and put my arm around her shoulders, leaning down to kiss her temple. "Everything is fine," I said quietly.

She relaxed into me and closed her eyes.

"Food is just about done. Who's hungry?" she called out when I let go and walked away. Matthew and I set the dining room table and a little bit later, we feasted like kings on Michelle's amazing dinner.

Michelle was exhausted, so once the kids were down, I told her I'd clean the kitchen and handle the Santa stuff and sent her up to bed, too. I helped Gam with the stairs one at a time and got her all settled into the guest room. Thankfully neither of them argued about going up without me. I cleaned the kitchen and dining room in record time, fueled by my excitement to lay out all the presents.

All the presents.

I looked around the kitchen, pleased with how it looked, and put my game face on. I couldn't wait till the morning!

"Momma! Momma!" Matthew's footsteps stomped down the hall and he flew onto our bed like a squirrel. "Viper!" he shook my shoulder. "Wake up! Do you think Santa came?"

I opened my eyes slowly. His words finally registered with my brain and I sat up. "I bet he did! You go knock quietly on Gam's door and I'll wake your mom and Maura, okay?"

"Deal!" He nodded and held his little fist out for me to bump. We did and he sprinted from the room.

"Hey." I bent down and kissed Michelle's cheek. "Sorry. My morning breath probably stinks, but who gives a shit. It's

Christmas, wake up."

She groaned and gave me a tiny smile without opening her eyes.

I put my hand on her small tummy and cupped my kid. "Santa even told me that he brought a couple presents for this guy, too."

Her eyes flashed open. "What? No, he didn't."

"I'm pretty sure he did," I said with a laugh.

She lowered her voice. "Viper, I bought all the Christmas presents, so I'm pretty sure I know what's down there."

"Uh . . . oooooor not." I shot her a playful grin. "It's Christmas. You're not allowed to be mad at me, okay?"

Her eyes narrowed. "What did you do?"

I kissed her cheek swiftly and then stood up. "I love you. I'll see you downstairs."

I scooped a sleepy Maura out of bed, changed her diaper, and met Matthew at the top of the stairs. Gam came out of the bathroom and I held her arm as we slowly climbed down with Michelle right behind us. We all walked through the kitchen to the family room together, and I watched as all of their mouths fell open at the same time, except for Maura's, who didn't quite get Santa yet and was back asleep on my shoulder.

"Holy crap," Michelle said under her breath as she stared at the pile of presents that covered all of the furniture and practically spilled out of the room.

Matthew started picking up boxes and shaking them as Gam cleared off a chair to sit.

Michelle looked at me incredulously, shaking her head slowly. She leaned in close. "When did . . . how did . . . You didn't have to do all this."

"I know," I said quietly and shrugged, looking back at Matthew who was sitting on a huge box in the middle of the room, grinning at us. "I *wanted* to."

Gam let out a quick laugh as her head fell back against the

chair. "Someone's overcompensating."

I glared at Gam as Michelle giggled loudly and moved boxes so she could sit down, too. It took the kids two hours to open all of their presents, one box at a time and the looks on their faces made it all worth it.

Best two hours I'd ever had.

Chapter
31

Michelle

Four Months Later . . .

"**U**GH!" I GROANED AS I pulled the Wild jersey over my belly. Maura sat on my bed and looked at me curiously, completely unaware of my struggles. "Maura," I sighed. "I'm almost seven months along, but I feel like I'm ready to pop. How much bigger is this thing going to get?"

Maura stared at me innocently and shrugged. Her blond hair was pulled into pigtails with hunter green ribbons tied at the top, and she was wearing a Minnesota Wild T-shirt, layered over a white long-sleeved shirt.

"Are you excited to go to the hockey game, baby girl?"

She nodded. "I want popcorn."

"You'll get popcorn." I giggled before calling out, "Matthew, are you almost ready?"

"Just a minute!" he called back.

A few second later, he came running down the hall and jumped into my doorway, putting his hands proudly on his hips and puffing his chest out.

"Oh. Wow." I stared down at him. He was wearing a Wild T-shirt and jeans, but his blond hair was spiked up with way too much hair gel and he had messy eye black under his eyes, something hockey players never wear, but apparently Matthew didn't know that. "You look super tough. Where did you get the stuff for under your eyes?"

"Your bathroom," he said nonchalantly as he climbed into my bed.

"My bathroom?"

"Yeah, the bag on the counter. I took the pencil to my room and drew it on."

"You mean my *eyeliner?*"

He nodded. "I used it all. Sorry."

I sighed and checked myself out one last time in the mirror. "Okay. You guys ready to hit the road?"

Viper had left the house a few hours before, and I don't think I'd ever seen him so nervous. He'd been medically cleared and it was his first game back, but it might as well have been the first game of his whole career. His hands had been shaking and I could feel his heart racing through his jersey when he'd hugged me good-bye. I'd known he was nervous the night before and when we woke up that morning, I'd dipped my head under the covers and did my best to relieve his stress, but it had only helped a little . . . and only for about two minutes.

Nonetheless, the kids and I piled into the car and headed over to pick up Gam. Then we were all on our way to the arena.

The stadium was buzzing. There had been a few stories on the news in the morning about Viper's return, and the kids and

I had watched him and Coach Collins do a big press conference the day before. The fans were excited to see Viper back out on the ice, and so were we. Viper was able to secure us some extra tickets to pass out, so I tried to pack the stands with everyone I could think of to come watch his return.

The usher directed us to our seats, which were right in front of Kacie and the girls. They waved at us excitedly as we made our way down the concrete steps.

Kacie stepped into the aisle and took Gam's hand, leading her into her seat carefully, then she came back and hugged me. "Are you excited?"

I nodded. "Excited. Terrified. Nervous. It's been a while."

She tilted her head to the side and smiled at me. "He'll do great."

The kids and I took our seats just as Andy walked up with enough popcorn to feed a small army. "I hear we have some hungry kids over here!" he called out playfully.

All of their arms shot up and he began passing out boxes.

As soon as our eyes met, we gave each other the exact same anxious look. "Did you see him yet?"

"Yeah, I was in the locker room a little bit ago." He paused and licked butter off his thumb.

"And?"

He shrugged. "And he's great. Nervous as hell, but I think after a few minutes, it'll disappear. Coach Collins did tell him he might not play long periods of time just yet, but that all depends on how his knee feels."

"Good. I don't want him to push himself too much."

"Please." Andy rolled his eyes. "This is Viper we're talking about. His knee could swell to the size of a basketball and he'd still insist he was fine."

"True," I said with a laugh.

The usher walked up behind Andy and waved at me to catch my attention. With him was a large man with dark, grayish hair, dark green and white polka-dotted sweatpants, and a huge smile on his face. I didn't even have to ask who he was. I already knew.

"You must be Sherman." I stepped past Andy and opened my arms wide. "It's so nice to finally meet you!"

He gave me one of the warmest, most comforting hugs I'd ever received in my whole life. "Nice to meet *you*, Michelle. I feel like I already know so much about you through that pain in the ass of yours, but it's great to finally put a face to the name."

"I feel the same about you. We both put up with a lot from him, don't we?"

He leaned in close. "That's an understatement."

I let out a quick laugh. "Here, come sit by me." I introduced him to everyone else and within a minute, the guys took the ice and the crowd started cheering.

I stood up and scanned the white and green jerseys, looking for my guy, who was skating straight for us. He came over and banged on the glass, grinning like a proud little kid. Matthew stood on the seat and pumped his little arms in the air, while Maura ran up to the glass and blew him kisses. Finally Viper looked over and shot me a quick wink. I raised both hands and pointed next to me. His eyes slid to Sherman and practically bulged out of his head as his mouth dropped open.

"I didn't know you were gonna be here!" he yelled, though we barely heard him over the glass and the crowd.

Sherman pointed to me with him thumb. "She did!" he shouted back.

Viper's eyes drifted back to mine and he pulled his brows down low, giving me a sweet, thankful smile.

"I love you!" he shouted as loud as he could.

"Love you, too!" I mouthed back quietly.

He winked at me one more time, punched the glass playfully, and skated away.

The game moved, fast and intense. The Wild won and Viper

even scored one of their three goals. As soon as he shot the puck and the red light turned on, the place erupted and I jumped out of my seat. Poor Maura covered her ears and started sobbing, but Kacie scooped her up and let me have my moment. Viper hugged and high-fived his teammates before skating over to us and giving Matthew a thumbs-up. Matthew, so proud of his Viper, started cheering and high-fiving complete strangers in the aisle.

"Matthew, get back here." I giggled, waving him back to me.

"Hang on, Mom. I'm telling them that my *dad* just scored a goal." He beamed proudly.

I froze and felt Kacie's hand on my shoulder. "Did you just hear that, too?" I asked her without turning around.

"I sure did."

"I don't know what to say about it." I started to panic. Matthew had never called Viper his dad before. I knew now that he was going to school he was going to start questioning it and maybe ask me about it one day, but I didn't picture it like that.

"You say nothing," Kacie answered. "Viper *is* his dad."

I turned back to her. "But not his real—"

Kacie closed her eyes and shook her head quickly, interrupting me. "It doesn't matter. That's all he's really ever known, so just let it happen. It doesn't mean he doesn't love Mike or that you can't tell him stories about him as he grows up. It just means he's a little boy who is very lucky to have two great daddies. One in Heaven, and one down here with him." Kacie squeezed my hand and I took a shaky breath.

She was right. Matthew was lucky. So was Maura. So was the baby kicking up a storm in my belly.

So was I.

Chapter
32

Viper

One Month Later . . .

I'D BEEN BACK ON THE ice full time for a month. Michelle and I were totally back to normal. We'd just finished decorating the baby's room—with a hockey theme, of course—and life was about as perfect as it could get.

I should have known . . .

I was just pulling into the parking lot for practice when my cell phone rang. It was Michelle.

"Hello?" I said as I pulled into a parking spot.

"Hey," she said with a heavy sigh.

"What's wrong?"

"Nothing, really . . . I guess . . . I don't know. I was at my doctor appointment and everything was fine and we were chatting and I told her that I felt like I was peeing my pants more than usual yesterday and she did this weird napkin test to make sure I wasn't leaking amniotic fluid and it turned blue."

My heart started racing around in circles inside my chest. "What does that mean?"

"It means it was amniotic fluid."

"Okay. Shit. So what now?"

"I don't really know. She's sending me over to the hospital for more tests and so they can monitor the baby. I might have to stay overnight."

I put my car in reverse and backed out of the parking space. "I'm on my way."

"Viper! No!" she argued. "I didn't tell you all this so you'd come home. Probably nothing is going to happen anyway, so there's no point."

"I don't care. I'm on my way. I should be there within an hour. I'll text you when I get close."

"Are you sure?" she asked, sounding guilty.

"Positive. I love you. Talk to you soon." My hands gripped the wheel tightly as I made my way to the hospital. Every muscle in my body, especially my shoulders and neck, felt tight.

I hit a button on my phone and called Coach Collins's office. After a handful of rings, his voicemail picked up. Without leaving a message, I hung up and called Brody instead.

"Hello?" he asked, his voice raised in surprise. I heard lots of voices behind him and figured he was already in the locker room.

"Hey, it's me. Do me a favor, please. Tell Collins I'm not gonna make practice. Michelle is leaking fluid or something and I'm on the way to the hospital to meet her."

"Holy shit. Okay. Keep me posted, please."

"I will. Thanks." I turned the phone off and tossed it on the passenger seat without waiting for his response.

I pulled into the hospital parking lot, found a spot, and grabbed my phone, dialing Michelle's number as I rushed across the pavement.

It rang and rang. No answer.

The hair on the back of my neck stood up.

She always answered her phone.

Following the signs in the hospital through the hallways to the Labor and Delivery Unit, I prayed that that's where they had sent her. It was a total guess between that and the ER, but with her not answering, I did the best I could.

I tried the door to get in but it was locked. There was a small intercom off to the side of the door, so I pushed the silver button.

"How can I help you?" a woman's voice asked.

"Uh . . . hi. My girlfriend was at the doctor this morning and they said that she was leaking something and so she came to the hospital. I called her, but she didn't answer, so I'm just trying to find out if she's here."

"What is your name, Sir?"

"My name is Vi—Lawrence Finkle."

"Okay, Mr. Finkle. What is *her* name?"

"Michelle Asher."

It was quiet for a minute, then the door made a clicking sound. "Come in, Mr. Finkle. Please stop at the nurse's station inside."

I pulled the door open and hurried over to the desk. "Hi. I was just at the door."

A woman looked over at me and gave me a small smile. "I know. I was the one talking to you. Do you have an ID on you, Mr. Finkle?"

"Yeah." I reached into my pocket and took out my wallet. "Here."

She looked down at it, back up at me, and then scanned it into the computer. A little machine next to me printed out a sticker with my information. "Put this on your shirt and this band goes on your wrist." She snapped a plastic band around my wrist and typed a few more things into the computer. "Okay, I'll take you to her."

"Did they decide to admit her?" I asked nervously.

She looked at me with wide eyes as she walked around from behind the desk. "Admit her? Oh, absolutely. She's in active labor."

"What?" I exclaimed loudly as panic shot through me. "What the hell is active labor? Our hospital visit isn't until next week."

"Next week?" She gave me a sympathetic look. "Mr. Finkle, I have a feeling you'll be holding this baby before the end of the day."

"Wait. Seriously?"

She nodded. "Ready to go in?"

I took a deep breath and listened to my body. It wasn't screaming and shaking and freaking out like I'd expected it to be. I was nervous, but more than anything, I was ready.

"Yep. Let's do it."

She pushed the door open and immediately, a loud, slow beeping filled the room. I moved to my left and peeked around her to Michelle who was lying in the hospital bed asleep. Other than the IV in her hand and the blood pressure cuff around her arm, she looked totally peaceful.

"Is she in pain?" I asked the nurse quietly.

She shook her head. "So far, so good. We gave her a little something to help with the pain and it made her sleepy. She came over because the doctor sent her, but by time we got her in here, she'd already started dilating and was past the point of no return."

"Isn't she too early?" I asked anxiously.

Looking back at Michelle, she nodded. "She's thirty-five weeks, so she *is* early, but the baby's survival rate is very high at this point. Sometimes they don't even need time in the NICU."

"NICU? Holy shit." I ran my hand through my hair and sat

in a daze on the chair next to Michelle's bed. The word NICU was so intimidating . . . and terrifying.

The nurse lifted up a strip of paper and read a graph on it. I opened my mouth to ask her what she was doing, but before I could speak, Michelle rolled over and groggily opened her eyes. As soon as she focused on me, a lazy smile crossed her lips.

"Hey," I said as I crept over and kissed her forehead. "Looks like we're gonna have our boy today, huh?"

She blinked for a long time and nodded.

"Are you in any pain?" I rubbed her cheek with the backs of my fingers. She looked so beautiful and so happy and I couldn't believe she was about to have my baby. My son.

"Nope. I feel good." She rolled her head toward the nurse. "Am I even having contractions?"

"You are. Pretty strong ones, actually." She crinkled her brow and looked down at Michelle. "The contractions aren't too bad?"

Michelle shook her head. "I definitely feel them, but they're nothing I can't handle right now."

"Okay. Dr. Avery is going to be over soon and she wants to check on you, so just sit tight for a little bit."

"Mmhmm," Michelle answered, and the nurse left the room. She turned back toward me. "Come here. Come sit by me."

"I *am* sitting by you." I scooted my chair closer to her.

"No . . . like on my bed with me."

"What?" I asked incredulously. "No way. I don't want to hurt you, or unhook anything—"

"Stop it, you big bonehead. Get up here." She moved all the way over against the far rail and I undid the one closest to me, lowering it quietly.

I lifted one leg onto the bed and sat down as gently as I possibly could, careful not to bump her. "Does this hurt?"

"No. Stop treating me like glass and get over here." She wrapped her hands around my bicep and pulled me tight against her. We both got comfortable and she rested her head on my shoulder. "Are you ready for this?"

"I am," I answered without hesitation. "I really am. I'm excited. As long as he's okay, and you're okay, I don't care about anything else."

I felt her smile against my arm. "I can't believe he's coming today. And what a weird morning. I went to the doctor, but now I'm in labor—even though I don't feel like I'm in labor. So strange."

"I hope I do okay."

She lifted her head and stared at me. "What do you mean?"

I shrugged. "For both of you. I hope I do everything I'm supposed to today and don't screw up. And then when he gets here . . . I just want him to be proud of me. I was never proud of my dad—not one single time in my life—and I don't want that with my son. I want him to be proud of me."

"He will be. That's the great thing about babies. All you have to do is love them and they love you right back. You got this, Finkle." She raised her fist and I bumped it, then rested my hand on her stomach.

We sat there in silence and stared at her stomach move and roll. It was hard to believe that in just a short while, that little bump would be on the outside of her, moving and breathing and crying. After several minutes, Michelle let out a soft groan and I jumped off the bed. "Did I hurt you?"

"No." She grimaced as she tried to sit up. I held my hand out for her to pull herself against. "My back feels like it's on fire."

"Uh . . ." I moved left then right then left again. "I'll get someone." I rushed out to the nurse's station and let them know she was in pain.

The nurse followed me back to the room and took a pair of gloves out of the box on the wall. "Dr. Avery should be here soon, but I'm gonna check you real quick, okay?"

"Okay," Michelle said as she lay down on her back.

The nurse moved to the end of the bed and pulled the blanket up, placing it on Michelle's stomach, where she rested her left hand while dipping her right hand under the blanket.

Michelle let out a soft moan and cringed as the nurse looked up at the ceiling and felt around. She pulled the glove back and there was blood all over the end of it. I felt woozy and had to sit.

"Okay, well . . . I'm gonna go page Dr. Avery and tell her to move a little bit faster. You're already at nine centimeters, which is why it's starting to hurt and you're pretty uncomfortable."

"Will I be at ten soon?" She grimaced.

The nurse raised her eyebrows. "Probably by the time Dr. Avery gets my text. I'm going to go send it now, then I'm gonna come back and start prepping the room. Get ready, guys. We're gonna have a baby soon!" She gave Michelle a big, tight smile and hurried from the room.

Michelle groaned again.

"Is it your back still?" I stood and walked up to the bed.

She nodded.

"Want me to rub it? Roll over."

She immediately rolled a way from me and I started massaging large circles into her lower back, right above her two cute dimples. "Does that feel okay? Is it helping at all?"

"Mmhmm," she answered. "It's starting to hurt though. Not my back, but my contractions. I think it's getting close."

With that the door swung open and in walked Dr. Avery.

"Whoa. You got here fast," I said.

"I was already in the elevator on the way up when I got Cathy's page." She walked over and pulled gloves from the box, too. "Guess this anxious little boy just didn't want to wait any longer, huh? Can you roll on your back for me, Michelle? I need to check you also."

Michelle pinched her eyes shut tight and bit her bottom lip as she rolled over.

Dr. Avery stared at the ground as she reached under the blanket and felt around. "Wow." She shook her head slowly.

"You're just about there. I'm gonna come back and break your water fully, then we'll probably start pushing, okay?"

As Michelle nodded, the nurse came back into the room, flipped the light on above a crib-type thing in the corner, started taking blankets and sheets out of a cabinet, and put more gloves on. Then she helped put Michelle's feet in stirrups and held a heavy paper gown out for the doctor to put on, arms first.

Everything was moving at warp speed and I was starting to feel overwhelmed. My heart rate sped up and I wiped some sweat off my forehead as my legs shook. I glanced behind me and was just about to sit in the chair as Michelle reached out for me and grabbed my hand.

I looked down at her. Her face had flushed and she had sweat on her head, too, but she was smiling . . . at me. She was about to push our son into this world, but instead of crying or yelling or swearing or hitting me, she was smiling at me. I had never been more in love with her in my whole life than I was at that moment. Her smile made all of my worry disappear, and in its place was excitement. I couldn't wait to hold my son.

After a few more minutes of chaos, Dr. Avery took her seat at the end of the bed and instructed Michelle to push when she felt the next contraction. I stood up near Michelle's head, holding her hand tightly in mine. About a minute later, Michelle's head lifted off the bed and her hand squeezed mine harder than I ever knew it could. Her chin dug into her chest and she groaned hard as her face turned beet red.

"Look at all that dark hair," Dr. Avery called out as she looked down at Michelle. "Dad, you wanna come down here and see this?"

Holy shit. Do I?

Without letting go of Michelle, I took a big step to my left and peeked over her knee. "Oh my God!" I called out involuntarily. You really could see a small tuft of dark hair just inside of Michelle. It was the most amazing fucking thing I'd ever seen.

Michelle's head fell back against the bed and she gasped for air.

"Michelle, as soon as you can, I want you to come back with one more big push, okay? He's right here. He's ready to be born. Come on, you got this! Give me one big one!"

Michelle let go of my hand and wrapped hers around her thighs, pulling hard against them as she pushed with everything she had.

Holding my breath, I watched in utter amazement as my son's head emerged from Michelle's body. With the next push came his shoulders and then the rest of him. He was tiny, but he was loud. The nurse sucked some junk out of his throat and my pissed-off little man let the whole hospital, maybe even the world, know that he was here. Tears rolled down my cheeks as I looked from him to Michelle, who was crying just as hard as I was.

I stepped back next to her and put my forehead against the side of her head and wept like I'd never wept before in my whole life.

The nurse laid him on Michelle's chest so that they were skin-to-skin and then put a blanket over him. The minute he felt his mom, he stopped crying and looked around. "I can't believe how wide awake he is," I said in awe.

"It's a weird newborn phenomenon," Dr. Avery said as she tended to Michelle at the end of the bed. "No one really knows why newborns are so awake after delivery, but it usually only lasts a little while, so soak it up while you can."

He wasn't really focusing on anything in particular, but his eyes darted all around and his tongue kept poking out of his mouth. "He's the cutest baby in the whole world, you know that?" I said to Michelle.

She laughed and nodded. "I think so, too."

I put my arm over her and gently pulled her toward me so I could kiss the side of her head.

"Does this cutest little boy ever have a name yet?" Nurse

Cathy asked.

Michelle looked up at me and gave me a small nod. We'd talked about it many, many times and always came back to the same name.

"He does," I answered proudly. "Our son's name is Michael Lawrence Finkle."

Several hours later, we were finally settled in our room and everything had quieted down. It was pretty late, so Taylor wouldn't be bringing Matthew and Maura up until the next day, and I was also going to go get Gam and bring her over, but we did have a couple of visitors that snuck up to see us.

"Knock, knock," Kacie said as she pushed the hospital door open and walked in with a big smile.

"Hey." Michelle smiled at her.

Kacie bent down and kissed Michelle's cheek. "You look amazing for just having a baby a few hours ago, you big brat."

Brody kissed the top of Michelle's head. "Congrats, momma." He walked over and held a hand out to me. "And you. Congratulations to you, too, pops."

My cheeks hurt from smiling so much over the last few hours, but I didn't care. I shook his hand excitedly and pulled him in for a bear hug. "Thank you, brother."

Kacie washed her hands quickly and squealed as she took Michael from Michelle's arms and sat in the chair next to the bed. "Did you guys decide on a name?" she asked.

"We did," I answered. "Michael Lawrence Finkle."

Brody's eyes flashed to mine. "Michael? Wow. That's . . ." His voice trailed off and he swallowed hard.

"Oh my God. You guys . . ." Kacie said softly as her voice cracked.

The four of us stood there with tears in our eyes, thinking about the exact same thing.

"Hey," I said with a nervous laugh. "Don't get any tears on my kid."

Kacie sniffed and chuckled as she bent down, nuzzling Michael's nose with her own. "By the way, how much did he weigh?"

"Yeah, your text was pretty vague." Brody punched my shoulder playfully.

"He's actually a good size for being a little early," Michelle stared at our son adoringly. "Five pounds, three ounces."

Kacie's eyes widened. "Wow! If you'd carried him to full term, this chunker would have been almost ten pounds."

"He felt like ten pounds," Michelle said with a quick laugh.

"So when's the next one coming?" Brody asked playfully.

Michelle and I looked straight at each other, a hint of sadness between us. "There won't be any more babies," Michelle said. "Because of the bleed I had during the actual pregnancy and then going into labor early, Dr. Avery thinks I shouldn't get pregnant again. So . . . I had my tubes tied."

Kacie's face lifted and her sad eyes moved from Michelle to me and back again. "Wait. Seriously?"

"Seriously." Michelle's gaze dropped to her hands where she played with her fingers nervously.

"Holy shit," Brody mumbled under his breath. "That's too bad. I'm so sorry, guys."

"Don't be sorry." Michelle lifted her face to Brody. "Michael's here and healthy and we're very lucky."

The room was silent for a minute.

"Yeah," I added. "And he's *also* lucky because since he'll be the last kid till grandbabies, we're obviously going to spoil the shit out of him." I shrugged.

"Wait a minute." Brody straightened up and raised his hands. "Did my best friend, Lawrence Finkle, really just say something about *grandbabies?*"

"Yeah, I did, asshole. You got a problem with it?" I teased.

"Shhh!" Kacie hissed. "No swearing in front of the baby. I really don't think you want his first word to be asshole, do you?"

"Hell no. His first word is gonna be *daddy*. I can feel it." I beamed.

Kacie glanced at Michelle and rolled her eyes playfully. "You really need to keep him away from your pain meds."

Brody and Kacie left a little while later and it was just me, Michelle, and Michael in the quiet room. Michelle had insisted that I climb into bed and sit with her again, but within seconds of me scooting up next to her, she was asleep on my shoulder.

Some people walk through the doors of parenthood with excitement and open arms. Others, like me, are dragged through it kicking and screaming in resistance. As I sat in that room with Michelle sound asleep against my shoulder, Michael sound asleep in my arms, and Matthew and Maura on my mind, I thought about the scars I had on my hands from white-knuckling the door trim as hard as I could.

Brody was right. Fate didn't ask permission and she didn't give you warnings, but she had a way of balancing your life when you didn't even know it needed to be balanced, and calming even the wildest of hearts.

Epilogue

Michelle

Two Months Later . . .

"EVERY SINGLE THING HURTS," KACIE whined. "My hair hurts. My eyelashes hurt. My whole body hurts."

"I don't even think I can walk to the car," I added.

We sat in the big, dark red booth at Brody and Viper's new bar, The Penalty Box. It was three o'clock in the morning after the big grand opening party, and we had all clearly underestimated how old we really were.

"Who's dumb idea was this bar thing anyway?" Viper asked. He was lying flat on his back on the wood floor, staring up at the ceiling.

"If I had the energy, I'd get up and kick you right in the junk," Brody said dryly. He had lined up four bar stools and was lying across them on his stomach.

"We were pretty packed tonight though, huh?" Viper said, a little more upbeat.

"Yeah." Kacie groaned as she sat up. "The line was out the door and around the block. I have a feeling this place will be like that for a while."

"I hope so. I really don't want to have to kill Viper to pay this loan off." Brody pushed himself off the stools and looked around the room. "Holy shit. This place is trashed."

I sat up, scooted to the end of the booth, and surveyed the damage. Confetti and streamers covered the floor. Dozens of glasses, half-full of beer, littered every table. There was even a random high heel abandoned in the corner. "It *is* trashed, but it's still so damn beautiful."

Like someone shocked his system back to life, Viper jumped up from the floor and looked around his new adventure with excited eyes. "It really is badass."

The Penalty Box was a sports memorabilia collector's mothership. Framed jerseys, hockey sticks, and bats covered the walls. Shelves with baseballs, golfballs, and basketballs sprinkled every corner and then some. Of course there was a heavy emphasis on the Minnesota Wild, but that was to be expected. After all, it was Brody and Viper's bar.

Without a doubt, the most amazing part of the entire space was the oversized booth in the far back corner. It was a place just for Brody, Viper, and their friends and family. Above the booth hung a place setting that read "Head of Our Table—Mike Asher #88" with one of Mike's old jerseys framed over it. I had no idea they'd planned that until I got there earlier that evening. I hadn't seen a lot of it, actually. Viper was so excited, and so proud, that he refused to let me into the bar until it was completely finished. Brody had done the same thing with Kacie.

When we got there tonight, an hour before the grand opening, we were both speechless as we walked around and looked at everything closely. Brody and Viper specifically skipped hiring a designer because they wanted to do all of the decorating themselves, and surprisingly they did an amazing job, picking out every single detail personally.

"Should we do anything before we leave?" Kacie asked through a yawn.

Brody shook his head. "No. I have a crew coming in to clean

up at eight o'clock because I figured it would be extra messy after the grand opening."

"Good." Viper clapped loudly. "Then I'm going to make sure everything is locked up in back and we're getting the hell out of here. I'm exhausted."

"I still can't believe you guys actually pulled it off," I said, still in awe, as Viper drove us home.

"I can't either," he replied. "Brody was so against it at the beginning, but the more we got into it, the more excited we got."

"I'm proud of you."

He reached over and grabbed my hand, pulling it to his lips. "I'm kinda proud of me, too." He kissed the top of my hand and put it down but didn't let go. "I have a surprise for you."

My head turned toward him. "What surprise?"

"Don't be mad, you promise?"

"Oh boy." I took a deep breath and let it out slowly. "Fine. I won't be mad."

"You know how Taylor was here with the kids? Well, I asked her to take them to her house and keep them overnight."

"You did?"

He nodded. "I was sure we were gonna be really late, and you haven't had a good night's sleep in months now, so I figured we could sleep in and then go pick them up at her house." He peeked at me from the corner of his eye. "You're not pissed, are you?"

"Not at all. I mean, of course I miss them, but the thought of more than two hours of sleep at a time makes me a little giddy." I rested my head against the seat and started counting down the minutes until I could climb into bed and drift off. "Taylor wasn't mad, was she?"

"No." He laughed as he shook his head. "She offered to keep them all day tomorrow, too, but I told her she'd have to talk to you about that one."

We pulled into the garage and he turned the car off. "Ready?" he asked.

Without lifting my head off the seat, I turned to face him. "I'm too tired. Just leave me here and come back in the morning."

He laughed. "Come on. It's only a few more steps, then you'll be to our bed."

"Fine." I groaned and pouted my way into the house and through the kitchen.

"Are you hungry?" he called out just as I got to the bottom of the stairs.

"What?" I called back incredulously. He didn't answer, so I went to see if I'd heard him correctly. "Did you ask if I was hungry?"

He stood at the island and nodded. "I think I'm gonna make something to eat. You want something?"

"Yes, I want sleep," I said sarcastically.

"Fine. You can go up to sleep. On your way out of the kitchen, can you grab the big pot from the cabinet and set it on the island?"

I rolled my eyes. "I seriously can't believe you're going to cook at four o'clock in the morning. If you were hungry, you should have said something. That's what Taco Bell is for." I bent over and grabbed the big silver pot and set it on the island . . . then I froze.

The pot was one I'd never seen before, and something was engraved on the lid. I squinted my eyes and leaned in closer to read it.

EVERY POT HAS A LID. YOU'RE MY LID.

WILL YOU MARRY ME?

282

My eyes shot open as I straightened up and looked over at a grinning Viper.

"What . . . how . . . when . . ."

"You do that stuttering thing a lot, you know that?" He walked over, lifted the lid of the pot, and pulled out a black velvet ring box. Opening it, he got down on one knee. He licked his lips, took a deep breath, and smiled up at me. "Well. Will you?"

Ten minutes ago I'd been exhausted and practically crawling up the stairs, but suddenly I was wide-awake and fighting back tears.

"Oh my God, Viper. Yes!" I put my hand over my mouth as he stood and wrapped his arms around me. "I don't even know what to say."

"You already said the most important thing, so you don't have to say anything else." We stood in the kitchen, hugging and swaying back and forth for at least two minutes as tears dripped from my eyes onto his shirt.

"Here," he said as he eventually pulled back. "I want to see how this looks on you." He took the ring from the box and placed it on my shaky left hand.

I stared down at the ring. It was a simple diamond set in a platinum, antique-looking band. "Viper, this is beautiful."

"I'm glad you think so. It's Gam's."

"What?" My eyes shot up to his.

"I told Gam a while ago that I was going to propose, and she insisted that I use the ring that my grandfather gave her. Well, the stone anyway. I had it reset."

"I already loved it, but that makes it one hundred times better."

"The only thing she asked is that we leave it to Maura one day. She wants her only great-granddaughter to have it after us." He pressed his lips together and lifted the corner of his mouth in a sweet, humble smile.

"Your grandmother is an amazing woman."

He nodded. "She is. And she helped raise me, so of course I turned out pretty amazing, too."

"I'll agree with that." I hooked my arms around his neck and pressed my lips against his. His hands slid down my sides and cupped my bottom as he opened his mouth for a deeper kiss. "Wanna go upstairs and show me just how amazing you are?"

"Fuck yes!" He grabbed my hand and led me around the house behind him as he locked the doors and shut all the lights off.

"By the way, what would you have done if I'd gone right upstairs and didn't get the pot for you?" I asked matter-of-factly.

He glanced back and raised a sexy eyebrow at me. "How do you know that ring hasn't been sitting in there for months already? It's not like you take the pots out to cook very often, so for all you know it's been sitting in there for a long time."

"You're such an asshole." I rolled my eyes.

He shot me a wink and tossed me playfully onto the bed. "I am, but I'm *your* asshole. Forever and ever."

Coming next from
Beth Ehemann

Single dad Andy Shaw loves his job as a sports agent, with one exception: it doesn't leave him much time for his kids. No parent likes being sidelined, so Andy decides to hire someone to share the workload. But when one of the hottest agents in the industry applies, Andy knows that this deal is definitely trouble.

Danicka Douglas works her butt off, but being an attractive woman in a testosterone-heavy industry isn't exactly a cakewalk. She guards her professional reputation fiercely, which means no crushing on her gorgeous boss. But the more they ignore that sexy little spark, the more it sizzles . . .

Just when it looks like romance might be in the game plan, Dani is threatened by a stalker with dark intentions. To keep her safe, Andy must cross the line between professional and very personal . . . because this time, he's playing for keeps.

Releasing September 6, 2016

About the Author

Beth Ehemann lives in the northern suburbs of Chicago with her husband and four children. When she's not sitting in front of her computer writing, or on Pinterest, she loves reading, photography, martinis and all things Chicago Cubs and Blackhawks.

Connect with her at-

www.bethehemann.com

authorbethehemann@yahoo.com

www.facebook.com/bethehemann

@bethehemann (Twitter and Instagram)